Faerie Misborn

TITANIA ACADEMY BOOK 1

Faerie Misborn

TITANIA ACADEMY BOOK 1

Samaire Wynne

Black Raven Books

Black Raven Books

Faerie Misborn.
Copyright © 2019 by Samaire Wynne. All rights reserved.
Cover illustrations copyright © 2019 by Melody Simmons
Printed in the United States of America.
For information, including permission to reproduce selections from this book, write to
publisher@blackravenbooks.net or to
Black Raven Books, P.O. Box 3201, Martinsville VA 24115

The text was set in 12-point Californian FB

ISBN-13: 9781948594202

First Edition: October 2019

10   9   8   7   6   5   4   3   2   1

Dedicated to the homeless children, and to all those living rough. May the magic they possess bring them prosperity and enrich the world.

Faerie Misborn

Chapter One
Thief

"Hey! COME BACK HERE!" The shopkeeper shook his fist at me as I ran. "THIEF!"

I was thirteen years old, skinny as a rail, and small for my size.

So I was fast. Really fast. I could run like the wind, even while carrying the two loaves of bread.

I heard a police whistle behind me, but I didn't stop to look.

If you stop to look, they catch you.

I raced down the alleyway, stuffing the bread into the sack hanging from my shoulder as I ran. They were hot on my heels; I could hear them breathing behind me.

More like puffing. Fat old man, you can't catch me.

I reached the end of the alley, and leaped, catching the top of the dumpster with both hands and swinging my feet up. Scrambling to the back edge, I jumped up and caught the side of the second-floor fire escape, and swung myself over the eight-foot-high chain-link fence to the next alley.

This alley led away from the street where I'd just swiped the bread, the deli that had the table on the sidewalk full of just-baked bread, to tantalize people with the smell and lure them inside. The soup they then sold to those customers was gross. I'd seen a rat fall into the vat last month, and the gross thing was, so did the cook. He hadn't fished the thing out; he'd left it in. I guess he figured, "more meat for the soup."

I didn't eat rat. Aunt Clare always told me they carried disease and to avoid them. We'd been lucky: We hadn't had to eat rat yet. Though things had gotten lean in the last year. Aunt Clare had gotten older, and she didn't really gather food anymore.

That was up to me. And I was good at it. She'd taught me well, after all.

But it was still hard.

"Being skinny will help you, Holly," Aunt Clare had said. "You can run faster, you can squeeze through gaps in fences better, and you can jump farther. Sometimes jumping rooftops is the only thing that'll get you away from the coppers, and it'll save your hide. So stay thin and lean and live to read another day."

Aunt Clare loved to read. She had two books she kept guarded and read to me most nights. She'd taught me to read from those books.

I ran down the alley, my feet padding the ground noiselessly in my sneakers.

Aunt Clare had procured the canvas sneakers one night six months ago, and they were already getting tight.

"You're growing like a weed, Holly," she'd said, smiling.

"I *am* a weed, Aunt Clare," I said ruefully, trying to brush out my wild hair with my fingers.

My hair was kind of white, at least after I went swimming in the canal. Most days it was grey, and wild. An untamed mess of tangles, Aunt Clare called it.

It flew behind me when I ran, a white/grey silvery beacon, and helped the coppers spot me in a crowd. It was not an asset, let me put it this way.

I wore a brown hoodie, the hood covering my head of crazy platinum hair, the drawstrings tied snugly under my chin. It helped to hide me in a crowd, and in dark alleyways.

I turned and ran down a sidewalk, slowing as I approached a crowd.

Slipping in through the edges, I lost myself in the throng of people walking, and I disappeared.

New York City was a great place to live if you were homeless, Aunt Clare had always said.

Whenever she would say that, I wondered why she didn't mention the winters, which were cold as ice, the rats, which managed to get in everywhere, and the dangers.

Dangers of being grabbed by coppers.

Dangers of being robbed by the others who shared the streets with you.

Dangers of getting sick.

Dangers of getting stabbed.

Lots of dangers.

I was now walking rapidly through the crowd, one hand firmly wrapped around my bag holding the precious bread loaves. Aunt Clare and I hadn't eaten since yesterday, and I had a hollow feeling in my stomach.

Ten minutes later, I turned down between two buildings and into a side door that led down to the subway system.

Ten minutes after that, and I was walking down a nearly dark subway tunnel beside tracks that had been abandoned before I was born.

I trotted faster, then ducked into an alcove, lifted a heavy metal grate, and slipped into our home.

The spot was barely seven feet square. It was lined with discarded coats, blankets from the shelters and giveaways, and a small, flea-infested old mattress Aunt Clare and I had dragged in five years ago.

"I'm back," I whispered, setting the candles I had swiped on the crate that served as a table. A button lamp sat there, flickering fitfully.

Aunt Clare had made it last month.

"Let me show you how to make a button lamp," she'd said. "My parents had these when I was a child."

She'd taken a small metal disk that we'd used to burn candles in, it had wax at the bottom, and she'd put a small tear of fabric from her shirt, threaded it through a large plastic button from an old coat long since lost, and stuck it in the wax.

Then she'd lit it.

It didn't give much light, but it lasted forever and stubbornly refused to go out.

"It will stay. It will stay for a long, long time," she'd said.

Aunt Clare was asleep on the bed, wrapped in an old tattered blanket.

I leaned over to her face and kissed her cheek.

Her eyes opened, fluttering softly in the dim light.

I pressed one of the loaves of bread into her hands, and she sat up and began to eat.

I sat facing her in my own little nest My back against the wall, and my knees drawn up to my chest, I began to nibble on my own loaf of bread.

She was all I had.

"Aunt Clare?" I whispered, rubbing her arm. "How are you feeling today?"

"Ohh," she yawned. "I think I'm feeling better, child." She took a bite out of the small loaf of bread. "Mmmm, this is delicious!"

The bread loaves were about ten inches long and crusty on the outside, baked to a golden brown. The inside was soft and fluffy, just the way Aunt Clare liked it.

I smiled.

"Mmmm, it *is* good, isn't it?" I crunched the bread with relish.

We ate in silence for a few minutes.

Our little corner of the world was small and dirty, and the walls were stained with old water runoff, and no matter how much I tried, I could never keep all the insects out, but one thing that set it apart from the other cubbies underground in this old subway tunnel was that it was warm.

A few years back, we'd had a woman who befriended us, and shared her food with us. She'd been homeless a few years and had learned the ropes from others in the city.

She'd been nice and asked to sleep in our cubby in exchange for sharing the food she stole, and we let her.

That had been a mistake.

After two months of this situation, she'd pulled a knife on us and forced us out of our cubby. "Yours is the only one that's not freezing!" she'd screamed.

It was true that the underground could be brutally cold during winter. But she was right: ours was the only cubby not freezing.

In fact, it was warm enough so I could take off my coat.

So, we'd grabbed our stuff and fled, while she'd brandished the knife at us and glowered.

We'd spent a day looking for a new space to sleep in, and finally found one, about a half mile down the tunnel.

It was another warm cubby.

I wasn't sure I understood what was going on, but Aunt Clare and I had spent the evening talking in whispers about it.

"Holly, sweet baby girl, you're the reason why the cubby was warm," Aunt Clare had hugged me and whispered, then put a finger to her lips. "No one can know."

No one can know.

I never understood this thing I did, but I did realize that it was because of me. When I left the cubby for a long time, the temperature slowly dropped until it was freezing.

Once, I had been gone for two days, because I got caught in a bad deal with several people chasing me and the coppers were around, and I just ran. I ran and ran and ran, then found an old coal chute I could hide in. I had some food in my bag since it'd been the end of my hunting-for-food day, so I was fine. Even though there'd been snow on the ground outside, I was able to huddle in the three-foot space and wait it out.

It had grown warm while I crouched there, and I'd decided to stay.

But when I finally emerged and was able to make my way back to Aunt Clare in the cubby, I'd found her shivering and the cubby had been freezing.

When I entered it, she'd been so happy to see me, and had hugged me for a long time.

"You're so warm," she'd said through her chattering teeth.

I thought about all these things as I ate the bread, chewing slowly, savoring every bite.

I glanced around our little cubby. It was our world. It was home. I always felt better when I was back home after a day of foraging for food in the city.

Food.

It was a constant worry. I usually went to the park or the fountain and watched people eat their lunch, waiting for one of them who glanced at their watch, realized they were late, and tossed the last half of their sandwich or meatpie into the trash. I was there like a flash, picking it back out and running off as I stuffed it into my bag.

Sometimes no one threw out half-eaten food, and I had to go hunting for something to eat. Then I'd walk down the streets and look for stores that had food out front, displayed to entice shoppers to enter and buy.

I could often get away with grabbing an apple or orange, a banana or a pecan pie, or a small loaf of bread without being seen.

But sometimes they saw me. That's when I ran.

They'd never caught me, not once. It was a point of pride.

A far-off noise rattled outside in the tunnel and brought me back to the present.

I finished the last bite of bread and began picking the crumbs off my coat and licking them off my fingers.

Chapter Two
Oral History

"Aunt Clare? Can you tell me the story of my mama again?" I whispered.

"Oh, my dear," she smiled. "You love that story, don't you?"

I nodded eagerly.

"Well, now. Let's see if I remember it." She thought for a minute, her finger tapping on her lips.

"Well, you know that your mama and I were best friends. I met her a week after she'd started on the streets. Her belly was just starting to grow, and that was you inside there." Aunt Clare smiled.

"Your mama was the prettiest thing anyone had ever seen. She had red hair — that was from her Irish side — and light green eyes that could dance with merriment. And she always had a wonderful disposition. I think that's why we became such good friends."

"We looked out for one another, too. It's always easier when there's two, you know that."

I nodded.

"Well, let's see. Your mama, Noelle, was just nineteen when I met her in a shelter. It was early fall, and the leaves were just starting to turn in the park. We became friends, mostly because we were so close in age, and had bunks near each other. And she told me her story."

"The Christmas before she'd gone on a vacation to Ireland, it was a graduation present from her grandmother, and they went together on this trip, along with some friends. Noelle had just finished high school, graduating with good grades, and was to start at the university that fall."

"Which university?" I asked, even though I already knew. I loved to hear the words from Aunt Clare.

"NYU, dear. She was to major in performing arts. She was a ballet dancer," Aunt Clare said.

I shivered in delight. I liked to dance, too.

"So, Noelle was in Ireland. She said she found it enchanting. She and her grandmother and friends had spent a few days in England and had visited Stonehenge, and Noelle had been enchanted. She had loved it. And then they had flown to Ireland where they were to spend a week. They visited many beautiful places and had had a wonderful time."

"And one day, when her grandmother had been feeling ill, because she didn't travel well and had come down with a cold, Noelle had left her in the cottage where they were staying and had gone for a walk in a nearby forest. It was a rural village, you see, surrounded by woods. Noelle had been on her walk when she'd come across a faerie ring."

"A faerie ring is a ring of mushrooms growing in a circle, right?" I said, knowing the story by heart.

"Yes, that's right. Noelle described the mushroom ring as being under the canopy of the forest, in a shaded glade, and in a circle of about ten feet. So it was pretty big. She said there was all sizes and kinds of mushrooms, from large brown flat ones, to smaller tall, white ones. Noelle said they were beautiful."

I listened raptly. I loved this story.

"Noelle said the sunlight coming through the trees was dappled and made everything look so enticing that she decided to sit down inside the mushroom circle. So she did. Well, the minute she sat down in that faerie ring, she felt so happy she couldn't describe it. Just the happiest she'd ever been."

"I wish I could see the faerie ring," I whispered.

"So do I. It sounds wonderful, doesn't it?" Aunt Clare said, smiling.

I nodded.

"So Noelle was sitting in the faerie ring, and she decided to lie back and look up through the trees. One thing about Ireland, my sweet child, the trees grow very tall and very full, and there are so many leaves! And the sight that met Noelle's eyes was so beautiful that she fell asleep in the faerie ring."

My jaw dropped open, thinking how wonderful it would be to fall asleep in a forest mushroom ring.

"Noelle said she had dreamed about a man, a man with ram horns and pale green skin, and red berries in his hair. She dreamed he came to her in the faerie ring and sat down next to her."

Aunt Clare paused then.

"And then she kissed him!" I supplied, clapping my hands.

Aunt Clare smiled. "Yes, in Noelle's dream, she kissed the man in the forest. She said it was the most wonderful thing in the world, and that he smelled of juniper berries and sunshine and that he treated her with a tenderness she had never experienced before. Noelle said it was a magical dream, and she wished the dream had lasted forever. But dreams never last forever, and we always wake up."

"And when Noelle woke up, it was nearly dawn. She had stayed in the faerie ring all night and she realized she had to get back to the hostel and check on her grandmother and friends. So she gathered up her things and ran back. When she returned, her grandmother was feeling better so they all went to eat, and then they continued the rest of their vacation in Ireland. And then they flew home."

I held my breath.

"And then, just a few months later, Noelle noticed her period had stopped. She told me she'd thought the first missed month had been a fluke, but the second time it happened, she went out and bought a pregnancy test and took it at home. And it was positive."

"She was frightened because her parents were extremely strict. They had only allowed her to go on her Irish vacation because her grandmother had insisted. But she knew they would become extremely mad when they found out she was expecting a baby. You see, Noelle was adopted, and therefore they expected more from her. "

"Noelle tried to hide her pregnancy while she prepared to start NYU in the fall. But she was very skinny, just like you, Holly. She wore loose-fitting clothes that summer, and she almost made it to the university without her parents finding out. But one morning, a week before she was about to leave, her mother walked in on her getting dressed, and saw her belly."

"Well, there was a huge fight. The neighbors even called the police, because of the yelling. Her grandmother tried to intervene, but Noelle's father was loud and rough, and he threw her out. She had just enough time to pack a small backpack with a change of clothes before her mother hustled her into the car and drove her to the bus station."

"Noelle was frightened. Her mother bought her a ticket to the city, told her to go to a homeless shelter, and left. And that was it. Noelle was alone. She took the bus, and it was an all-night ride from Buffalo to New York City. Noelle said she cried all the way. When she arrived at the bus station in the middle of the city, she asked directions to the nearest homeless shelter and walked there. It took her hours, she said. But she made it, and we met there, and became best friends."

"Aunt Clare, why did Mama's parents kick her out? Didn't they love her?" I asked.

"They probably did, in their own way, child. But sometimes people put pride and appearances before family, and that's a shame. Because Noelle suffered, you see. She was small and skinny, and that winter, while she was in the homeless shelter, she caught a cough. And then you were born. And two days later Noelle was gone."

I felt tears gather in my eyes. My heart constricted with loss.

I sniffled. Aunt Clare bent forward and gave me a hug.

"I know, Holly, I know." She sat back again. "But what you must realize is that your mother loved you, more than anything else in the world. She loved you and she fought to get better and live, so you'd be together. I was with her in the shelter, I stayed beside her the whole two weeks after she had you. In the end, she was too weak, she just couldn't hold on any longer."

"And you adopted me," I said, wiping my eyes.

Aunt Clare took a deep breath. "Yes, after a fashion. We had told the shelter workers and counselors that we were sisters. And I had been taking care of you since almost the beginning. So they knew I was your aunt. I think they were relieved. It was the end of fall, winter was coming and with it the snow and ice, and the overcrowding at the shelters."

"The shelters," I spat. Aunt Clare and I did not like the shelters. They didn't let you keep your stuff. They were dirty and overcrowded, they always asked questions and they turned people over to the coppers just because they were hungry and had gone foraging.

"The shelters," said Aunt Clare, "Are good for some people, but not for us. I stayed in the shelter for almost a year after your poor mama died. I finally had to leave."

"They were mean to you!" I said.

"Well, mostly because it's hard to be in a shelter. They toss you out in the early morning, and don't let you back in until night, and they don't let you have anything. We lost a lot to the shelters. We lost your mama's stuff, and my stuff, and it was bad," Aunt Clare said.

"But then you met Bobby!" I said.

"And then I met Bobby. My goodness child, you know this story by heart, don't you?"

"I still want you to tell it."

"Okay, I will tell it." Aunt Clare thought for a moment. "Bobby. Yes, Bobby. Bobby was an old man I met when I was in the park after foraging. I had you strapped to my back; you were such a little thing. And quiet! My goodness, you were so quiet. Well, Bobby saw me on a bench, and you were on my back. I had you covered, to keep eyes from prying."

"Bobby told me about the subway lines that were abandoned. He said there was places, places the people had found. Places to find that were okay. That I could stay in and shelter in. Bobby led me down there, into the subway, past the throngs, and down the line, and showed the way to get past the metal door, and through the tunnel they didn't use anymore. And he showed me the cubbies. And I picked one out, and we've been down here ever since," she grinned.

"I like it down here. No one can find us. The coppers don't come down here," I said.

"I don't think they want to come down here, to tell you the truth," Aunt Clare said.

"And we don't want 'em down here, no way, no how," I said.

"No, we don't want them down here," said Aunt Clare. "We want to be left in peace. And that's all anyone ever wants, to be left in peace. To live our life the way we see fit, to forage..."

"To forage!" I said, my voice growing louder.

"To be silent, so we stay safe," Aunt Clare whispered.

I nodded solemnly. I had forgotten.

"To forage and be silent," I whispered.

"To stay hidden is to stay safe," Aunt Clare patted my hand.

"Safe," I repeated.

My eyes closed, and I lay down on the blanket, and held my bag close. I fell asleep to the sound of Aunt Clare's wheezing.

Chapter Three
Alone

I woke up to the sound of Aunt Clare's coughing.

"You're getting sick again, Aunt Clare," I said, sitting up and rubbing my eyes.

"Maybe, child," Aunt Clare coughed again.

The candle had almost gone out, and I grabbed another one to light from the first.

"Oh, my," Aunt Clare said as soon as the new candle caught, flaring into life in the small cubby.

I glanced over.

"Oh!" I exclaimed.

The rag Aunt Clare had been using to cough into was spotted with bright red blood.

"We need to get you to the clinic!" I said softly.

"No, no, I won't go. They'll just poke and prod me again, and I don't need that trouble," she said.

I looked at her, worried.

Another hour passed. I heated some water over the candle flame and added an old, used teabag, and gave it to her to drink. I had to hold her hand steady while she sipped at the chipped cup, but finally she drank it and lay back down on the mattress.

"I'm going to go forage. Will you be okay?" I whispered, worriedly.

Aunt Clare waved her hand at me. "I'll be fine, child. I always get better after you make me tea," she smiled weakly. "I hope you get more bread this time, that was delicious."

I hugged her, then left to go.

The streets were cold. I ran through the park and down to the docks to see if anything interesting was going on there.

Then I made my way to the street with all the markets, and was able to gather an apple and a loaf of bread, and a real treat: a brownie out of the trash, with only one bite taken out of it.

Pleased, I made my way back underground.

The subway was loud and crowded, and as I slipped under the bar and started around the corner, a copper grabbed me.

Panic!

I tried to run, but he held on. He hadn't grabbed much else but the shoulder of my coat, and I immediately dropped to the ground and rolled a few feet, shimmying myself out of the coat and down onto the track depression.

"Hey!" he called out, blowing his whistle.

But I was already gone.

I ran down the tracks and away from the station, hopped back up onto the walkway about a hundred yards down, and slipped through a fence.

Tears formed in my eyes as I crouched behind a wall. The copper had grabbed my coat, and winter was coming. But worse of all, when I'd shimmied out of my coat to get free, I'd had to let the bag of food go, too. It had been hanging off my coat on the other shoulder he hadn't grabbed, and it had dropped onto the railway depression when I'd slipped away.

Now I had no food. After foraging for the whole day.

I crouched and allowed myself to cry. I was silent, and the bitter tears that ran hot down my face made no noise at all.

I decided to wait and try to go back when night fell. Maybe the bag was still there.

I walked down the tracks for several hours, unwilling to go back to the cubby empty-handed. Aunt Clare needed food, and would be crestfallen if she had to go hungry again, like that time last month when I was robbed.

Four boys had caught me in an alley and had teased me, and taken my bag off my shoulder. They'd laughed when they saw there was just a few bananas inside and no money, and had thrown the fruit as hard as they could, up over the rooftops.

The bananas had been lost.

They'd thrown my bag back to me, and called me 'Little Orphan Annie', whatever that meant.

I'd gone back home empty-handed that night, and both me and Aunt Clare had fallen asleep with growling stomachs.

This time would be different, I hoped.

I walked a long way, then turned around and headed back. I thought enough time had passed, but when I crept back and peeked around the corner, some people were still standing on the subway platform.

So I backed out of sight, and sat waiting on the side walkway another hour. I even curled up and dozed off at one point. Then I woke up, the passing train making a huge sound right in my face.

More than an hour might have passed.

I rubbed my eyes and peeked back around the corner. The coast was clear. The platform was empty. Everything was still.

It seemed like it was very late.

I crept back to where I thought I had fallen, and there it was: my bag of food!

It had gotten blown to the side of the depression, and hadn't been run over by the tracks, thank goodness. I grabbed it and turned and ran.

"Aunt Clare? I'm back," I whispered, lifting the edge of the metal grate and slipping inside the cubby.

Aunt Clare was asleep on the bed, and the candle had gone out.

"Why did you let it go out, Aunt Clare?" I fumbled in the dark for one of the precious matches we kept in a crack. "There's only three more left," I mumbled, feeling cross.

Matches were hard to come by. Candles were easier to find, though I wasn't sure why.

I struck the match and held it to the next candle and the wick flamed to life, filling the small cubby with light.

"I got some bread and an apple, Aunt Clare," I said, digging in my bag for the food.

I put it all on the blanket by the mattress and then put my hand on her shoulder, shaking it to wake her.

She wouldn't wake up.

Something was wrong.

I carefully brought the candle over to her. The blanket was covering her face, and I had to lift it.

I gasped.

Aunt Clare's eyes were closed, and there was blood on her mouth. Her hand clutched the rag she used to cough into, and I saw there was a lot of fresh blood on it. I looked back into Aunt Clare's face, and touched her cheek.

It was cold.

"Aunt Clare?" I whispered. "Wake up, Aunt Clare!"

I set the candle down and turned her on her back, and listened to her chest. I couldn't hear anything, though I listened for a heartbeat for a long time.

Finally, I sat back, stricken.

I just stared at her form, lying on the mattress.

She looked like she was sleeping.

"Aunt Clare," I whispered, reaching out to touch her hand.

I didn't want her to leave me.

I didn't want to leave her.

I stared at her a long time, until my stomach rumbled loudly.

"Here," I said softly, putting the bread on the blanket covering her form.

I sat and slowly ate the apple, and watched her, waiting, hoping she would wake up.

Finally, I curled up, and closed my eyes and fell asleep.

I slept for a long time, and I had no dreams that night, although I normally dreamed every night.

"Dreams are your imagination making up stories for you to hope for," Aunt Clare had said. I could almost hear her voice.

I opened my eyes, thinking I *had* heard it. "Aunt Clare, oh, my goodness, I had the worst dream," I said, sitting up.

The candle was barely lit, it was down to just a stub.

I looked over at Aunt Clare.

She hadn't moved at all.

The bread was still on her; it hadn't moved or fallen off.

I stared at her face for a long time, and the tears finally came, running copiously down my cheeks and making my shirt all wet.

Snot ran down my lip and I did nothing to stop it.

Aunt Clare...

I cried for a long time, the apple, half eaten and forgotten, in my hand, which had dropped to my side.

Finally, I lapsed into silence, my gaze unfocused and a thousand miles away.

My chest felt tight, and I found it hard to breathe.

It was still as death in the cubby, and I realized: *I have no one.*

I am all alone now.

I felt a twinge of fear in my chest.

I glanced up at Aunt Clare's body and felt mesmerized as the reality of the situation dawned on me.

I cannot move her; she is too heavy.

Well, maybe I could try.

I got to my feet and cleared the blankets away from her. I carefully set the bread aside, it would be madness to waste food. Then I stood back and considered the situation.

It was a long way to the tunnels still in use. But I knew of a place I could put her, where she would remain undisturbed, possibly forever.

I lifted her and moved her blanket underneath her. She had always loved this blanket, though the once-vibrant colors had dulled to a mottled brown and grey.

I thought for a moment and then took the apple, and with a dull knife Aunt Clare had kept in her bag, careful carved two perfect slices.

They were beautiful, and Aunt Clare would have loved to eat them. She always loved to eat slices of apple.

Food was the most valuable thing we had, food and each other.

We had no money, no coins. Carving the apple slices was like carving coins out of the apple.

I placed the two perfect apple slices over her eyes and stood back, surveying my work.

It will have to do.

I then carefully wrapped her in the blanket and then fished around in her bag for the old needle and thread she kept there, for fast repairs. I had no idea where she'd gotten hold of sewing supplies, but she'd always had them, for as long as I could remember.

The needle was dull, but would still do. I unwound the thread, a strong corded black thread made for sewing on buttons. It would do.

I carefully sewed the blanket, taking great care to keep my stitches small, as she had taught me.

Tears fell from my eyes onto the old, rough material as I worked. Aunt Clare had taught me everything I knew. Everything. From how to read and write and sew, to how to avoid the coppers, how to run the fastest, and how to jump a fence without tripping up.

Finally, I was done.

I propped open the metal grate, turned and grasped Aunt Clare by the feet, and, backing out, managed to slowly pull her out onto the walkway that ran along the deserted subway line.

It was backbreaking work.

I turned to look and get my bearings.

The tunnel was deserted, most of the people who lived here were asleep or off foraging or something.

I didn't know and I didn't care.

My mind was on the task at hand.

I turned and began pulling her farther down the walkway, away from the civilized world, and deeper into the underground. It was hard work, but the blanket made it easier: It slid down the old cement smoothly, and didn't catch on anything.

At one point, there was a dip in the cement and as I pulled her, I saw her head, wrapped in the blanket, drop with an audible 'thunk'. *Without thinking, I apologized.*

"I'm sorry, Aunt Clare."

I stopped short of asking if it had hurt her head.

Nothing can hurt her anymore.

The tears fell anew as I realized she had been sick for a while. She would always say it was nothing, that she would be just fine in the morning, but I realized she had known.

I'd offered to take her to the clinic many times in the last month, but she'd always insisted they would *'do more harm than good'* and that she *'just needed to rest'.*

Her cough had gotten worse in the last few weeks, and she'd been coughing up blood more and more.

She knew she was dying.

I sobbed and straightened, and wiped my nose on my arm. After a minute, I bent and continued my task.

It took several hours.

I finally got to my destination: an old coal bunker, still coated in black soot. I opened the hatch and crawled in, pulling Aunt Clare in after me.

It was a small compartment, not much more than five feet square. But it was sealed. The steel sides had no cracks, no chinks, nowhere for the coal bits to fall through.

Aunt Clare and I had always said if there was any disaster, we'd hide in there. Even water couldn't get in.

I pulled her all the way in and to the back, settling her against the side of the wall while I dug in the coal.

I had to move a lot of heavy pieces, some of them quite large, but finally I cleared the space against the back wall. I moved her carefully into place, and hugged her one last time.

I knelt there, my candle flickering, and lost myself in thoughts of what a wonderful aunt she had been to me.

Then I bent over and kissed her head through the blanket, and began to pile the coal on top of her.

When I was finally done, the pile of coal looked the same as it had before, maybe just a bit taller.

Aunt Clare had been a tiny woman, and thin as a rail.

I backed out of the coal bunker, and carefully wedged the hatch shut, leaning all my weight on it and making it screech one last inch, so I knew it was tight.

No one would come here and disturb her.

She would be able to rest here for always, in peace and quiet.

Just how she always preferred.

I trudged back the way I'd come, my shoulders down and my head tired. My eyes had a dull feel to them, and I felt ancient.

Burying the dead is the last kindness we can do for them. The last act of love.

Chapter Four
Chance

The next day found me in a terrible gloominess, mixed with real fear.

What am I going to do without her?

I had no idea.

That morning, I had gathered most of my stuff, which was to say, two extra shirts and one extra pair of pants. I still hadn't found a new pair of shoes, although the old tennis shoes I wore were getting tight. I stuffed the clothes, my thin blanket, the last candle, the matches, and the knife in my bag, threw it over my shoulder, and started walking.

I knew good places to sleep were hard to come by, but I did not want to stay in our old cubby. It was full of old ghosts, old memories which made me so sad that I had a hard time sleeping last night.

I didn't want to repeat that over and over.

So off I went.

I walked out of the old, abandoned tunnels, down the track depression, up onto the walkway, and into the subway central.

No one paid me much attention, I was covered in grime from the coal bunker.

Even though I had lost my coat, the coal dust had coated my platinum hair until it looked the color of grey flotsam. My shirt and pants were dun colored.

I kept my eyes downcast, and walked in a plodding manner that invited no conversation.

No one bothered me.

Sometimes it was good to be small and grey and plain.

I walked for a long time. Hours, it seemed.

I reached an old loading dock near the wharf, behind all the fancy stores, where street folk gathered around 55-gallon drum fires, to talk and socialize.

I trudged up to the nearest fire and held out my hands, warming them.

"Holly, isn't it?" an old man on the other side of the metal drum asked.

I nodded.

"You're with Clare, aren't you?"

I said nothing, made no movement. I felt miserable and numb at the same time.

"How is Clare doing these days?"

I shook my head, and a fresh course of tears ran down my face.

"Hello? You okay?"

I finally raised my face to look at him.

He saw my tears and put two and two together and sighed heavily.

"Oh, man. Ohhhh, no. I am so sorry. God."

We both stood there for a several minutes in silence.

Then another person walked up to share the fire, and he had a paper bag bottle.

"Hey man, want some?" He asked, himself halfway drunk.

The homeless shared so much.

The first man took the bottle and drew a healthy swig from it.

"Yeah, that's not bad. Whiskey, isn't it?"

"Whiskey! Makes the world go 'round."

"Thanks. I just heard an old friend is no longer with us, and I'd like to toast her."

"Awww man, that's too bad about your friend."

"Holly? Want a taste?"

I shook my head, and moved off to another fire.

I left the two old men drinking and sharing and laughing, reminiscing about lost friends.

My stomach grumbled loudly.

"Sister, you okay?" A pair of old women were huddled by the new fire, and one of them was looking at me kindly.

I shrugged.

"Oh, she's crying. Honey, why're you crying? What happened?"

"Shush Donna, leave her to her tears, don't bother the grieving."

"The grieving?"

"Yeah, Batt and Tod over there said Clare died."

"Oh, man, that's tough."

"I think this girl was with Clare. I've seen them together before."

"Is that so? Honey, were you and Clare traveling together?"

I nodded, feeling miserable.

My stomach growled again.

"Oh, listen to that. She's hungry."

"You hungry, Honey?"

I ignored them.

"Got anything to eat, Donna?"

"No, no. I had a half a sandwich yesterday, but it's gone now."

"Ah, pity that. Honey maybe you can go to the soup kitchen over on 6th Avenue?"

"That's St. Joe's. They've got good soup, and if you get there early, they usually have bread to go with it."

"Honey, want us to walk you over there in the morning?"

I turned and walked away from the fire and the two women. I wanted to be alone.

As I left, I could still hear them: "Donna, I have a wad of chewing tobacco. Just a small one left but do you think she'd want it?"

"No, Donna, she's just a kid."

"Well, I started when I was ten. You never know."

I walked over to the water and looked into the black depths. The sun had set, and the moonlight reflected off the small waves made by multiple ships and boats.

I could hear the water lapping against the dock.

I turned and walked over to the wall fronting one of the loading docks, and sat down, my back against the cement.

Knees up, my hands on either side of me, I bowed my head. I had no idea what to do, and I was rapidly feeling like I didn't care.

I felt dull and lost, and my head felt utterly empty of thought.

I held my bag under my legs, and cradled my knees in my arms, and fell asleep.

My eyes opened the next morning to the beeping sound of a truck backing up.

The fires were gone, the oil drums pulled off to the side, and everyone had left.

A semi-truck was backing up near me.

Several men on the loading bays were waving the truck back, back, back, helping it to back up onto the ledge so they could unload it.

I got to my feet, grabbed my bag and walked.

Taking deep breaths and waving my arms back and forth to wake up, I decided to walk to the fountain and wash.

It was very early. The sun had just come up maybe a half hour ago. I could still see the moon in the darker western sky.

It took me an hour to walk to the fountain. A couple of street folk were already there, washing their hands and face.

I bent and began washing.

Aunt Clare had always told me not to get any of the water from the fountains in my mouth.

"It'll make you sick, Sweetheart," she'd cautioned.

I remembered every single thing she'd taught me.

Boy, I'm filthy.

I washed my face and hands, and tried to wash my hair out a bit, but not too much. The coal dust camouflaged the color well, and I still didn't want to draw attention to myself.

After a half hour of splashing, and getting myself soaking wet, I decided it wasn't going to get any better than this.

I stood up, my bag slung over my shoulder.

My stomach was so empty it felt hollow.

I still felt tired and sad, and in no fit state to do any running, so I found a piece of cardboard in a dumpster, and a discarded crayon in the grass, and made a sign.

"Hungry. Please help."

I decided to try begging. Aunt Clare had taught me, although she did not recommend it. A lot of people would rob you if they knew you carried cash, and that's what begging brought.

I'll just get enough for some breakfast, then I'll stop.

I went to sit under a tree near the fountain. The plaza was a crossroads; a lot of people passed by on their way to do important things.

I sat, my sign propped up, and waited.

After an hour, people started to fill the plaza, most of them walking rapidly toward their destination. Not many stopped. I was still mostly invisible.

But a few stopped and tossed coins at me.

I forgot to get something to hold the coins.

I grabbed the loose change tossed my way, sticking it under my leg until I could count it.

Then one man tossed me a dollar.

It fluttered down, and landed a few feet away.

I leaned over and reached for it, and another man, who had been begging about thirty feet away, knocked me in the head, grabbed the dollar, and ran off.

I fell over, my head ringing from the blow.

I saw stars.

I sat there, holding my head, for a while.

My sign lay face-down and forgotten a few feet away, no one able to read it.

I sat there a long time, holding my head.

"Hey, are you okay?"

I looked up.

It was a boy, a few years older than me, bent over, looking concerned.

I took a deep breath and looked at him.

He had green eyes, messy brown hair, and ...

Did I see this correctly?

... pointed ears??

I closed my eyes.

I must've got hit harder than I thought. This is the last time I go begging. From now on, I'm stealing my food.

I looked up again. He was offering a hand to help me to my feet. And his ears were not pointed, they looked like normal ears.

Now.

I frowned internally.

I reached out and took his offered hand, and slowly got to my feet.

"Here. I think this is yours," he said, handing me my bag and a handful of change.

"Oh, thanks." I took the coins and dropped them into the bag.

"Is your head okay?" he asked.

"Huh?"

"I saw the guy club your ear and take the dollar," he said.

"Oh, yeah, that." I looked around for the guy who'd hit me, but he'd left.

"He's gone. I saw him run off. I think he realized it was best not to stay at the scene of the crime."

"The crime?" I asked, still feeling fuzzy-headed.

"Yeah, it's against the law to hit someone in the head, you know. I think the charge is assault."

"Oh, yeah, I think it is." I looked up at him. He was about a foot taller than me.

I was short for thirteen.

He looked tall, and maybe about fifteen. His brown bangs hung over his eyes, and he kept jerking his head to the side to swing the hair out of his eyes.

He was looking down at me with an easy grin on his face.

"I'm sorry. Um, thank you for helping me," I said.

"My pleasure," he stuck out his hand. "My name's Chance. Pleased to meet you."

I slowly took his hand. "Holly."

"Holly, would you like some breakfast? I was just about to get a roll and a latte over at the cafe. I'm on my way to school, and I forgot to eat at home."

My stomach grumbled again.

I looked up at him sharply.

He was still grinning, but pretending he didn't hear my stomach growl.

"Umm, I guess so. Thanks." I grinned back at him. I was trying to blend in.

"Awesome," he shouldered his backpack, which I had not seen until now. It was blue and gold. He jerked his head. "Come on," he said, and started walking.

I fell into step next to him, happy to have made a friend.

Chapter Five
The Letter

"So Holly, pick out what you want. I'm getting a bagel and some hot cocoa."

I looked over what the coffee shop offered. I had never tried a bagel before.

"Those look good. I'll have one, too."

He nodded and ordered, and we made our way to an open table.

My bagel was rainbow colored. Pink, purple, blue, green and yellow stripes wound their way in curving lines around it. Chance had gotten them toasted and split open, and we spread pink cream cheese over the open halves.

"It tastes like strawberries!" I said, chewing the bite of bagel slowly, to savor it.

"Yeah, that's strawberry cream cheese. Isn't it great?"

I nodded.

"They also have blueberry, lemon, and plain. Oh, here, I almost forgot." He handed me a cup of hot cocoa.

This was also something I'd never tried before.

"Be careful, it's hot," he cautioned.

I took a sip. The most wonderful taste in creation slowly spread through my mouth. I closed my eyes in ecstasy.

Could this morning get any weirder?

Apparently, it could.

"So, Holly, how do you like your bagel?" Chance asked.

"It's wonderful. I love it!" I said around mouthfuls. I took another sip of hot cocoa.

"Listen, remember how I said I was on my way to school?"

I nodded.

"Well, it's kind of a fib, but not really a fib. Call it a white lie, in a roundabout way."

I stared at him. What was he talking about?

"I came to find you, Holly."

A river of fear began to wind its way down my back. Aunt Clare had warned me against getting trapped, getting picked up by the coppers or the counselors, or any number of people who wanted to snatch you.

They wanted to snatch you badly.

I realized I'd been staring at him without blinking when my eyes started to burn.

He put his hands up, palms facing me. "Hey, whoa, don't look at me like that. I'm not going to force you to do anything, I swear. And I'm not with any authorities or anything. I'm from the school."

Huh?

"Whatdyamean?" I choked and took a sip of hot cocoa, then swallowed my bite, cleared my throat, and tried again: "What do you mean?"

Chance smiled.

"I am from the school I attend. I'm in my second year. It's an eight-year school so I've got a long ways to go. I'm one of the youngest recruiters they've got on staff. And it's not really a proper job. They give me free lunches and extra school work credit for doing this."

"So ... you're a recruiter for your school?" I asked.

He nodded.

"And why did you come talk to me? I'm barely thirteen. I've never really gone to school before, er ... I mean, I've been homeschooled my whole life." I remembered Aunt Clare and her lessons, and felt tears spring up in my eyes.

"Here," Chance handed me a napkin.

Had he seen my tears?

I wiped my eyes.

"No, um, you've got cocoa dripping out the corner of your mouth. Just there." He pointed at my cheek.

"Oh." I dabbed at my mouth and was rewarded with a smear of brown, along with a healthy bit of black coal dust.

Guess I didn't get it all.

"So, back to the school. I've got a list of people I'm supposed to talk to, and," he pulled a piece of paper out of his pocket. "Your name is second from the top, see?" He showed me the list.

Sure enough, there it was: Holly Ó Cuilinn.

"Huh," I said softly, looking down at the paper. I hadn't known my own last name.

"Well, but why, um ... why am I on the list? There's only, like, fifteen names on the list total," I asked.

"That's a very good question, and I'm going to answer it. Our school only accepts very special students? The kids who go there have to be of a certain type of ... of ... "

I stared at him, waiting.

He cleared his throat and tried again.

"The school is, um, a boarding school, that um, well." He looked at me and took a deep breath. "Our boarding school includes a room you live in, with a bed and a frig and a TV. And all your meals are supplied."

This made me sit up straighter.

Free food? Free bed? Free room?

There's got to be a mistake.

Aunt Clare had taught me nothing came free. That you either had to have money or you had to steal it.

I thought for a minute.

But here I was eating food and drinking hot cocoa, and Chance had bought it. This was free!

But he had paid for it. It wasn't free at all.

I looked around. People were eating food and drinking out of coffee cups.

I looked over toward the counter. People were ordering and handing over dollar bills and coins, and in some cases, a little plastic card, that got handed back to them after a minute.

This food wasn't free. Chance had bought it for me. He had paid for it, then given it to me.

"Chance, who pays for the school? The rooms and beds and food?" I asked.

"Different people. Parents mostly," he said.

"But I don't have any parents, not anymore. My mother died when I was born, and just yesterday my Aunt Clare died. I've got no one."

Chance took a deep breath.

"There are special scholarships set up at the school. Money in accounts to pay for some students, so they don't have to pay. That's what the list is for. That's what the school is offering you, Holly. A scholarship."

A scholarship?

I thought for a minute.

"What do I have to do in return?" I asked slowly.

There had to be a catch. Someone always has to pay.

"All the school is asking you to do it come, try it out, try to learn what they're teaching. Make some new friends. That's it." Chance looked at me, a smile on his face.

" 'Try to learn what they're teaching'?" I asked.

He nodded.

"What do they teach in this school?"

Chance took a drink of hot cocoa, lifting the cup high, draining it completely. He set it down and smacked his lips. "Boy, those are good. I will never get tired of hot cocoa." He looked at me. "You know I hardly ever get it? "

I grinned and took another sip out of my half-full cup. "This is the first hot cocoa I've ever tasted, and I think I'd like to drink nothing else, from now on. Forever."

Chance threw his head back and laughed.

"Okay, okay, you asked what they teach at the school. Well, they teach things like lessons on history, on plants, on chemistry, on physics, on all sorts of things. And the classes are fun!" He grinned.

"And the food is free?" I asked.

"All you can eat!"

"ALL YOU CAN EAT?! I can eat a lot, you know. Sometimes, I'm so hungry I wish I could eat all day and all night!"

"Holly, I know things have been hard, and I know you've been hungry a lot. I've been over your file. I know all about you and what your life has been like. And I'm here to tell you those days of scrambling for your existence are over. If you want them to be."

I took a deep breath. It sounded too good to be true.

"Chance, what's the catch? You're saying this school wants me to have lessons, food, a bed, a room of my own, all of that, all paid for by some scholarship I never knew existed. What's the catch?"

"You're suspicious. I get it. But Holly, there's no catch. I swear. No one's going to force you to do anything you don't want to do." His eyebrows rose in a plea.

"You want me to come with you, don't you? You want me to go to the school?"

"Well, yes. I do."

"Why?"

"Why? Because I get credit for bringing in another lost aos sí, um, I mean, another lost child of the Faefolk. Because I get a work credit for bringing you in."

"For bringing me in? You make me sound like I'm wanted by the coppers."

"No, it's not like that. Holly, the school is only for certain people, people that have a certain ancestry, people with certain gifts." Chance looked around. "Look, have you ever read those books about the boy wizard? The one that goes to the school of magic?"

I thought for a minute. "I haven't read the books, but I saw a newspaper talking about the movie. I haven't been living under a rock, you know. The picture showed a boy with glasses and a lightning scar on his forehead."

"That's the one," said Chance. "You know how that school he goes to, only certain kids can go, right? Only

49

witches and wizards can go to that magical school. And he didn't even know he was a wizard, until he got his letter asking him to go to the school, right?"

I nodded.

"This is exactly like that." Chance sat back, folding his arms together in front of his chest, a satisfied look on his face.

I shook my head. "Not so fast. There's no such thing as magical witches and wizards. That's all made up, out of that book that lady wrote."

"Very true, Holly. There's no such thing as witches and wizards, and no such place as a magical wizard school. But!" he held his finger up. "It's the same kind of thing. We're saying you're a certain kind of person, and this school we run is only for those certain kinds of people. People like you." He spread his fingers wide. "Not just anyone can attend, you know."

He looked around the coffee shop. Some people were sitting and drinking from coffee cups and eating bagels and croissants and other things, and they were wearing school uniforms. They were clearly students.

"Do any of them go to your school?" I asked.

"Oh, no, no, no. None of them do," Chance answered.

"None of them?"

"Not a one."

"How can you be sure?"

"For one thing, the school is not nearby. It's very far away."

"Far away? Wouldn't it make more sense for me to go to a school nearby? Isn't that what kids usually have to do?" I asked.

"They do if they're hum... uh, if they're going to regular school. My school is not a regular school. Not by a long shot," he said.

"But the subjects you said were taught. History, chemistry, physics, those all sound like regular subjects."

Aunt Clare had taught me the basics of some of them. I knew what a regular school taught.

"Okay, Holly. Let me put it this way. The school I go to is very specialized. It only teaches a very select few people, people who have a very certain background. The scholarship I offer to you will pay for everything you need. Books, school supplies, room, board ..."

"What's that?"

"What's what?"

"You said 'board.' What's that?"

"Oh, that means food and stuff," Chance said.

"Oh."

"So, like I was saying ..." He put out his hand and started ticking off each finger as he listed things. "Books, supplies, room, board, all lessons, uniform, everything you'll need." He wiggled his eyebrows.

"Everything I'll need?"

"Everything."

"What about toasted rainbow bagels?"

"Uh, those we don't have. But if you'll come with me to the school, I'll buy a dozen here, and you can bring them with you."

My eyebrows rose.

"What about hot cocoa?"

"School's got it."

"And strawberry cream cheese spread?"

"We'll bring some from the shop, along with your rainbow bagels."

I thought about it.

Were there any drawbacks? I couldn't think of any.

Wait.

I looked at him.

"What if I go with you to the school, and I don't like it?" my eyebrows rose in a question.

"You are always free to leave, at any time," he said without hesitation. "You are not going to be a prisoner. That would be against the rules. Um, against the law."

I thought about it, turning the idea over and over in my head.

I took another bite of toasted rainbow bagel with strawberry cream cheese spread.

I took another drink of my hot cocoa.

"Okay, one last question, and you have to answer truthfully," I said.

Chance nodded.

"What kind of very special people does the school only accept?"

He blinked. Then he leaned forward.

"We only accept those of faerie blood."

It was my turn to blink.

A glowing happiness began to spread in my heart.

"Okay, I'll go," I smiled.

He nodded. "Wise decision, Holly." He reached inside his coat and drew out a long cream envelope, and handed it to me.

"What's this?"

"Your letter of acceptance into Titania Academy."

Chapter Six

Head Injury

"I *thought* I saw pointed ears when you first came in," I said as we walked along the grass. A large bag full of rainbow bagels and strawberry cream cheese packets bounced against my leg.

"I keep my glamour on so no one can tell I'm different. There's safety in blending in with the crowd you happen to be in," Chance said.

"Boy, do I know that well," I said. "Aunt Clare taught me that lesson before anything else."

I was in a fantastic mood. I could not believe everything that had happened to me in the last two days. It was like I was waiting to wake up from a wonderful dream.

Now that would be a nightmare.

I pinched the side of my leg, to be sure.

Nothing happened. I was still walking with Chance, still on my way to the Academy, and still carrying more food than I'd ever eaten in a week, in my whole life.

I puffed as I walked. Chance was not hurrying, but my legs were shorter, and I had to hurry to keep up.

"Chance, you said you're in second year?"

"That's right."

"And how do you like it? I mean, are the classes hard? Is there a lot of homework?"

Aunt Clare had gotten me a notebook and a pencil, and we'd done lessons in the cubby. She'd taught me well. She would teach me a lesson, then have me go off on my own to practice it. I'd learned my multiplication tables that way. And a whole lot more.

"There's not too much homework, but I won't lie: there is some every day," Chance said. "The important thing is not to fall behind."

I stopped.

Something was wrong.

"Hey," Chance had stopped walking and come back to where I was stopped. "You okay?"

"Yeah, I ... I'm fine." A blackness came over my eyes and I lost consciousness.

When I came to, I was lying down on my back in the grass. Chance was kneeling next to me, my feet in his arms. He was raising them up off the ground. They were about two feet high.

"Wha ...what happened?" I said, still groggy.

I put my hand to my head, then to my ear, which tickled.

"You conked out. Right in front of my eyes. Good thing we were walking on the grass," Chance said.

My ear felt sticky now, and the tickling increased. I heard a roaring sound. I put my finger in my ear and wiggled it around, then lifted it to my face to look.

It was covered in blood.

"Ohhh dear. Oh, my. Okay. That's a ... um ... right. That's blood. That dude must've hit you harder than I thought," Chance raised his head and scanned the area. "Okay, um, we need transport to the gate. Um, I mean, we could use some help ... er. ..." His voice trailed off.

He was still holding both my feet up in the air.

"Hey, put my feet down. I want to get up," I said.

"Okay, okay, but ... um... okay." He gently lowered my legs and got to his feet, then extended his hand to help me up.

I grabbed it and rose to my feet.

I was instantly overcome with another wave of dizziness.

"Whoa there," Chance said, catching me as I swayed forward. "Hold on, don't take another tumble." He held my arms and continued to look around.

We were about a hundred yards from the edge of the great park.

"Holly," Chance said. "Can you walk at all? If we can just get to the gate, I think we can summon help."

"I ... I think so. I'll try. Help me?"

"Of course," Chance moved one arm to support my shoulders. I took an unsteady step, then another.

"Grab ... Chance? Grab the bagels, we can't lose them," I murmured.

"Okay, hold still. Don't move," Chance said, balancing me on my feet and then racing back to grab the bag of rainbow bagels.

I swayed but didn't fall.

Then he was back, holding me under my arm. He began to walk slowly forward.

"That's it, let's take it slowly. You're fine. We got this."

I walked slowly forward and didn't pass out again, so at least that was progress.

"Okay, okay, good. Almost there, allllllmost thereeeeee ... Huh? What's that?" Chance stopped.

"What's what?" I asked, looked up at him.

"Oh, gosh, oh my. Ohhhh dear. Holly, your ear is dripping blood," he said.

I put my hand to my right ear. It came away even bloodier than before.

"Does it hurt?" he asked.

"Not really, but there's a low roaring that sounds funny, right there in my ear. It's weird. ..." I murmured.

My legs buckled.

"Uh oh, here we go." Chance caught me halfway to the grass. "Easy there, easy. Can you ... can you ... okay." He lowered me to the grass.

"What is wrong with my legs?" I mumbled.

"Holly, I think you're lightheaded because of the blow to your head, and because of the blood you're losing." Chance thought for a minute. "Listen, I'm going to go for help."

I looked up into his eyes.

"You're leaving?"

There it was. I knew it was too good to be true.

"I'm not leaving you, Holly. I'm just going to be a few minutes, probably less than ten, and I'm coming back with help. 'Cause you need help." Chance squeezed my hand.

I did not feel reassured.

"Chance, please don't go. I want to go to your school. I want to go ..." my voice trailed off. Tears formed in my eyes.

Another drop of blood splattered down from my ear. I looked at my shirt. It was a mess. "There's blood ..."

"I know, and I'm going to help you. Holly. Look at me."

I looked up at him.

He stared into my eyes for a minute. "I will be back in ten minutes. I give you my word."

I felt tears run down my face.

"Okay," I whispered.

What choice did I have?

"Look." He pressed the bag of bagels into my hands. "Hold on to this. I can run faster without it."

I looked down at the bag, mesmerized. My fingers curled around the loop of plastic.

"Here." Chance was removing a necklace from under his shirt. He lifted it, and up out of his top came a green-and-gold enamel leaf, dangling from a gold chain.

"My mother gave me this on my birthday last month." He pressed it into the palm of his hand. "This is my promise to you that I will return. You hold this for me, and you give it back when I come back, okay?"

I nodded, staring at the leaf and chain. I looked up at his face, nodding. "When you come back," I whispered.

"When I come back." He stood up, nodded to me, then turned and ran fast toward the park. I watched him go and held tight to the leaf and chain.

Minutes passed.

I shivered, my head feeling drowsy again.

I thought for a moment, then lifted the gold chain and put it over my head and down on my neck. The leaf looked shiny and brilliant lying on my shirt. I stared at it for a second, then tucked it into my neckline, out of sight.

"Hey. Hey, Holly, wake up."

I opened my eyes.

My face was cold.

Chance was bent over me, gently patting my shoulder.

"Hey, kiddo, you okay? I guess you passed out again, huh?"

"Guess so," I mumbled, raising my head. "You came back." It was a statement of fact.

"Well of course I came back. I told ya I would, didn't I? I've only been gone about ten minutes, just like I said."

He helped me sit up.

There was someone behind him.

"This is my friend, Brendan. He's going to help lift you and carry you, Holly." Chance bent low and whispered in my ear. "We're going to do this fast, so we don't garner much attention, okay?"

I nodded. Chance moved to the side and Brendan came into view.

Oh, my God.

Brendan was ... he was ...

"You're ..." I murmured weakly.

"Yes," said Brendan. "I am. Now I'm just going to pick you up, kid. Don't kick me or anything, okay?"

"Okay," I whispered. I couldn't stop staring. Brendan was a dwarf. But not a little person, he was an honest-to-gosh dwarf. He was almost as wide as he was tall, and his arms and legs were ridiculously thick. he looked like he could lift a tree.

Brendan bent over and gently scooped me up in his arms like I was nothing.

"Chance, she weighs nearly nothing. Did you even *try* to pick her up?" Brendan teased his friend as he turned around and began walking to the trees.

"Brendan, just walk. You're such a wise guy. Dr. Farryn said you should be helpful, not helpful and insulting," Chance said as they walked.

I felt myself jounced and jostled, and my ear began bleeding again.

"Oh hell, she's bleeding," said Brendan. "Why didn't you say she was bleeding, you ridiculous faun?" He began to run.

"Er, ER ... happy thoughts and secret pots, Brendan. Go faster. The quicker we get back the quicker we can get her medical help and stop dropping secrets. Yeah, okay, okay, hmmm ..." Chance began to trot.

They were almost to the trees.

What had Brendan said?

My head began to ring. I put my hands up to my face and tried to hold my noggin together. It was rough being carried while someone ran, but it couldn't be helped, I guess.

We entered the park and it got darker. Brendan and Chance ran between the trees, straight into the middle of the park, and I held on for dear life, while bleeding all over the nice young man, er ... dwarf, who was carrying me.

"Ughhhh ..." I murmured.

"Hold tight, Holly girl. Hold tight. Almost there ..." Chance said in a quiet voice.

I guess we're trying to sneak.

Central Park was often full of people even when it didn't look like it was full of people. Not only were there all kinds of paved walkways running through it, there were pathways through the grass, many worn down to the dirt. There were animal paths through the thickets and trees, and the park was teeming with life.

There were people everywhere.

"HEY!" A strange voice yelled.

Brendan and Chance kept running, and we soon left the voice behind.

Who was that?

"Hurry," Chance said under his breath.

"Through here," said Brendan. "It's a shortcut."

He ducked around some trees and down a path that curled around some large bushes. I could see a lake on the left as he ran.

Suddenly, Chance stopped beside a huge hedge, and stuck his arm out to bend the branches back. Brendan ducked through the gap, wiggling me sideways so I wouldn't get scratched. I ducked my head to help.

We were through the bush, and I felt a warm shimmer, and suddenly we were in a massive tree.

The inside was huge.

"Where should I set her down, dear?" Brendan said.

"Just there, on the lounge," came another voice. This sounded like a woman's voice, it was kind and high and soft.

"Hi, Jess," Chance said, coming through right after us.

"Shut the gate, Chance," said the female voice. I guessed this was Jess.

"Yes m'am," Chance turned and pressed a lever on the inside of the tree trunk. I heard a low 'thunk'.

"She's bleeding, Jess," said Brendan. "The lounge."

"Here, I'll spread a blanket over it."

I heard a rumpling sound, then Jess came into view.

Now I was certain I was delirious. Jess looked very elfin, and she had wings. She flipped a thick blanket up and let it fall onto the lounge, then straightened the corners a little.

"Set her down now, Brendan.

Brendan set me down gently on the wide lounge, being careful with my head. The blanket Jess had covered the lounge with was very soft.

"Her ear is bleeding," Brendan's voice rumbled. I looked up at him and saw he had tears in his eyes.

I put my hand out onto his. "Thank you for helping me. I'm sure I'll be fine."

Brendan smiled and pulled a huge red-and-white polka dot handkerchief from his pocket, and blew his nose noisily.

"There, there, now, little miss. I'll help thee." Jess came up to me and delicately brushed my hair aside, trying to see my ear.

I turned my head to expose the side of my face.

"Some guy hit her on the side of the head," said Chance. "I saw the whole thing. It knocked her to the ground."

"Oooh, oooh," purred Jess. She reached for a basket and withdrew a white cloth and a bottle of clear liquid. "Here now, I'm just going to wash the wound a little," she murmured.

I took the opportunity to examine the girl.

Jess looked not much older than Chance, although there was no way to know how old she really was. She acted like Aunt Clare had when I'd gotten hurt.

The similarities ended there.

Jess was of normal height, but her skin was tinged a pale green. Her pale cream-and-pink dress looked like it had

65

been woven from feathers or leaves. She had platinum hair much the same shade as my own, although mine was far bushier. Jess's hair was wispy and floating around her face.

She had green eyes, and pointed ears, and wings.

She had wings!

The two transparent wings had a light green tinge to them, and they looked very much like what you'd see on a lacewing. They lay flat and loose against her back.

I looked at her face. It was a human face, for the most part. She had no insect antenna sprouting from her forehead, although I wouldn't have been surprised if she had.

The wings were ethereal, why not the rest of her?

I felt a cool sting on my ear, and I jumped slightly.

"There, there, coooo, coooo," she said softly, easing my tension.

Chance pulled a stool over and sat down at the end of the lounge.

"You're going to be just fine, Holly. Jess is one of the best." He patted my shoulder gently.

"Anyone want anything to drink?" Brendan hollered from the other side of the tree.

"Shhhhh, you're going to startle the poor miss," cautioned Jess.

Jess continued to work on my ear, and a little while later she had me sit up.

"There now. I've stopped the bleeding. Your ear was cut by the blow. Thank goodness the blood wasn't coming from inside." She smiled at me.

"Why was she dizzy?" Chance asked.

"I expect it was the blow to her head," said Jess. "You need to get her to the school, Chance. Right away."

"Term doesn't start for another week," Brendan said.

"Yeah, but we like to get the new students there and get them settled in first. Gives them time to get accustomed to everything," Chance said.

Brendan shrugged.

Chance turned to me. "I think you need to rest until you can walk without falling down, Holly. You need to go with me to get your school supplies, and I can't have you falling over every few steps."

"She can sleep the night here, and leave in the morning," said Jess. "You, too, Chance."

"Oh, no. Me and Brendan will go home. We'll come back in the morning."

Panic filled me at this statement. I tried to sit up. "Chance ..."

Jess turned to me and pushed me back down, smoothing the blanket and patting my hand.

"I promise I'll be back in the morning, Holly." He looked at me. "You still have my necklace?"

I put my hand to my neck. It was still there. I nodded.

"Good. I'll be back for it in the morning. Jess'll take good care of you. You're in good hands." He picked up his backpack and turned to Brendan. "Come on."

"I can't stay?" Brendan said in mock horror.

"Come onnnn," Chance grabbed his friend's sleeve and yanked him to the door.

"Bye, Holly. See you tomorrow."

I watched as the door shut.

Jess turned to me. "There now, they'll be through the gate and gone now. I'll make a thick stew. And some homemade bread. You stay right there. I'll bring you everything."

Chapter Seven
The Market

I slept fitfully and dreamt of Aunt Clare. At one point I half woke, my head throbbing. "Aunt Clare!" I cried out.

Jess was there in an instant, settling me back to sleep.

In the morning, she made a sweet porridge for us; we were just finishing up when we heard a knock at the door, and Chance poked his head in.

"Anyone home?"

"Come in, dear. She's feeling much better today, aren't you, Holly?" Jess said.

I sat up on the lounge and swung my feet to the ground. I'd already been up and down several times, and the dizziness was gone.

Chance walked into the room.

I stood up and walked to him, steady as a rock.

He beamed. "Much better, that."

I nodded and smiled, and slung my bag over my shoulder.

"I'm ready to go."

Jess came then, and handed me a bag. "Here's some fresh bread, dear. And a thermos full of stew, enough to share for two." She patted my arm. "Come visit me again soon?"

"I will," I smiled.

"It's lonely here, living on the edge of the forest, right up against the barrier," Jess said.

"Thank you for taking care of her, Jess. I owe you one," Chance said.

"Oh, posh. I was just happy to be able to meet the king's ..." Jess stopped abruptly.

I looked. Chance had his finger to his lips. When he saw me looking, he moved his finger to his cheek.

"How does your ear feel today, Holly?"

"Still sore, but the dizziness is gone," I said slowly, wondering what they were hiding from me.

"Well," Chance hugged Jess. "Thank you again. I guess we'll be off."

"You do that, Chance." Jess walked us to the door. "Holly, have fun at the school. You're in for a treat. I think you'll like it." She winked at me.

"Thank you," I hugged Jess, careful not to squish her wings. "I'll always remember you," I whispered in her ear.

We turned and left, and Chance touched the lever as we went, closing the gate.

We crouched and walked back out of the bushes into Central Park.

I looked back as I emerged from the hedge.

"That's not really where her tree home is, is it?" I asked.

"No," Chance said.

I was accepting every bit of magic that showed up to me, and it felt natural to do so.

I took a deep breath and looked around.

"What time is it?" I asked.

"About a half hour after dawn. Come on, let's go."

We walked out of the park and across the same grassy area we'd walked over the day before.

It felt like a lifetime ago.

So much had happened since that guy knocked me down.

I turned as I remember something.

"The bagels! I forgot ..."

Chance lifted a bag he was carrying. "Got 'em right here." He smiled.

"Oh good. Okay, Chance, where do we go now?" I asked.

"Over this way," he gestured.

We walked to the other side of the grassy area and into the other end of the park, then through the trees and out onto the plaza.

"Through here." Chance led the way into an indoor mall area made entirely of bricks. "This is a very old market. This gate has been here for over a two-hundred-and-fifty years. The folk have been using it since the days of Benjamin Franklin."

"Aunt Clare taught me about him."

"Did she, now? I'll bet she didn't tell you he was one of us." Chance smiled as he turned to open a small wooden door half hidden on the side.

He led me through to a dark passageway, about twenty feet long, which ended at another door. This door was carved with intricate symbols I did not recognize. The door handle was of the lever kind, a round bar that was pushed down to open the door.

"See here?" Chance indicated the different symbols. "These are the various marks of the fae tribes. Most of them are here. The sigil in the middle is actually a spell. No human would even see this door, let alone be able to open it." He reached for the door latch, which looked like it was carved from bone, and turned it ten degrees down.

The door opened with a soft click, and we stepped through. With the first step, there was a small drop of an inch or two to reach the floor, and the jolt of the drop was startling without being dangerous.

I stood just beyond the doorway and looked out.

It was a huge market, and what a market it was!

The middle walk was paved in old stones, they felt rough through the thin sole of my shoe, but had clearly been worn smooth by tens of thousands of feet walking over them for many, many years.

The walkway was filled with people of all descriptions, exploring various shops on both sides of the center plaza. The buildings that housed them were made of stone with old wooden doors and thick glass storefront windows.

Ribbons of vivid pink, orange, and yellow fluttered above one doorway, beckoning shoppers in. The window alongside it displayed school colors and clothing in every color imaginable for any type of magical being. Among them was the same type of dress Jess had worn, in a brilliant shade of green.

"The ribbon shop was where my mother used to take my little sister. Every birthday and every holiday, she'd come and buy her another ribbon," said Chance. "She must have dozens by now."

Another window was filled with brown and green colored shirts and pants. I peered inside, and saw the whole shop was decorated like an enchanted forest, with a tree growing up the outer wall beside the door, from a hole in the paved stone. There were all types of wood boxes and toys in this shops window as well, and I could not stop looking.

I glanced at Chance and then back at the shop. "Did you buy your shirt there?" I asked.

"You bet. They have the best clothes anywhere for blending into the forest," he said. "You'll see when we're on the way, but the Academy is surrounded by a beautiful, dense forest."

"I can't wait," I smiled.

Chance beckoned me on.

A juggler stood in the plaza center, on a raised brick platform, somehow managing to keep a dozen eggs spinning in an arc above his head, all while balanced on stilts several feet high. His pantaloons were brightly striped with metallic greens, blues, oranges, and purples, and his face was painted in yellow and red circles.

I was captivated.

"You know, he's been doing that here ever since I can remember," said Chance. "Want to hear something embarrassing?"

I nodded eagerly, grinning.

"When I was nine years old, I was here with my mother and several friends and we were horsing around. ..." He stopped.

"Please don't tell me you tripped the juggler," I said. "He's on stilts!"

"I ... um ... we tripped the juggler," Chance looked sheepish. "It was an accident!"

I laughed.

There was a shop off to the side, rising several stories high, and in its window was a platform. On this platform crouched a massive lion. An elaborately costumed circus trainer stood next to the great maned beast and held up a large hoop, and the lion jumped through the hoop to another platform, roaring loudly and making the crowd gasp.

"I can't believe how close we are to a live lion!" I exclaimed.

"It's very cool," Chance admitted.

"And he's not even on a chain or behind a fence or anything!" I said. Aunt Clare and I had snuck into the NYC zoo at least once a year, and I loved seeing the lions, but they were always so far away, behind chain link fencing ..."

"I think the trainer's got the lion really well disciplined," said Chance. "She's got the lion under control."

"It's amazing. I never realized how incredible it was to see such a thing so up close." I stared, my jaw dropped open.

Everything was just so amazing!

A pyramid of acrobats, all dressed in lilac, stood atop one another, and at the apex of their human tower, there was a small, bright green gnome-like creature, balancing on its head. It chattered down at the crowd and giggled madly as if it were insane.

"Oh my God! Ha ha ha!" I clapped my hands in delight.

Chance leaned close to my ear. "You wouldn't be that happy if you knew that thing was a gremlin."

I turned to look at him. "A what?"

"A mischievous imp that loves to cause trouble," said Chance. "My friends and I once locked one in a classroom, as a prank. It caused so much destruction we were suspended for a month, had to do community service the whole time, and our parents had to pay for the damage. I lost my allowance for a year."

I stared at him, wide-eyed.

He nodded knowingly. "Stay away from them, if you can."

"Whoa!"

Around the next corner there was an illusionist who held a long stick with a slick black ribbon on the end. The stick was maybe ten feet long, and the ribbon was three times that length. He twirled the stick so that the ribbon fluttered in a circle, then he threw a handful of gold glitter into the circle.

The air inside the ribbon immediately began to darken, then swirl in a smoky clockwise pattern. As the smoke began to clear, the circle of ribbon became a window onto a meadow as it was at night, even as the sun shone all around us.

The meadow was filled with fireflies and the moon shone brightly down on the meadow. I was mesmerized as I saw a great dance played out on the nighttime meadow within that ribboned circle. It was as if the ribbons had generated a portal through which we could witness a scene from a great celebration playing out.

"Chance? What is that?" I whispered.

He bent low to whisper back. "It's a spell. Pretty cool, huh?"

"So, it's not really a portal?" I asked, glancing at him.

He shook his head no.

I shrugged.

Pretty spectacular for an illusion.

We kept walking.

I saw a virtuoso, dressed in a fabulous dress of iridescent purple. Gold threads were woven in a corkscrew pattern, accenting her deep ebony arms and face. Her voice rang out in a tune that had us gasping with its beauty. She handed out small flowers to any who would place a coin in the basket at her feet.

I had never wished for a coin more in my life. I was entranced.

Chance nudged me. I glanced at him. He was handing me a silver coin; it had strange patterns on it, and was about the size of silver dollar.

I looked at him, questioning.

"It's a faerie penny. Worth about fifty cents in the human world," said Chance. He nodded to the singer. "Go on. Go put it in her basket."

I smiled broadly, and walked over shyly, then plunked the large coin in her basket.

She bestowed the most beautiful smile on me, and for a few seconds, sang her aria just for me. She bent down and handed me a small white flower from the bunch in her hand.

I walked back to Chance, smelling the flower and feeling enchanted.

Chance bent to whisper in my ear again. "That's a snowdrop. Keep it, it's valuable. It's got magical properties you'll learn about in your first-year classes."

I glanced at him, my mouth open in surprise, then carefully tucked the little flower into a small pocket in my bag. It would be safe there.

There was a wizard in a brilliant midnight-blue robe, wearing a tall pointed hat, half-moon glasses perched on the end of his nose. His long, flowing white beard was tied with trinkets that dripped of stars and moons and glittering tendrils of a plant I could not recognize. I stared into his eyes, and he met mine with a secret wink, then continued to peruse the wares on a table outside a small shop brilliantly painted in blue and gold, where he was shopping.

I beckoned to Chance, and when he brought his head close, I motioned toward the wizard and asked, "Is that one of the fae?"

Chance grinned and answered, "Every person at this market is one of the fae. That old man is an elder; he just likes to dress in an olde fashioned manner." He grinned at me.

I chuckled.

I saw a shop run by an enchanter, who boasted he could bespell any object, and then proceeded to make a lizard obey his command to run up his sleeve and perch atop his head. Then he took a small cup, balanced it on the palm of his hand, and said some mystical words over it. He blew, and the cup transformed into a giant moth, with a five-inch wingspan. He raised his palm, and the moth took flight and fluttered its wings, rising higher and higher until it disappeared above our heads.

"Chance," I asked. "Is that something I can learn how to do at the school?"

"You can, as an elective," said Chance, nodding, "But you should know he's an illusionist, not a transfigurer. And the class to learn that sort of thing is called 'Trickery and Sot.'" Chance winked.

"Ha ha ha!" I couldn't help myself.

There was a man dressed all in dark greys and browns sitting in the window of his shop, where all manner of crystal balls and divination tools were displayed. He wore dark brown robes with runes appliqued all over them, and he held an urn, and whispered over it. A mist rose out of the urn and took shape in the form of a ghostly face, which the necromancer proceeded to ask questions of its former life. The mist dutifully answered.

I glanced at Chance. "Another Illusionist?"

Chance shook his head, his face serious.

My mouth dropped open.

Chance threw his head back and laughed.

"Ohhh you!" I pushed him playfully, grinning, secretly relieved.

I glanced back at the man and the ghost coming out of the urn as we walked past, and I swear he winked at me.

Something tells me this world is going to keep me on my toes.

We kept walking and looking at everything.

A few paces farther on, we encountered a grey-haired witch in a shop with a window entirely covered in leaves, where dozens of potion bottles were displayed, all with different colored liquids within. She called out to us, beckoning us to come and try her wares, then picked up a vial, seemingly at random, and drank the contents, and her hair changed from long grey and white, to a short cut in a brilliant leaf green color. She blinked her eyes and laughed at us, and we saw her eyes had also changed, from dull blue to piercing and endless black pools that looked like huge pearls.

"That's amazing!" I said.

"It is, but it only lasts an hour, if that," said Chance. "Your own hair is rarer and more special than anything she can enchant.

I blushed.

Next to the witch's shop was a large ring of stone that enclosed a deep pool of water in the ground, surrounded by seaweed and smooth stones gathered from the sea. Inside the pool was a large boulder and sitting on this boulder was a siren. Her hair was wet and the color of the seaweed, greenish-black. Her skin was tinted green, and her piercing eyes followed us as she sat there. The man calling out to me from the side of the pool implored me to throw coins in the water to free the siren, so she could return to her people. At one point, she opened her mouth to sing a few notes, and a shiver ran down my spine at the sound.

"We won't waste a coin on this. It's all an act," Chance whispered.

"I don't have any coins," I mumbled.

There was a store selling herbs and tinctures and mushrooms and balms and every type of dried plant you could ever want. It smelled wonderful and enticing, but Chance pulled me away from that as well. I vowed to come back to the shop sometime and investigate what they had to offer.

Then, there was a witch doctor with shrunken heads in his shop window. His hair was gathered in a topknot, and a bone pierced his septum. His dark brown skin was tattooed with dots and spiral patterns everywhere. He smiled as we passed, and we could see his teeth had been filed to points. He beckoned us to come closer, and I saw each of the shrunken heads he was selling had a third eye in the middle of its foreheads, to foretell the future.

"Too weird," I said.

"Agreed," said Chance. "That guy always gives me the creeps."

We hurried past.

We saw an astrologer whose shop was covered in depictions of the stars and constellations, who promised us she knew of a massive rock that would plummet from the sky and blast through to the ground, wreaking massive destruction. She assured us she had been sent by the king's top magician to the fae marketplace to warn the people, who were urged to take cover before the next full moon.

I glanced at Chance, who rolled his eyes and whispered, "The king does not employ any magicians." He shook his head, beckoning me onward.

A dozen more shops sold every type of antique and collectible. Dealers held out objects and called out to shoppers, enticing them to approach. One shop window displayed taxidermied pigs, deer, cows, and goats, and even a huge taxidermied sasquatch that I stared at for a long while before Chance murmured in my ear that we had to move on.

"Was that real?" I asked in a low tone.

Chance glanced back. "You mean the sasquatch?"

I nodded.

He shrugged, then grinned.

I chuckled.

We saw a large shop whose window was devoted to the sale of musical instruments. Inside, several shop musicians were playing. They played in unison, and the result was highly pleasing to the ear. Harps played alongside lyres, and flutes played alongside small drums, all serenading us with music.

"That's where I got my first flute," said Chance. "When I was eleven. Wellllll, my first serious flute. I don't count the toy flutes I had as a child.

I turned to him. "You play the flute?"

He nodded. "Maybe I'll show you some time." He smiled.

Chapter Eight
School Supplies

Chance led us to a corner shop with school uniforms. We entered, and a lady came toward me with pins sticking out of her mouth, held by her lips. She beckoned me forward to the rear of the shop.

Chance pointed to the uniform, and she nodded. Then I had to stand on a dais wearing the white blouse and skirt while the seamstress hemmed the skirt to reach to my knees.

The skirt was a deep blue purple, with pink lines, making a tartan.

"It's the tartan of the Academy," Chance said, smiling.

It was beautiful.

There were special socks to buy, and several pairs of shoes.

"The shoes are regulation, too," said Chance. "Every day you are at the school, you must wear the same uniform. This is why we are purchasing so many sets."

I could not believe how much he was ordering. All of it hemmed and adjusted just to fit me.

I had never in my life seen so many clothes, and I had only ever owned three shirts and two pairs of trousers, all used and worn and fished out of a dumpster.

I looked down at my worn-out, too-small shoes.

"Don't worry, you'll be getting three new pairs of leather school shoes," Chance said.

We moved on to the chemistry shop. Chance indicated the letter I had received. "It says what you need on that, read it to me."

"Let's see," I said, concentrating. "One cauldron, one set of spell books, two sets of varying potion bottles ...," and we were off buying chemistry supplies.

After a while, I noticed we didn't bring anything with us.

"They'll be delivered to the school by tomorrow morning," said Chance. "See? This is why we've brought one of the uniforms with us." He indicated the paper-covered clothes hanging from the wooden hanger over his shoulder.

"There's so much to buy. I had no idea," I said, my mouth open.

"It's mostly because it's your first year," said Chance. "The second-year supply list is shorter."

"Hmmm ..."

"Okay, what's next?"

I studied the letter. "Books."

"Ah, yes. My favorite shop." He eagerly led me to the other side of the plaza, opposite the chemist.

The old bookshop was stone and old wood, and the bell over the door tinkled as we passed through.

"Wow," I whispered.

The bookshop was covered in old wood paneling, which stretched from floor to ceiling. Bookshelves reached high on every wall. A thick maroon carpet cushioned my footsteps as we walked in.

Rare, old books were on display behind glass.

"This is one of my favorites," Chance whispered, as he stared at a small hardback book with a blue-and-gold cover, sitting on a velvet cushion in a glass case.

" 'The Book of Hallow ... Halloween' hmmm," I read slowly. "By Ruth E. Kelley." The cover art depicted a big yellow setting sun next to some bushes and a tree. Six bats flew over the moon, silhouetted against the blue twilight sky.

Chance led me to the back, where a man stood at a counter.

I handed him my letter, which he took and peered at through square eyeglass lenses.

"Ah yes, Titania Academy," he said. He glanced at me over the rims of his glasses. "First year?"

I nodded.

"Oh, you're in for a treat," he said, smiling. "Well, I've got the set here, let me just check them."

He turned to rummage in the back room, through a blue curtain.

Chance turned to me. "We'll have all the books shipped to the school except one."

"Which one?" I asked.

"The Book of Halloween."

I turned to look back at the glass covered case. "The one you just showed me?"

Chance nodded.

"But, I thought you said you wanted that one."

"I already have a copy. It was given to me by the queen herself," he said proudly.

"By the queen herself?"

"Yes. It was in reward for completing a very special task last year."

"Last year was your first year?" I asked.

"Yes."

"Did all the first-year students perform this task?" I asked.

"Oh, no." Chance shook his head. "I was the only one she asked. She asked me because I was the best for the job, and her chosen champion. The globe I retrieved for her had been lost for ages. I brought it back for her and lived to tell the tale." He rocked back on his heels, pleased with himself.

I blinked my eyes. There was so much to absorb. And Chance completing a task that had seemed dangerous when he told it.

I looked at my toes. I didn't think I would be strong enough or good enough for any special tasks the queen might ask me to do.

The shopkeeper returned and set a stack of books on the counter. "There we are, all of them but one." He moved out from behind the counter, lifting his keys from his waistcoat.

We watched as he went to the glass-enclosed book Chance had indicated.

Before he lifted the book from the black velvet, he donned white cloth gloves, snapping them onto his fingers snugly.

Then he carefully picked up the little book and brought it to the counter.

"I trust you've told her how special this book is?" He looked over his spectacles at both of us.

"I have," Chance said, a twinge of indignation in his voice at the very thought of him not fulfilling his duty to keep this sacred trust.

The shopkeeper nodded in satisfaction and carefully slipped *The Book of Halloween*, by Ruth E. Kelley, into a small, soft cloth bag, then folded the edges over, and brought out an expanse of brown wrapping paper, set the book on it, and wrapped it into a neat brown paper parcel.

"I'll have these other delivered to the school this evening, but I expect you'll want to carry this one yourself."

He handed me the brown paper-wrapped book.

I took it carefully and began to slip it into my bag.

"No, don't put it in there," said Chance. "Put it on your person."

"On my person?" I asked.

"Put it under your shirt, in the waistband of your trousers," said Chance. "Do you have pockets?"

"I don't think they're big enough," I said, feeling around the side pockets of my pants.

"Waistband it is, then. And you'll be happy to find the school uniform skirts have large pockets. Big enough for that book. In fact, I think the pockets were designed especially *for* that book to fit."

The shopkeeper nodded.

Wow, I can't wait to put on my school uniform.

I carefully stuck the small paper parcel in the waistband of my pants, then pulled my shirt down over it.

I turned to Chance. "How do I look?"

"It's hidden." Chance nodded in approval.

He turned to the shopkeeper. "This will go on the school account, Barnsby."

"Very good, sir. I'll mark it down."

We nodded and left the store.

It felt a little funny walking around with a small paper-wrapped book down my trousers. I felt like I was hiding a treasure, smuggling it to safety. I told Chance as much when we stopped for an early lunch.

"You are," he said. "That book is extremely valuable. There's only a handful of them left in the world. Most were destroyed by one means or another."

I sat straighter, and patted the hard rectangle in my waistband.

We ate sandwiches. I had roast beef. They were delicious.

"I've never eaten until I was full before," I said.

"You actually haven't eaten all that much," said Chance. "I expect we'll have to fatten you up a bit, once we get to the Academy."

I grinned. "I look forward to that."

By the time the sun set, we were exhausted. We'd been to eleven different shops and had spent the whole day there. We'd walked a thousand miles, or so it seemed to my feet.

"Okay, we'll catch the first flight in the morning to the Academy. For tonight, let's get a room in the old inn here," he indicated a large inn next to an ice cream shop.

The sign swinging from the metal hook above the door read, "The Green Dragon Tavern and Inn."

Sounds interesting.

We went in. It was a busy establishment, filled with a mixture of students and adults. Chance had informed me that anyone under the age of twenty-one attended school, and then was apprenticed for a period of four years to the trade that best suited their abilities.

We sat at a rectangular wooden table in the back that was thick and rough, but worn.

"This inn has been here for nearly four hundred years," Chance said. "It was built at a crossroads, and the humans used it for about a hundred and fifty years, give or take a decade. Then the marketplace was enshrouded by the Fae counsel, and it became ours. The owners were fae, you see, so they were very happy when the counsel decided to make this neighborhood into our marketplace." He stood up. "I'm going to get us some dinner. You stay here, okay?"

I nodded.

I watched him go to the front counter and talk with the waitress.

Probably ordering food.

The smells coming out of the kitchen on the side were so good my stomach started rumbling. I felt odd because on a normal day, I usually was happy to get one meal, be it an apple and some bread, a half-eaten sandwich out of the trash, or something else.

I guess I was extra hungry because of all the walking and shopping we'd done.

I looked around. A wizened old man was sitting alone three tables away, and he was looking at me.

I slouched in my seat, trying to make myself look smaller. He kept staring. I scowled and wished I hadn't lost my coat; I'd have pulled the hood over my head if I'd had it on.

The hubbub in the restaurant rose suddenly to a high volume, the larger party at the table in the corner all laughing at something someone had said. I stared, not used to being around so many people.

"Hello, is this seat taken?"

I swung my head around and stared.

It was the old man.

I scowled again and said, "Yes, it's taken." I put my bag on Chance's chair so the old man couldn't sit in it.

He shrugged and pulled another chair from the next table over, first asking the old women sitting there if he could take it.

I was alarmed.

Why is this old man sitting at our table?

He sat in the new chair, scooted it closer to the table, put his elbows on the wood and considered me silently.

My eyes went wide, and I looked down at my hands folded in my lap.

I felt very small.

"So, I noticed you when you came in," the old man said. "My name is Boothby, and I work at the school."

I looked up.

He nodded. "Yes, I'm a groundskeeper at Titania Academy."

Okay, old man, I'm listening.

"There's not many who come to the school who look like you," he said.

A small inkling of worry blossomed in my stomach.

Where is Chance?

"You know, you shouldn't be ashamed of who you are. It's not your fault."

I blushed red. I had no idea what he was talking about, but I felt alarmed and vulnerable. And worried.

"I think I might ..."

"Hi," Chance arrived at the table holding two flagons of cider.

"Chance!" I sounded relieved and eager, even to my ears.

Chance glanced at the old man. "Boothby, you need to leave the table."

"Mister Faunus," the old man got to his feet. "How are you this fine evening?"

"Boothby, I'm on Academy business, on order from the queen herself. And you're interfering with that business."

The old man went white. He bowed his head, backing up, and left.

Chance set down the flagons of cider.

"Thank you for getting rid of him," I mumbled.

Chance sat down.

"I wouldn't worry about Boothby. He's a gardener at the Academy. Pretty harmless."

"He didn't feel harmless," I scowled.

"Here, take a sip of this. You'll like it," Chance pushed over the flagon.

"What is it?" I asked.

"Have you ever had apple juice?" Chance asked.

"No."

"Well, hmmm. Okay. Well, this is fizzy apple juice, without the extra sugar. Try it."

I took a sip. It was delicious.

"Mmmmmm," I said, wiping the mustache of foam the drink had left on my upper lip.

Chance smiled. "Now tell me what Boothby said."

"He said he was groundskeeper at the school. He said he noticed me when we came inside. He said there weren't many who came to the school who looked like me, and that I shouldn't be ... ashamed of who I was." I looked up at Chance. "He made me feel bad, and I don't know why. Do you know what he meant?"

Chance stared at me for a minute, considering. Then, he spoke. "Why do *you* think he said that?"

"I don't know," I answered. "Did he mean because of my clothes?" I looked down at my shirt. It still had dried blood on it from my ear. My pants were filthy. I blushed and scowled.

"Holly," Chance took my hand. I looked up at him.

"He didn't mean your clothes. He meant ..." Chance took a deep breath. "I guess you'll find out sooner or later," he mumbled.

"Find out what?

"Your hair, it's platinum. And so are your eyes," Chance said.

"My eyes?" I asked.

"Don't you know what color your eyes are?"

"No. Aunt Clare just said they were beautiful eyes. I guess I never asked her what color they were."

Chance smiled. "Your eyes are platinum, ringed with black."

"Okay. So?"

"So it's a rare color for eyes. In fact, no other student at the school has eyes like yours. And none of them will have platinum hair, either," Chance said.

"Why not?" I asked.

"Because different types of fae have different hair and eyes, depending on their lineage. The colors are different for different bloodlines."

I blinked, not understanding.

He tried again. "You see my hair? It's brown with gold streaks."

"Gold streaks?" I squinted at his head.

"They show up in the sunlight. And my eyes, notice them?"

I nodded. "Green, aren't they? Aunt Clare had green eyes, though not as light as yours."

"Well, my hair color and eye color are only found in the faun strain of the fae. So, what Boothby meant was, your hair and eye color are rare, so rare you won't find them in anyone else at the Academy."

"Okay. Again, why not?"

Chance took a deep breath. "Because your strain of the fae is very rare. Holly, you're *very* rare."

"I am?"

"Yes." He stared at me for a long minute. Then he sighed and leaned closer. "Holly, only fae of royal blood have platinum hair."

I sat back and stared at him doubtfully. "I'm descended from royalty?"

"After a fashion," Chance said.

"What does that mean, 'after a fashion'?" I asked.

"Well, you're ... um ... you're misborn, Holly. That's why you have that eye color."

"What's misborn?"

"Born out of wedlock."

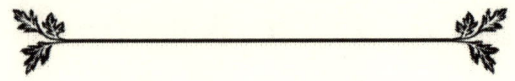

Chapter Nine
Misborn

I scowled.

Born out of wedlock.

"That's ... that's kind of ... kind of rude. Don't you think?"
I asked.

"Yes, it is. The manner of your birth is not your fault.
And it's an old, archaic tradition. And black rims around
your irises don't always mean you were born out of
wedlock. Sometimes it means your father died before you
were born."

"Huh?"

A server brought our food.

Two steaming bowls of thick stew and warm bread,
split and slathered with butter.

We spent the next ten minutes narfing down the delicious repast. I cleaned my bowl, and sat sopping up the leftover gravy with the last piece of my bread. I'd never done that before, but Jess had taught me, and I found it delicious.

"Okay," Chance pushed his bowl back and looked at me. "I'm going to give it to you straight."

I nodded slowly. I wanted to know.

"Your platinum hair color is the mark of the royals. No other fae line has that hair color. And the royals don't have many children at all. That's why it's so rare."

I nodded. "Okay."

"Now, your eye color means two different things. One," he ticked off his fingers as he spoke. "The color is an indication of the royal line, the platinum color. But," he pushed down a second finger. "The black rim around your eye means your father was not handfasted to your mother when you were born. It means he either died, or left."

"Okayyyy," I wondered why any of this was significant.

"In other words, your eyes tell people you were misborn. That you were born out of wedlock," Chance said.

"Get to the point," I scowled.

"You have the eye color of a bastard, Holly."

"So?"

"That's what Boothby meant. It's not that big a deal being a bastard, but a bastard of the royal line means you lost out on a lot. Plus you've been homeless your whole life.

He could probably guess that from your appearance," Chance said.

"So it *is* about my clothes. I knew it." I felt my face go red yet again.

"It's your clothes, your hair, your state of being. Look." Chance picked up my hand.

I looked. The fingernails were torn, and two had dried blood on them.

"That is one neglected hand," said Chance. "All these things tell people about you."

The corners of my mouth turned down. I took a deep breath.

"So what can I do about it?"

"I'm glad you asked," he smiled. "You're not the first homeless orphan faeborn I've met. I suggest that tonight you have a good long bath. Scrub every inch of yourself."

"A bath." I said flatly.

"Yes. A bath. In a tub. With soap. You've had baths before, haven't you?"

"Aunt Clare and I visited the fountains in summer and splashed all the dirt off ourselves," I said.

Chance closed his eyes.

"No." He opened them again. "Okay, I will show you what to do. Tonight, we work on this. Then tomorrow, we get you a haircut, a manicure, and a toothbrush."

"What's a manicure?"

"Come on," he stood up, his chair scraping the wooden floor. "Let's go upstairs to our room. I'll explain everything as it happens."

I got up and followed him.

Our room was actually two beds, each in its own cupboard, with a central space.

My cupboard was decorated with carved flowers, painted pink and green, on the doors.

Chance opened the doors and showed me how to put my bag on the shelf at the bottom, and how to climb up to the bed on the top.

The bed was a dream. I'd slept on the mattress Aunt Clare and I had used; when I was smaller we'd both fit on it. It was better than the floor, but the springs poked out in several spots and stuck me. I ended up on the floor half the time, because I'd roll off the mattress trying to avoid the metal wires. Once, I woke up with a red, bleeding scratch from them.

This bed was soft, and had sheets! And several blankets, and a pillow!

I started to climb up onto it, but Chance stopped me.

"First, a bath." He led me to the bathroom, which was a separate room all its own. A large tub and a washbasin, and a toilet! I couldn't believe it!

"Here, see? You turn on both faucets, and feel the water temperature until you like how warm it is," he said. "But you don't want it too hot, see?"

I watched as the bathtub slowly filled with water.

"Here, I'm going to add some soap to the water, and you use a little on your hair, too. Okay?"

He poured a small drop of soap out of a bottle onto the water crashing out of the faucet.

It frothed into the water and filled the top of the tub water with so many bubbles!

"These look clean," I said.

"Yes, they are clean. And they will make *you* clean." He turned the faucets off, and the water stopped pouring in.

"You want to leave room for yourself, because the water level will rise as you get in and sit down in the water," Chance said.

I looked at the gleaming white bubbles in the tub. I'd only ever seen bubbles in the canal, and they had been brown and greasy.

I touched a bubble with my finger. It popped and sprayed my face, and I laughed.

"Okay," Chance smiled. "I'm going to leave you in here. Now listen: Take all your clothes off, every bit, and get into the water. And be careful: the bubbles make the tub slippery. Don't fall and conk your head."

I nodded, still looking at all the bubbles.

"Hey," he bent over and lifted my chin with his finger. He looked into my eyes until I focused on him.

"I mean it. Be careful of the slippery tub."

I nodded solemnly.

He stood up and walked out, closing the door behind him.

I looked around the bathroom. It was bright and clean and smelled good. I looked at the toilet, then started taking everything off.

I placed my shoes and clothes on the floor in a neat line, then turned to the tub. As I walked up to it, I caught the sight of myself in the mirror. I'd never seen a mirror before; that's why I'd never known what my eyes looked like. Now, I saw more than my eyes: I was filthy.

I had dirt smeared everywhere. There was a line around my ankles, where my sneakers ended. My feet were a little dirty, but from my ankle upward, my legs were covered in grime.

The same thing had happened on my arms.

And on my neck. I could see the line where my shirt collar ended. My neck above it was filthy.

I turned my head and looked at my ear in the mirror.

I could see where Jess had cleaned away the blood and grime from my ear. The bandage had half come off where she'd stuck it.

I reached up and slowly peeled it away, cringing as I pulled.

I leaned closer.

My ear was a mess. The cut was across the outer edge, and there was a small tear in the flesh.

I touched it gingerly with my finger, and it stung.

I shivered.

I was getting cold standing there, so I turned back to the tub and sat on the edge.

I lifted my feet over and slipped them past the bubbles and into the warm water, and closed my eyes in pleasure.

I carefully slipped the rest of the way into the tub, and sunk down into the water.

Oh, it was bliss! Sheer bliss!

How had I ever not known of this?

The fountain Aunt Clare and I washed in had been cold, and we'd always been careful not to get any of the water on our face. Not in our mouth, nor in our eyes.

Aunt Clare had told me about microbes and bacteria: tiny creatures that could enter through your face and make you sick.

The water in the fountain had been so cold you couldn't stay in it for any length of time without starting to shiver.

This, however, was pure joy.

I could not help myself. I slipped all the way in. I put my entire face into the warm, bubbly water.

The feeling was fantastic.

I stayed lying in the bathwater for a very long time. The water started to grow cooler.

Then I remembered. Chance had said to put soap in my hair and wash it.

I dribbled a small bit of the slick soap on my hands, then massaged it into my hair.

It felt great!

My head felt so good as I washed my hair.

Brown grime mixed with the bubbles and dripped into the water.

"Wow." I *had* been filthy.

I dipped my head into the water to rinse it. I had to dip it into the water over and over and over, until the soap was mostly washed out.

Then I soaked some more, lying back in the tub, my hair piled up on top of my head, and my eyes closed.

I felt like a queen.

I lay there for a long time. The bathwater grew cool.

There was a soft knock at the door.

"Hey in there. Are you okay? It's been over an hour," Chance called through the door.

I sat up, splashing myself in the face.

Almost all the bubbles had popped. The water was dirty.

"Um, I'll be done in a minute," I called.

I stared at the water.

All the dirt that had been on me was in the water.

I looked at my arms. They were pale, and clean, scrubbed and pink from the warmth of the bathwater.

I grinned.

I felt wonderful!

But the water was growing positively cold, and was no longer fun. I had to get out.

I stared at the edge of the tub.

I'll just get out how I got in.

I tried to stand in the tub, and halfway up, my feet slipped out from under me and I plopped back down into the bath, and the water sloshed over the edge of the tub and onto the floor.

I tried again, this time gripping the sides of the tub.

I almost made it all the way up before falling down again.

More water splashed out in a great wave.

A great Holly wave.

I considered my predicament.

This is not as easy as I hoped.

I decided to try something new.

I turned over in the tub until I was on my knees, then, gripping the edge, slowly brought my shoulders up out of the water.

Success!

Okay, now try the next step.

I slowly brought one knee up and put my weight on it.

It slid sideways, hitting the edge of the bottom.

"Ow."

"You okay in there, Holly?" Chance said through the door. "Did you slip?"

"Um, I'm just having a bit of a hard time getting up out of the tub, Chance," I said.

"Be careful. Do you need help?"

"No, no. No, no, no. I'll be fine," I called out.

"I hope," I muttered under my breath.

I was still on one knee, with my foot braced against the bottom side of the tub.

Okay, slowly now. Balance!

I leaned my weight on the foot again, gripping the side of the tub, steadying myself when I felt the foot slide.

Careful ...

Then I brought the other knee up.

So far so good.

I gripped the edge of the tub, and slowly stood up.

My foot slid twice, but I caught it in time so I didn't fall.

I finally put one foot over the side to the floor.

Success! Whoops!

As I transferred my weight to the foot on the floor, my foot still in the bath slid.

I leaned forward and grabbed the towel hanging on the rod next to the bathtub, and stumbled out of the tub.

I stood there, breathing hard. I had never concentrated so hard in my life.

After taking a deep breath, I wrapped the towel around me. It was so big and fluffy!

I glanced at my clothes lined up on the floor and was filled with an intense repulsion. I did not want to put those filthy clothes back on.

Glancing down and my squeaky-clean feet, I decided I loved being clean.

"If I can, I want to be clean all the time," I said under my breath.

"What?" Chance said through the door.

"Nothing," I called over my shoulder.

I turned and opened the door.

Chance almost fell through.

"Were you leaning on the door?" I asked suspiciously.

"Oh. Oh, me? No. No, no, no. No."

I grinned.

"You look ..." he said, considering me, his head turned to the side

"I look what?" I asked.

"You look clean," he said. "It's a good look for you."

He moved out of the doorway.

"Sorry. Come out," he said.

"Thanks. Um, I really don't want to put those dirty clothes back on. But I don't have anything else to wear."

"I thought of that," said Chance, handing me a paper bag. "Here's a change of clothes for tomorrow, and a nightgown and socks for tonight."

"Oh, thank you!"

I was lying in my bed, in my new nightgown, wearing my new fuzzy socks, looking at the paper-wrapped book.

"Chance?" I called over to the other side of the room.

"Yeah?"

"Do you think I could unwrap this book? To read?"

"Oh, *The Book of Halloween*?" Chance asked.

"Yeah."

"Holly, that's *your* book. You're allowed to unwrap it and read it."

I smiled, then carefully unwrapped the brown paper, setting it aside to put the book back in when I was done.

My hands were still scrubbed pink from the bath. My fingers were wrinkled and pruney. I knew I was clean enough that I didn't need white cloth gloves to touch the book.

Besides, I had decided to add a new quirk to myself: I was going to be extra careful with all my own new things. My new clothes, my new shoes, my new books. Everything.

I carefully pulled the little blue and gold book out of the soft cloth bag the shopkeeper had wrapped it in, and opened it to the first page.

"The Book of Halloween," I read softly. I turned two more pages in. "The Book of Halloween. By Ruth Edna Kelley, A. M. Lynn Public Library."

I turned to Chance. "Chance?"

"Yeah?"

"What's a library?"

Chapter Ten
Happy Birthday

"Wake up, sleepyhead."

The voice came to me in a dream.

I was lost in a meadow made of pink cotton candy. I kept dipping my hand down into the pink grass and stuffing it into my mouth.

There was dark pink sticky stuff all around my lips and on my cheeks.

I heard a bird calling and looked up.

It was a raven, pure black and flying low, coming toward me fast.

Too fast.

I ducked.

The bird skimmed the top of the pink cotton candy grass, squawking loudly.

I stayed low, not wanting the bird to see me.

I'm not sure why, but I knew the bird represented danger. A danger I wanted no part of.

"Wake up, wake up, wake up ..."

There was the voice again. I swung my head around, searching for the source.

The pink wispy cotton candy smelled delicious, and my tongue flicked out and grabbed a few strands, lifting them to my mouth as I hid.

Is it safe to stand up yet?

I couldn't be sure.

I lifted my head to just below the top of the cotton candy grasses, and tried to look out on the pink meadow.

CAW! CAW! CAW!

I ducked down again. That had been close. The raven's cries sounded almost directly overhead.

I decided to lie flat on my stomach.

There was so much cotton candy grass it still hid me.

I tried not to breathe, tried not to make any sound.

My heart beat faster in fear.

The raven must not find me!

I stayed down like that for many minutes, and did not hear the raven again.

I should be okay down here. Maybe I'll just stay down on the ground for the rest of the afternoon. It should be safe, unless it rains ...

Almost on cue, I heard thunder overhead.

Oh no!

Fat drops began to fall, splattering on the cotton candy, tamping it down over and over until I was lying in a wide field of dark pink sticky-sweet goo.

I kept my head down.

The sticky cotton candy was now only three or four inches high, and I knew I was not hidden any more.

I heard the cawing of the raven, and my heart fell.

CAW! CAW! CAW!

I heard the sound of feather and then a *THUMP!* on my arm.

I uncovered my eyes and looked.

It was the raven!

My heart raced.

It had found me!

OH NO!

Panic!

I hid my face in my hands and closed my eyes...

"Holly, wake up, wake up, sleepyhead ..."

I felt a hand jiggle my shoulder.

I opened my eyes and saw I was in bed at the inn.

My heartbeat began to slow as I realized it had been a nightmare. I sat up in bed, rubbing my eyes.

"Happy birthday, Holly." Chance handed me a small box wrapped in shiny gold paper.

"It's my birthday?" I asked, still sleepy.

"Yes," he smiled.

I blinked and yawned.

I had never known exactly when my birthday was. I knew it was in the early fall, and that I was thirteen.

I opened my eyes wide.

"So I'm fourteen today?" I asked.

"That's right," Chance said from the other side of the room. "Now get dressed. We have a lot to do today.

I looked down at the box Chance had given me. It was about two inches square, and wrapped tightly, with a red ribbon tied around it.

"Is this from you?" I asked.

"Nope. That," Chance came close and pointed down at the box, "Is from a secret admirer." He winked.

A secret admirer?

I slowly unwrapped the box. Underneath the red ribbon and gold paper was a black velvet box containing a ...

"Oh!" I lifted the gold chain out and held it high. A tiny figure of two green spiky leaves and three red berries reflected in the light. The green leaves and red berries were composed of tiny faceted gems clasped tightly by gold prongs. The whole thing was about half an inch wide. It was amazing.

Chance walked up and peered at the delicate piece of jewelry. "Wowwww."

I was speechless.

I had never ever owned anything remotely as pretty and obviously valuable as this.

"Want me to put it on you?" Chance whispered.

I nodded and held it out to him.

"Move your hair."

I reached up and pulled my hair to the side.

Chance latched the chain to my neck and straightened it.

"Holly, that is really gorgeous and special," he said.

"But who gave it to me?" I whispered.

"I have no idea, but you are one lucky girl." Chance nodded.

We had breakfast down in the inn's dining room, and I stuffed myself full of eggs, sausage, and bacon.

Chance smiled as I tried to stuff a triangle of toast smeared with butter and jelly into my mouth all at once.

"Take is easy, Holly. You're wolfing your food down too fast. You're going to make yourself sick."

I slowed down.

I had tucked the birthday necklace down under my shirt, and given back Chance's necklace. He'd taken it gratefully, latching it around his neck and patting it.

I looked down at my uniform. It consisted of a starched white blouse with a Peter Pan collar, and a navy blue and pink tartan wool pleated skirt. Black knee-high socks and brown leather shoes completed the ensemble. I felt so incredible! I had never felt this good in my life.

I felt secure, well fed, happy, clean, and well dressed.

It was amazing!

"Before we catch our plane, I want to go shopping in the fae marketplace one more time," said Chance. "Tell me, Holly. What would you like from me for your birthday?"

I blinked.

"You're getting me a present too?"

"Well, of course I'm getting you a present. I'm your first fae friend, aren't I? That's a position of privilege and importance." He beamed happily.

I giggled.

"Hmmm, well ..." I thought for a few minutes. "I did recently lose my coat. I feel weird without one ..."

"Done. Let's go coat shopping," Chance stood up from the table and put out his hand.

I stared at it. It was a smooth light brown, and looked strong and sure. I looked up at Chance. He *was* my first fae friend. My *only* fae friend. I rose from the table and took his hand, and he led me out into the marketplace.

It was sunny and bright, and a gentle breeze blew through the plaza.

Chance led the way to a store that had multiple types of coats in the window.

There were yellow coats with white fluff around the hoods. Blue coats with black fluffy collars, and green coats with purple fluffy collars.

I stared. There was a dark red jacket in the window, on the side. It had a detachable collar with a soft brown fluffiness all around it. I had never seen such a beautiful coat.

"You like the red one?" asked Chance. "It nice! I think it would look great on you, Holly. Shall we go see if it fits?"

I felt dazed. I never thought I would have such a jacket, all to myself. Chance led the way into the shop, and talked to the shopkeeper, who left and returned shortly with the jacket.

I stared at it.

It was a dark red/purply/pink color that matched my plaid skirt, and I felt a happy glow at the sight of it.

There were zippers crisscrossing it, and snaps, and the collar could flip down after the fur edge was detached.

"Try it on," Chance said.

The shopkeeper helped me into the coat; it was a perfect fit.

It was made of a buttery soft leather I couldn't stop touching.

"That's lambskin, Miss," the shopkeeper murmured.

"Oh, it's lovely!" I said enthusiastically.

"We'll take it," said Chance. "And she'll be wearing it. Maybe we can detach the fur edge of the collar and put it in a bag?"

The shopkeeper nodded and shortly thereafter, I was walking out of the shop in the jacket, looking so nice I doubt Aunt Clare would have even been able to recognize me.

"Okay," said Chance, checking his watch. "It's time we headed to the airport."

"The airport?" I asked.

"Yes. The Academy is in Ireland."

"Can't we just magic there? Like the tree Jess lived in?" I asked.

Chance laughed. "No, no. Jess does live on the edge of Central Park, her tree home is just behind a gate. The gates lead from the human realm into the fae realms. But they don't go over distances. For that, we have to use regular old transportation."

He stopped.

"What?" I asked.

"That's my favorite ice cream shop. I'd hate to leave North America without having a scoop of my favorite flavor," said Chance, grinning. "Let's go!"

We ducked into the ice cream shop, and emerged ten minutes later with ice cream cones.

Chance licked his, which was a scoop flavored like German chocolate cake, and I licked mine.

I'd never had ice cream before, so this was another new experience to add to my growing list.

My cone was strawberry cheesecake, and I could not stop licking it. It was the most delicious thing I'd ever tasted.

"Okay," Chance said.

We continue walking slowly.

"Okay what?" I asked.

Chance laughed. "Sorry, this is so good it's distracting me. Um ..."

I licked my ice cream in relish, completely understanding him.

"Oh, I almost forgot," he said. "We need to get you a haircut."

I stopped.

My hair was bushy and unruly, and a mass of wild wavy hair that tumbled down to my waist.

Chance looked around, then said, "Come on."

I followed him around a corner and down a side lane that was lined with various shops selling hairbrushes, combs, shaving kits, other personal grooming items, and makeup.

"Here we go," Chance stopped at a shop with a striped candy cane pole twirling in the air. I looked in the front window and saw several people in chairs, with other people holding scissors and combs and snipping away at their hair.

"Haircut," said Chance. He looked at me. "Maybe just a trim and a style, to get it under control. He opened the door and ushered me in.

I finished my ice cream cone and immediately wanted another one. I made a mental note to ask if there was ice cream at the school.

Chance spoke to the receptionist, and a few minutes later, I was in a chair that reclined back toward a sink, and a nice lady was spraying warm water in my hair from a faucet.

Ten minutes later I was seated in another padded chair, and she was asking me what I wanted.

I wanted another ice cream cone.

Chance leaned over to us.

"Just a trim, and some conditioner. Get it under control. She starts at the Academy this week," he said.

"Gotcha," said the hair stylist, and started combing my hair into sections. "You have really lovely hair, Sweetheart."

"Oh, thank you," I said uncertainly.

"So, how old are you? twelve? Thirteen?"

"I just turned fourteen," I said.

"Oh, you're petite for your age. That's very cute!" She started snipping the ends of my locks with her scissors. "And are you looking forward to starting school soon?" she asked as she cut my locks, a small bit at a time.

"Um, yes. Yes, I am."

"That's nice ..."

I closed my eyes for just a second; the snipping sound and the warm water had made me sleepy. I think I must have fallen asleep, because the next thing I knew, she was turning my seat and saying "All done, Sweetheart. And I trimmed your nails, too."

She handed me a mirror and I looked at myself.

I blinked.

I was clean. My face was clean and pretty. My hands looked clean and neat. My hair was tamed! She had cut the length significantly, and now, instead of reaching to my waist, my hair reached just halfway down my arms. It was drying in the air and starting to get wavy.

"I put in some conditioner, Sweetheart. And your boyfriend bought a bottle of it, for you to take home."

I blushed furiously. "He's not my boyfriend, he's just my friend," I said in a quiet voice.

"Oh? Well, that's a pity. You two make a cute couple," she said, turning my chair and gently taking the hand mirror from me. "There you go, that's done."

I slowly got down from the cushioned chair and stepped away from the stylist. I glanced back once, and caught my reflection in the large mirror against the wall.

"Hey," said Chance, meeting me at the front. "You look great."

"Thanks," I said, grinning.

"I paid and we can go," he said. A small bag bounced against his leg.

"What's that?" I asked.

"A bottle of conditioner. The stylist said it would help keep your hair tidy. Oh, and a hairbrush," he said.

"A hairbrush?"

"Yeah. You've got a lot of hair. You need to brush it several times a day," He said.

I made another mental note. Brush hair morning and night.

"Chance?" I looked around. "Is this the last time we're going to be in this marketplace for a while?"

"Pretty much," he said. "We fly from New York to Ireland in a few hours. We should go to the airport now."

"Okay." I looked around. I was growing very fond of the fae marketplace. The stone buildings, the people shopping, I was going to miss it all.

"Don't worry, we can come back to visit soon. Maybe at Christmas."

I nodded.

Chapter Eleven
Arriving at the Academy

I slept on the plane the whole way. Something about the hum and the cozy seats just put me straight to sleep.

When we landed, Chance and I made our way to the desk where everyone was stopping.

I felt a nervous tension in my stomach.

"Chance," I whispered. "They are giving that man a booklet and he's letting them pass. I don't have a booklet. What am I going to do?"

"Don't worry," Chance whispered back. "I have all the necessary documents. The counsel made sure."

"But ..." I fell silent. The man at the desk was looking at us.

I ducked my face and looked at my shoes.

I was in love with my new shoes. They were a brown leather, and the soles were hard and new, good soles, no holes at all.

In the past, I'd had shoes that others had discarded. They were stained and damaged, and there were often holes in the soles.

Everything is new.

We stepped forward.

"Passports?" The man asked in a disinterested tone.

Chance handed the man two booklets, which the man opened and stamped, then handed back.

We stepped through and walked into the airport terminal.

"See? I told you it'd be okay," Chance whispered.

I shrugged.

Inside, I could feel the tension slowly drain out of me.

"This way," said Chance.

We took a taxicab out of the city and into the countryside of Antrim. Chance had the driver let us off at a petrol station.

I stood there, my bag on my shoulder, the knowledge of the paper bag of rainbow bagels inside comforting me.

Chance stood beside me, his own bag on his shoulder, talking on his cell phone.

"Yes. Yes. No. Okay. Thank you." He ended the call and slipped the phone into his bag. "Just so you know, cellphones don't really work in the fae realm. Which we are about to slip into. Look."

An old wooden wagon loaded with hay and driven by an old man was coming into view on the dirt road that led back around the petrol station.

"Did you just summon that on your phone?" I asked.

"Yes," Chance said with a grin, stepping forward to meet the wagon.

The old man had a big, bushy beard and an old floppy hat that looked like it was crusted with dried manure on the rim. He was driving two huge brown shire horses. They had the most enormous feet I had ever seen on a horse.

Aunt Clare and I had watched the horses in Central Park, that pulled the small carriages around the paths, giving people rides for coin. They had been good sized, but nowhere near as large as these gentle giants.

As the team approached, I couldn't help myself, I walked up alongside Chance and stretched my hand out to the closer steed, who dipped his head and nuzzled my palm.

A thrill of happiness traveled down my back.

"Holly? Time to climb up," Chance said, holding out his hand.

I turned and looked up at the old man, and did a double take.

He had pointed ears, and his smile was just a little wider than normal.

He had a pipe in his mouth, and a thin curl of smoke rose lazily from it.

Chance led me to the other side of the front seat and climbed up to sit beside the old man, then bent and offered me his hand.

I stretched and took it, and between Chance's pull and my climb, I clambered up and sat beside my new friend.

"Here'm," the old man rumbled, handing us an old woolen, and very hairy, folded blanket to lay across our laps.

One we were situated, the old man clucked to the horses, who turned around and began ambling back down the dirt road.

It was such a contrast: I watched us leave the modern petrol station behind, with its paved parking lot, its tall floodlights, and its modern cars parked all in a row, and turned to look forward over the ears of the shire horses as the old wagon creaked down the dirt road.

Huge trees, their brilliant green leaves fluttering madly in the breeze, seemed to welcome us as we rode along.

It was clear we were leaving the modern human world behind and traveling to the olde world of Enchanted Faerie.

The wagon wheels trundled along, and we swayed back and forth with the wagon's movement. The horses were glorious: very strong, they didn't seem to strain at all to pull the wagon, which must have been heavy, loaded down as it was with both hay bales and three people.

I looked around us. The trees on the left were very tall; on the right we soon left the petrol station far behind us.

Then the trees on the right began, and we were no longer riding down a dirt lane on the side of a forest, but entering into the deep wood.

The forest was all around us, its sights and sounds mesmerizing to me.

I'd lived on the city streets all my life. The closest to a forest I'd ever been was Central Park, which was very nice, but it was a park, not a forest.

This wood was wild and untamed.

About a hundred feet into the deep forest we passed a barrier of some sort. I felt it as a cool hum that made my hair stand on end.

"What was that?" I asked.

Chance smiled. "We just passed into the land of the Fae."

I turned and looked back over my shoulder, but could see no difference along the path we'd just traversed.

Wait.

Actually, I could: I saw a shimmer at the edges of my vision, almost like pavement on a very hot day.

I turned back around and eagerly faced forward again. I wanted to see what was coming.

"Chance," I whispered. "Tell me about the school? What does it look like?"

"Well, it's a castle the Queen converted ages ago," said Chance. "Made of stone, it can get quite chilly in winter, but don't worry, there are fireplaces in nearly every room. And the dorm rooms have tapestries hung on the walls, to make them cozier."

I tried to imagine a school in a castle and couldn't.

After about ten miles, the dirt road the wagon was following turned down a slope and to the left.

The forest sounds got louder.

"What's going on?" I asked.

Chance smiled. "We're getting closer to the school. There's more wildlife as we get closer."

"Why is that?"

"It's because of the allurement spell that covers the grounds," said Chance. "The spell extends to several miles outside the school and acts as an umbrella protectant for the wild animals, among other things."

"I don't understand," I said.

"You'll see, said Chance. "It's a part of orientation, and also your Enchantments class, I believe."

"Okay," I sat back.

The forest was getting darker, and I could see fireflies through the trees.

The wagon wheels suddenly changed their tone, and I saw the dirt ruts had given way to a road paved with cobblestones, with lampposts on either side.

It was enchanting.

"Look there." Chance pointed through the trees. I leaned and looked, and just through the trunks I could see a doe with her two fawns was drinking from a pond in a glade illuminated amidst the dark forest.

"Ohhh," I smiled.

"We'll be coming 'round a bend in the road and then up to the grounds of the school, and you'll see it from far away at first," Chance said, nodding to the front.

I watched the road expectantly.

The trees slowly gave way as the road we were on emerged onto the Academy grounds, which were expansive.

Green grass grew everywhere, and the road was now lined with small trees that grew about twenty feet high.

As the lane curved, the school came into view.

The great dark stone structure rose at least five or six stories into the sky. I saw many lit windows, and I could make out the shadows of people moving back and forth in some of them.

There were about two dozen other kids on the front lawn of the school, all in uniform.

They were playing with balls on the grass, running back and forth, and kicking the balls to each other.

"Football, which Americans call soccer," said Chance. "It's a big sport at the school."

The kids stopped what they doing to watch as the wagon approached the front of the school.

I whispered to Chance, "Is it a rare thing, the wagon bringing students to the school?"

Chance nodded. "Somewhat rare, yes."

I felt instantly self-conscious.

"Don't worry, you'll do fine," said Chance. "Everyone starts at year one. You'll be what's called a 'freshman' and they'll tell you everything at orientation."

I suddenly thought of something.

"Chance? Are you going to be there?"

"At what? Orientation?"

I nodded.

"I'll be there, but behind the scenes," he said. "You probably won't see much of me today after I check you in."

"Check me in?"

Chance nodded as the wagon pulled up to the front steps of the school and came to a stop. "That's where we're going now."

I gulped, worried.

I had followed Chance all the way from the city I knew and the underground and the cubby, to this far-away land. We'd flown overnight on an airplane, and come all the way out here, and I felt comfortable with him. But I hadn't given any thought to what would happen when he had to leave.

A sinking feeling began to grow in the pit of my stomach.

"Don't worry. My sister's best friend's little sister is in your class," he said. "She knows the school, from tagging along with me, and she got here a week ago. Her name is Liesl, you'll like her."

"A week ago?" I asked. "When does the school year start?"

"It starts in three days. Today is Thursday, and it'll be dark in a few hours," said Chance. "Then there's the weekend. Then your first class starts Monday morning, bright and early." He winked at me.

"Bright and early?" I asked in a small voice.

"First class for freshmen is at eight a.m. Breakfast is at seven. Your dorm supervisor will help you get used to the routine."

I fell silent, a thousand worries in my head. A million more crowded in the lump in my throat.

Buck up, Holly. You didn't expect him to stick around with you the whole time you were in school, did you?

"My dorm is on the other side of the castle, and my classes are in a different area than yours as well," said Chance. "But don't worry, I'm sure we'll see each other around."

I had never been able to figure out how to stop worrying. I wondered if this was a skill they would teach me at the school.

Chance had hopped to the ground and was holding his hand out to help me down.

I stood and took his hand.

Then I heard them.

There was a group of about ten schoolgirls off to the side, pointing and laughing at me. I stood on the top wagon step and stared at them.

Chance swung around and addressed them.

"HEY, CUT IT OUT, YOU LOT!" his voice rang out across the grass.

I blushed furiously and jumped down. Thank goodness I didn't trip; they would have had even more to laugh at then.

I stood next to Chance as he pulled our bags from the wagon. I glanced all around me, but the other girls had run to another part of the lawn.

Chance patted my shoulder. "I have the authority to alert their dorm supervisors and to assign punishment," he said. "They ran off probably because they didn't want any trouble."

This sounded even worse. I worried the girls would tease me whenever Chance wasn't around, and he'd just explained that he wasn't going to see me much anymore.

The sinking feeling in my gut deepened.

"Chance," I swung around and took his arm. "You said anyone is free to go, right? That we're allowed to quit the school?"

He nodded, a serious look on his face.

"What happens if I decide I don't want to stay?"

He glanced in the direction the other girls had run, then back to me.

"Holly, give it a week. If you're still thinking of leaving the school after a week, come see me, and we'll talk."

I opened my mouth to protest, but he held up his hand to stop me. "And," he said. "if it does come to it, I give you my word I will return you to the exact spot where we first met."

I stared at him. There were a million feelings in my heart and mind, and I felt so ... so FULL of indecision I could barely breathe.

"Come on. I'll show you where you need to go, and get you checked in."

Chapter Twelve

Orientation

We entered the Academy through huge double doors that creaked as they swung open.

Chance led the way to the center hallway, then through a door on the left and into a smaller waiting room.

"Sit here. I'll check you in," he said, indicating the chairs against the wall.

I sat down, my bag at my feet, and started fiddling with the straps of the bag to release my worry. I watched Chance talk with the man at the desk. The man looked through a sheaf of papers, found what he was looking for, and made a checkmark on the page. Then he nodded at Chance, and indicated the door behind him.

Chance walked through and closed it behind him.

I waited. And waited.

"Would you like a drink of water while you wait, Miss Ó Cuilinn?"

I stared at him.

That's my last name. I'd better get used to it.

"Uh ..."

"He may be a long time in conference with the headmistress," the man said.

I took a deep breath. "Yes, thank you. Water will be fine."

He nodded and left the room, and returned a few minutes later with a glass of cold water.

I sipped it and was surprised. It tasted delicious, and faintly of lemon and mint. I looked down into the water and saw a leaf at the bottom.

The water was cool and crisp and I drain the glass in less than a minute.

I set it down on the table off to the side and continued to wait. I put my hand to my neck to make sure my birthday necklace was still there, and felt reassured when I touched the chain and charm through my blouse.

It was another half hour until the door opened again and Chance came through.

"Okay, she'll see you now," he said.

I rose from the chair. "Are you coming, too?" I whispered.

He nodded. "Yes, I'll introduce you. Come on." He put his hand to my back, and I walked forward into the headmistress's office.

"Miss Ó Cuilinn," the older lady behind the desk rose and extended her hand. "It's a pleasure to finally meet you."

I took her hand in mine and move it slowly up and down. Her palm was cool and dry and pleasant.

She smelled of evergreen and plumeria. I knew what those smelled like. The park was full of evergreen, and I loved that smell.

Aunt Clare had one found a small, mostly empty bottle of perfume. She'd said the words on the bottle were "sample" and "plumeria" and she'd let me smell it once.

It had smelled like this lady.

Her white hair was streaked here and there with grey, and it was swept up in a hairdo that looked very elegant.

Her dress was a royal blue, and she wore white gloves.

She also wore a scarf with peacock feathers painted on it.

She reminded me of the people Aunt Clare and I had seen from across the street as we'd sat on a bench and watched people go into a building. They'd been all dressed up.

Aunt Clare had said they were going to something called "opera."

I'd called such ladies "fancy ladies" when I was younger.

"Please, sit down. Make yourself comfortable," she said. "I am Professor Ó Baoghill. I teach History here at Titania Academy. I'd like to formally welcome you to our school." She smiled.

I felt cheered.

"Thank you. I'm happy to be here," I said.

"Now, Mr. Mac Craith here tells me you have never attended a formal institution of learning, is that correct?" The headmistress asked.

I glanced at Chance.

Chance Mac Craith huh?

I smiled at him, and he nodded his head.

I cleared my throat. "Yes, that is correct."

Professor Ó Baoghill began leafing through the papers on her desk. While still looking down at them, she asked, "And you have lived in America your entire life, is that correct?" She looked up at me.

"Yes, that is correct," I answered.

She continued consulting the papers.

"Very good. Now, I see here the proof that you are indeed of fae heritage, and so you have the legal right to attend the Academy. In fact," she glanced up at me, "In fact, we have a legal and moral obligation to accept you here. The facts of your heritage have guaranteed you a small inheritance, as well. I have the box right here."

She bent and unlocked a drawer in her desk, brought forth a long metal box, and placed it on her desk.

"Now, make no mistake, Miss Ó Cuilinn, we are extremely pleased you are here." The headmistress took a deep breath and looked very serious. "The mere fact of your presence brings certain ... ah ... effects to not only the school, but the land around it. Now, this box contains that part of your inheritance that was bestowed upon you so far. Would you like to examine the contents?"

I blinked.

An inheritance? I have an inheritance??

"I ... I guess so," I said softly.

Without a word, she lifted the box and swung it around to face me, then handed me the key.

I stood up and took a step forward, taking the key from her.

I gulped.

"Uh," I looked up at the headmistress. "Can you tell me ..."

She waited for me to finish.

"... who it was that left me this?"

She nodded. "Your father has bequeathed this to you, Miss Ó Cuilinn."

I nodded and slowly fitted the key into the lock, then turned it.

The top was hinged in the back, and as I lifted it, it swung backwards.

Professor Ó Baoghill gently grabbed the lid, and swung it all the way back.

The box had a second metal top, with a half-moon cutout on the side. I put my finger in and lifted this second piece, and looked inside.

There were a number of objects I couldn't identify, a leather pouch, a paper check, and a ring.

The headmistress and Chance both stayed silent as I took the time to go through the contents of the box.

It took a while.

"All right, Miss Ó Cuilinn, as you have instructed, we will keep this in the student section of the school vault," said the headmistress. "Now, you have been assigned to a dormitory that you will share with six other girls. There are five dormitories in each wing, and each wing has a house mother who will look after you all and take care of the issues that arise in your dormitory wing while you are here at the school. I will show you to your dormitory at this time. Your belongings should already be there, we get deliveries every day." She stood up and came around to stand in front of her desk. "Are you ready to come with me?"

I stood up and turned to Chance.

He stood and met my eyes, a look of resignation on his face.

"Well, this is where we part, at least for now, Holly."

He stuck his hand out for a handshake. I looked at it, then rushed into his arms and hugged him.

He hugged me back, squeezing me tightly.

"You're going to be okay, Holly," said Chance. "You're a good person."

"I wish you didn't have to leave," I said.

"I'll be nearby. We'll bump into each other, I promise," said Chance. "I'm just going to be in the blue wing, with the other second-years."

I loosened my hug and looked up at him. "Thank you for all you did." I whispered.

He grinned. "I would do it all again in a heartbeat."

He handed me a bag. "Here's the rainbow bagels."

I laughed and took the bag.

"Thank you."

He stayed where he was as I walked out with Professor Ó Baoghill, and waved when I looked back at him.

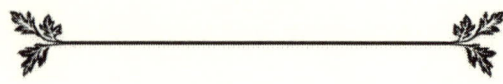

The headmistress led me on a winding path up some stairs and down a few corridors to the dorm room. I passed multiple other students in the hall. Some seemed friendly, most just stared, their jaws dropped open.

"Professor Ó Baoghill, why are they looking at me that way?" I asked, when we were alone again on a stairwell.

"What do you mean, Miss Ó Cuilinn?"

"I mean," I jerked my head back down the stairs. "Those girls in the hallway, they were staring at me like this." I dangled my jaw and opened my eyes wide.

"Oh, well, let me look into that." She turned and continued up the stairs.

I put my head down and followed her. I didn't want to make trouble at my new school, but really, I hadn't *done* anything. I'd just been walking. The other girls were looking at me strangely. It wasn't my imagination. I knew it.

At the top of this staircase, Professor Ó Baoghill led me down a short hallway and through an ancient wooden door.

"Here we are, dear, she said. "Oh, look, Miss Becker and Miss Penner are already here.

I looked over at the other beds. Two were occupied. One of the girls was pulling on the bag the other one was holding, and the first girl was breathing hard.

The second girl had tears in her eyes.

I glanced at the headmistress, who seemed to be studiously avoiding the obvious conflict between the two girls.

"Here, I think this is your bed," the older woman indicated the bunk on the other side of the teary-eyed girl.

I slowly approached and sat on the bed, laying my bag next to me.

"And see? Your belongings have already been delivered, my dear. Well, I have a hundred other duties. Remember to come down for The Assigning, dear. All of you must attend. Until then, ta!"

And the headmistress left.

The second the door shut, the first girl started yanking the second girl's bag.

"LET GO!" the first girl screamed.

The second girl, on the bed next to mine, held on tightly to her bag as tears spilled out and ran down her cheeks.

I didn't know which girl was which, but I could recognize a bully when I saw one. I was already feeling bullied by all the looks and snickering behind my back, and I felt an instant kinship with the unknown girl getting picked on.

"Leave her alone," I said in a steely voice.

The girl with the bag glanced at me, a pleading look on her face.

The girl trying to take her bag ignored me.

Without a word, I walked over to the bully and gave her a hard shove.

She let go of the bag she was trying to take from its owner and fell back onto the next bed, rolled off, and landed on the floor.

"AHH!" she cried.

Her head bumped the bedpost, and her hand knocked against the floor.

She immediately grabbed her head, moaning.

"Ohhh, my head! You're going to get in trouble for this," she said.

I walked over to her.

"Oh, stop. You're not hurt." I stood over her, my hands on my hips.

"Shoving is against the rules," she scowled.

"If shoving is against the rules, then stealing is, too," I said in a quiet voice. "What do you think you were doing when we walked in? Reciting poetry?"

She stood up and faced me, her fists balled.

I took a step forward. I was now just a few inches from her.

"If you ever bully her, or anyone else again, I *will* hurt you. Understand?" I said.

Her face went red and her eyes scanned me.

"I should have known you were misborn," said the bully. "Skinny little ruffian, you don't scare me. I've seen your type before. How'd you even get into this school anyway? You're probably poor ..."

CRACK!

She fell back down.

I flexed my fist. It hurt like anything, but I wasn't about to show it.

Her hand went to her nose, and came away bloody.

"You broke my nose! YOU BROKE MY NOSE!" she shrieked.

"You nose isn't broken," I spat. "But I can break it for you if you'd like."

"I'M GOING TO TELL THE HEADMISTRESS." she cried.

"Go ahead. You tell your side, and I'll tell mine," I said quietly. "And I've got a witness."

The girl got up and ran out of the dorm room, holding her nose as she hurried out.

I turned to watch her go.

Chapter Thirteen
The Assigning

Just as the mean girl left the dorm room, four others entered.

"Why was Jessica bleeding?" asked the tallest of the girls in a thick French accent. The other three just shrugged.

I sat on my bunk and began to put my things away.

The girl who'd been bullied came over and gave me a soft smile. "I'm Liesl," she said in a thick German accent. "Thank you," she said shyly.

I nodded and smiled. "I'm Holly."

"Hi, Holly," said Liesl. "Want to sit together at dinner?"

I nodded. "Yes, definitely."

"Hey, you two," said the tall girl. "I asked you why Jessica was bleeding." She stood there, hands on hips, waiting for our reaction.

I shrugged and continued to sort through my meager belongings.

Liesl shrugged as well, and climbed back onto her bunk.

The tall girl stood there silently, tapping her foot, then glanced at her three friends, who were gathered next to her.

I unwrapped the boxes that had been delivered to my bunk and put them away, then consulted the paper schedule the headmistress had given me.

It was a good ten minutes before tall girl and her three barbie sidekicks made rude sounds and went to their bunks to unpack their own belongings.

It was clear: Liesl and I were the same, and the other girls wanted nothing to do with us.

"Dinner is soon, want to go now?" whispered Liesl.

"Maybe. Do you think our stuff is safe to leave?" I whispered back, glancing at the other girls.

Liesl looked over at them. They were talking among themselves and ignoring us. She shrugged.

The door opened, and in walked an upperclassman. She was dark and apparently in an extremely good mood.

"HI, EVERYONE!" She stood there with an expectant air.

After a few seconds, Liesl and I said "hi" shyly.

I guess we're going to be the shy brigade.

"Hello."

"Hi."

"Hi, Sarah!"

The upperclassman waved at everyone.

"My name is Sarah Goodheart, and I'm your dorm supe. Before we go down to dinner, I need to go over a few things."

"Miss Goodheart, Jessica isn't here. She left a while ago, and she was BLEEDING." The taller girl said, distressed.

"Yes, I know, Naomi. I've already talked with her," said Sarah. "That's one of the things I wanted to address now."

Naomi glanced over at Liesl and me, smirking.

"Now, every single day, including weekends, breakfast is at seven a.m. sharp. First class is at eight a.m. sharp. We don't dawdle. At all. I do not want any of you reported for being late." She fixed us with a serious look.

"Okay, continuing: lunch is at half past twelve. Classes resume at half past one p.m. and go until half past four p.m. So, there are five classes Monday through Friday. The weekend is yours, but the meals are at the same time, so don't miss them."

She fell silent, thinking for a moment. Then began speaking again.

"Curfew is nine p. m. You *will* be abed on the stroke of nine. Do you understand?"

We all nodded.

"Now, I understand Jessica had a mishap earlier. Tell me: who was present at the time?"

I stayed silent, though my eyes grew wider when Naomi and her friends all pointed at Liesl and me.

"I see," said Miss Goodheart in a firm voice. "Then you four," she pointed at Naomi and the other three, "leave now while I have a private word with the other two. Go down to the dining hall. We will be down shortly."

They left, solemn expressions on their faces.

When the door shut behind them, Miss Goodheart turned to Liesl and I. "All right. Tell me what happened."

I looked down at my hands.

"Jessica was trying to take my bag. She had grabbed it and was trying to pull it from my hands," Liesl said in a quiet voice.

"Go on," Miss Goodheart said.

"We were alone. Then the headmistress came in with Holly, said a few words, and left. Oh, and she completely ignored Jessica with her hands on my bag."

Liesl frowned. "Not sure why. Anyway, when the headmistress left, Jessica began pulling my bag again, and started screaming at me to let go. Holly came and told Jessica to leave me alone. Jessica ignored her. Holly shoved her onto her bed, and she rolled off the bed to the ground, where she bumped her head. Then she got up and said something to Holly about … about being misborn, skinny, and poor." She stopped, and looked down.

"And how did she get the bloody nose?" asked Miss Goodheart.

I finally spoke. "Because I punched her."

The older girl looked at me. "You punched her in the nose?"

I nodded.

"Because she was disparaging you, Holly?"

I nodded. "I punched her, and she fell back to the ground. I guess that's when her nose started bleeding." I looked down, feeling ashamed, but not sure why.

I looked up at Miss Goodheart. "I'm sorry I made her bleed, but I'm not sorry I stopped a bully from stealing Liesl's bag."

"Miss Goodheart, Jessica was trying to take my bag. The handle started to rip. See?" Liesl held the bag up and showed the older girl, who took a good look at the partially ripped handle.

"Take that to housekeeping. There's a seamstress who can mend it for you," Miss Goodheart said quietly.

Then she looked up and folded her hands.

"You probably have questions. I'll try to answer them. First of all, the headmistress does not get involved with petty disputes and bullying. It's not because she isn't supposed to, it's because she is of sprite ancestry, and is nonconfrontational by nature. It's in her genes. Kind of silly that she's in charge of this school, but she lets the disciplining fall to the dorm supervisors."

Miss Goodheart took a deep breath.

"Jessica came to me and told me her version of what happened. I sent her to the nurse and thence to the dining hall."

I looked up sharply. "Wait. 'her version'?"

The older girl shook her head. "What Jessica told me happened does not get people bloody noses."

I felt a small bit of relief.

"I understand the situation, and I'm going to ask you to, from now on, please handle it without drawing blood, if at all possible." She looked at me, her head to the side. "Holly, I am afraid we don't often have misborns here at Titania Academy, so you may be the target of some adverse attitudes, despite your royal heritage. I will try to make things better when I see this happening, but I can't be everywhere.

"People can be cruel, and students often group themselves into cliques. I just hope things don't get too bad." She patted my hand as she rose. "Please keep me posted on things?"

I nodded, feeling dazed.

Liesl stayed silent and wide-eyed during this exchange.

Miss Goodheart paused by the door. "Well, what are you waiting for? It's dinnertime."

We followed her out and down the stairs.

Liesl whispered "So, no punishment? That's really good!"

I nodded. I was expecting at least a reprimand and detention or something.

The dining hall was very crowded. Liesl and I stood in line with our trays, got our food, then took seats at the end of a table full of giggling girls. Jessica, Naomi, and the other girls were nowhere to be seen.

Hopefully they're on the other side of the room.

The dinner was delicious, but I kept glancing around, hoping to see Chance.

As we were finishing, two strange girls came up to us.

"Hi," they said in unison.

"Hi," I replied.

"Are you really of the royal line?" The shorter girl asked.

"Uhhh," I didn't know what to say. "It's what I've been told ..."

"Yeah, that would be the case with a misborn, huh?" The girls dissolved into giggles and stumbled away.

I scowled into my water glass.

"Holly," Liesl had put her head close to mine. "Don't let them get to you. None of that's your fault."

"I know, but ever since I got to the school, literally before I got off the wagon that brought us here, people have been doing that," I said.

"Making fun of you?"

I nodded.

"They're just stupid and ignorant," said Liesl. "It's what's inside that counts, not who your parents were."

"Then why am I a joke to them?" I asked in a low tone.

"I told you. Because they're stupid and ignorant."

I couldn't help it, I grinned.

Liesl suddenly looked up and blushed.

"Hi, stranger," said a voice from behind me.

I turned to look.

"Chance!" I rose and grabbed him in a hug.

"Oh, hey. Easy, easy," said Chance, working to remain standing. "Is everything okay?"

I wiped tears from my eyes in horror. I had not meant to cry. It's just that seeing him again made me feel so much. "Yeah, I'm fine. Just went off balance is all." I turned to my new bunkmate. "Oh, Chance, this is Liesl, my new friend. Liesl, this is Chance."

Liesl got to her feet, blushing furiously. "Hi."

Chance bowed, "Please to see you again, Liesl. I'm glad you're making friends with Holly." He stuck his hand out.

Liesl put her hand out to shake his, a silly grin on her face.

Chance took her hand and brought it to his lips. "Enchanted."

I though Liesl was going to pee her pants. I kid you not, her face was so red she looked like a strawberry.

I smiled and ducked my head.

"So Chance, do you eat in the dining hall every day, too?" I asked.

"Most days, although I'm usually over there," he waved vaguely through a set of double doors where I spied more tables of students.

"Huh," I said. "Well, would you like to start sitting with us?" I put my head to the side, smiling up at him.

He chuckled. "I suppose that would be fine."

I glanced at Liesl and she looked pleased.

Suddenly, there was the sound of a hunting horn outside, and everyone started getting up, their voices rising to a loud hubbub.

"What's that?" I asked Chance. "What's going on?"

"Oh! It's The Assigning. It's where first years get assigned their familiars," Chance said.

Their what?

Liesl clapped her hands in delight. "Oh! Grandma told me about the familiars, I can't wait! I hope I get a cat!"

"What is a familiar?" I asked.

Liesl looked at me with a shocked expression.

"Holly didn't grow up in a magical household, Liesl," Chance explained.

"Oh," Liesl said softly. "I'm sorry," she said to me.

I shrugged. "It's okay. I'm here now." I grinned.

Liesl laughed.

"Holly, a familiar is a magical animal that is bonded to you," said Chance. "It's a spell, so the headmistress will cast the spell over you, and your familiar will appear beside you. And they're connected to you for life. They are mostly invisible, until you need them."

I looked at him, my jaw dropped in surprise.

"I was raised by my grandmother. She had a large black cat as her familiar, said Liesl. "I really miss them." She smiled wistfully.

I stared at Chance. "What's your familiar, Chance?"

In response, he said several magical words that fled my memory as soon as I heard them. A hawk appeared on Chance's shoulder.

It was magnificent.

"Ohhhh," I exclaimed.

"Chance, that looks so cool," Liesl said.

Chance grinned, said the words again, and the hawk disappeared again.

"Is he still there, just invisible?" I asked.

"No, he's not there. He is back in the forest," said Chance. "He appears when I call him or need him."

I nodded, still amazed.

"Well, come on, you two. Let's head out to The Assigning." Chance led the way out to the front lawn.

There were tiki torches erected on the boundaries of the large grassy expanse.

Headmistress Ó Baoghill stood on a large boulder with a parchment scroll.

She was calling a name out.

A boy rose and approached the professor and held out his hand.

She shook it, then gestures for him to walk into a ...

What was that?

It looked like a big rock arch, with white mist in the center. The mist was swirling and curling, but it never left the arch.

It was as if the mist was enclosed.

"Chance, what is that?" I asked.

"Watch and see," he replied.

So I watched. We all watched the boy take a step up into the arch ...

And disappear ...

No one was reacting with fright or horror. Most of the upperclassmen seemed to be waiting, with bated breath, for what might happen next.

Then the mist cleared, and the boy stepped out the other side.

But he was no longer alone.

A rabbit hopped after him, and stayed by his feet. As the boy walked around and back to his classmates, the rabbit followed close behind.

I stared, not sure what to make of this.

"Where did the rabbit come from?" I asked Chance.

"The magical realm," he answered.

I still didn't understand, but I realized it was sometimes okay to not understand, to just observe and take it all in.

The next student was called. This time it was Jessica, I realized with a start. She had on a small white bandage over the bridge of her nose, and I felt a twinge of guilt.

I had done that to her.

Jessica walked into the arch, which was roiling with mist once again.

A few seconds later, Jessica reappeared on the other side, followed closely behind by her new familiar.

"What is that?" I whispered, craning my neck to see.

"I think it's a duck," Chance said.

I felt so confused.

"How is your familiar chosen?" I whispered.

"It picks you, according to your personality and needs," said Chance. "Usually, the fiercest familiars pick the boldest faeborn."

Two more students went through the archway, coming out with a badger and a fox.

Then the headmistress called up Liesl.

I thought she was going to faint.

"You'll be fine. You got this," I whispered as she passed me.

Liesl slowly walked to the misty archway and stepped through. Ten seconds later, she walked out followed by her ...

"What's that?" I whispered.

"An ermine," answered Chance.

The animal was sleek and white. It hopped onto Liesl's shoulder and rode there all the way back to us.

Sooo beautiful. I hope I get a beautiful familiar. Something white...

"Holly Ó Cuilinn."

Oh god, oh god, oh god ...

I felt a gentle push on the small of my back, and took a step forward.

I glanced back, and Chance winked at me and gave me a thumbs up.

I took a deep breath and walked to the archway.

Up close, the mist swirling about wasn't white, it was pearly, with pastels mixed in it.

"Go on, then," said the headmistress.

I took a step into the arch. I could see nothing but the swirling mist. I raised my hand in front of my face, but I could not see anything.

Wow, thick mist. Magical mist.

Greetings, little faeborn. Welcome to the archway.

"Huh ... hullo," I said.

"I see you are of royal lineage. You will need a strong protector. Hmmm ..."

I waited. The voice took a long time.

"Well, it seems we have two familiars who are vying for the honor of being tied to you. Tell me, do you accept these two sisters?"

Two images formed in my mind. Not of what the familiars would look like, but rather, what their minds held.

The two familiars were happy and enthusiastic, joyful and energetic, strong and regal.

My heart warmed to them immediately.

I felt a lick on my cheek from one of them, then another on my other cheek.

"That's how they kiss, in case you're wondering."

I laughed out loud in delight.

"You have been matched. You may take a step forward, faeborn."

I stepped out of the archway, grinning broadly, and walked back to where Chance and Liesl waited.

Two arctic wolves followed me.

Chapter Fourteen
Familiars

We slowly walked back inside, the whole group with new familiars hummed with chatter.

"They'll disappear when you fall asleep," said Chance. "They go to the magic faerealm, and they appear when you call them or if you are in trouble."

"So, we just bring them with us wherever we go?" asked Liesl.

"That's the idea," Chance smiled. "They are a very necessary part of being an adult fae."

Hmmm.

I somehow felt much safer with my two wolves walking on either side of me.

They were huge, coming almost to my shoulders when they sat with their ears pricked up.

I buried my fingers in their thick, white fur. The felt warm and soft and wonderful.

"Why did Holly get assigned two familiars?" asked Liesl.

"Not sure," said Chance. "It happens once in a while."

I swung my head around. "So it *has* happened before?"

"Oh, yes. I have heard tell of this happening before," Chance said.

"You've *heard* of it?" I asked. "So you've never seen this happen? There's no other students at the school that have two familiars?"

Chance shook his head. "But I have definitely heard of it happening."

"When? In what circumstance?" I asked.

"Chance, hey buddy, come on, we're going to be late." An upperclassman grabbed Chance by the shoulder and pulled.

"Yeah, okay," said Chance. "Listen ladies, I have to go. I might see you tomorrow, though."

"Well, definitely you'll see us at lunch, won't you?" Liesl said, smiling shyly.

"Oh, yeah, right. Lunch. See you then," Chance said, grinning and waving as he left with his friend.

"That was weird," said Liesl. "It was almost as if he were trying to avoid your question."

"Yeah," I said, distracted. "Hey, ha ha ha! You like him, don't you?"

"What do you mean?" Liesl said.

"I mean, you likkkkeeeeee himmmmm, don'tttttt youuuuuu?" I grinned.

Liesl blushed furiously, her face bright red.

"Ha ha ha ha ha!" I laughed.

"Oh, shut up," said Liesl, shoving me playfully.

"Ha ha ha ha!"

We returned to the dorm with our familiars, joking back and forth the whole way.

The other girls had not returned when we entered our dorm and sat on our beds. My wolves sat down between Liesl's bed and mine; her ermine curled up on her lap and promptly fell asleep.

"He is utterly adorable, Liesl. Seriously adorable." I said.

"Thanks," she smiled, petting the sleek white little animal softly snoring on her lap. "Your wolves are fantastic!"

I grinned, petting each wolf with one of my hands.

They sat upright and looked very regal. I could not believe they were mine, and I said as much to Liesl.

She shrugged with a smile, "Or you're theirs."

"Ha!" I lean and kissed each wolf on the head. "I hope I am."

"It's nearly nine. Lights out will be soon. I wonder where the others ..." Liesl never got a chance to finish, because the five other girls entered the room and went to their respective beds.

"Oh, Holly," Jessica came to stand at the foot of my bed. "They're so wonderful! Aren't you lucky? I heard it's very rare to get two!"

Friendliness? Weird, but I'll go along with it.

"Thanks! Yeah, I heard it was rare." I looked at the bandage on her nose. It was white, and stood out against her tan skin. "Hey, listen. I'm sorry about your nose."

Jessica shrugged and smiled. "Water under the bridge. Let's just move forward."

I smiled.

Something isn't right, but I can play along.

"Your duck is so beautiful, Jessica!"

"Thanks!" Jessica hugged her large, white duck. It was quite big for a duck. "I love her, I lived on a farm before coming to the Academy. I love ducks!"

I smiled and nodded.

It *was* a very handsome duck.

The lights flickered off and on.

"Oh!" Jessica turned and returned to her bunk. "I'd better get into my PJs!"

"Me, too," I said as I rummaged in my drawer for them.

I waited and then took a turn in the bathroom, changing into my sleepwear and brushing my teeth.

I was in love with my new toothbrush. I hadn't had one in years. It was a luxury I appreciated.

A few minutes passed after I returned to my bunk, then the lights flickered off and on again, then turned off for the night.

Moonlight filtered in from the window. There was a nightlight in the far corner, and what illumination entered the room lit up my arctic wolves as if they had been painted with fluorescent lights.

I lay down in my bed with one hand in the fur of one of the wolves.

We all tucked ourselves into bed, and Liesl and I whispered way into the night.

Other than the fight I was in, it was a good first day.

I lay on my side, watching my familiars. Both wolves had moved to the space in between Liesl's bed and mine and were fast asleep next to each other. But they had not disappeared, and I was curious.

The moonlight coming through the window made everything appear ethereal.

Liesl lay there too, waiting.

I watched as Liesl's eyes got drowsier and drowsier, and finally shut. As she fell into a sound sleep, her ermine, cuddled in the crook of her arm, shimmered and then disappeared entirely.

Amazing.

My wolf familiars were huge and an intimidating sight, but to me they were perfect. And adorable when they slept.

I heard a low, gentle snoring coming from them, and smiled. I reached down and plunged my fingers into their fur. It was warm and comforting.

I fell asleep like that.

"Holly, wake up sleepyhead."

My mind wandered up from the dream I'd been having.

I'd been down in the underground again, and sleeping in Aunt Clare's old cubby. Echoes of some kind of commotion above had been filtering down to me, traveling on the metal pipes and plates that lined the abandoned subway corridor.

There had been a menacing noise, and I was listening against the door.

There'd been a growl, then a shriek.

Suddenly, something had kicked in the door, something huge.

The metal door had been latched, the barrier secure. It would have taken something very strong to push it open, breaking the latch and coming in.

I screamed as a huge alligator pushed its snout into the cubby. My heartbeat was fast; I knew this thing wanted to eat me. I was terrified.

I was backed up to the far wall, trying to avoid those massive jaws and sharp teeth.

Suddenly, seemingly out of nowhere, two arctic wolves had leaped at the alligator, snarling viciously as they bit down on the monster's head. The wolves, their white coats flying, had attacked the alligator, and forced it to back out of the cubby we were trapped in, and had followed it out and onto the ledge.

"Wake up, Holly," a voice whispered.

I opened my eyes.

"Wha? What's going on?" I said in a groggy voice.

"You were having a nightmare," Liesl said.

I sat up in bed. The sun was just coming up, its first light creeping into the room. My two wolf familiars were there, by my side, looking up at me. One of them whined uncertainly.

"Wow," I said, rubbing my eyes. "Have they been here all night?"

"I don't know. I was asleep," said Liesl.

I put my arms around the wolves. "I'm okay, I promise. It was just a dream."

"They must appear when you're scared or something, huh?" said Liesl.

"I guess so. Real or imaginary dangers. That is good to know," I said.

"So," Liesl said, rubbing her eyes and yawning. "I guess my ermine is still in the fae forest."

"Guess so," I looked at my two wolf familiars. "I don't know how to send mine there. I hope we'll learn that soon."

"I heard there's a class on magical creatures, and that we'll learn all that in the class," Liesl said.

"You would have thought they'd have told us a useful thing like that when we got the familiars," I said.

"Yeah, ha ha! That would've been useful," Liesl said.

"What time is it?" I asked.

"Around six, I think." Liesl yawned again.

"Breakfast is at seven. So we still have almost an hour to wait." I looked around.

Most of the room was still in dim light, the sun was barely rising. I looked over at the other girls. They were still asleep.

I thought of something. "Hey, did I wake you? When I had the nightmare?"

"Uh huh. I heard you moaning in your sleep. Then the wolves appeared, and one tried to get into bed with you." Liesl smiled. "They're so big, though."

I looked down at the wolves. "I wonder if we should name them?"

"That sounds like a good idea. Or," said Liesl. "They might already have names."

"Huh, that actually sounds more likely." I leaned over and buried my face in one of my wolves' fur.

It smelled of pine forest and wind.

Later, at breakfast, Sarah, the dorm supervisor, came around and handed out our schedules.

Liesl and I studied the papers.

"Hi, ladies," Chance walked past. "I can't stay, but wanted to say, have a great Saturday! Two more days until classes start!"

"Hi, Chance. Bye Chance," I said, chuckling.

"He's so dreamy," Liesl said in a soft voice.

"I knew it! Ha ha ha!" I said.

"Oh, look: at the bottom of the page. The spell to make your familiar return to the forest," said Liesl. "Holly, you should practice it. Something tells me you're going to be using it the most, because of how big the wolves are."

"And there are two of them, don't forget," I said.

"How could I forget?" Liesl giggled.

We hurriedly finished, then returned to our dorm room to practice the first spell.

It took me two hours, but I finally got the intonations right.

The two familiar wolves popped out of sight.

"You did it!" Liesl clapped her hands.

Something caught my attention at the corner of my eye.

It was Jessica, Naomi, and the other girls. They were whispering on the far corner bunk. Whispering and glancing my way.

Liesl came onto my bunk and crouched, whispering in my ear. "Pay no attention to them."

I turned to look at her. "But last night, I thought everything was okay?" I whispered.

Liesl just stared at me and shook her head no.

Then movement and sound, and I turned back to the far bunk. They were getting down and walking over.

"Holly, Liesl, we're going to a bonfire celebration tonight. Want to come too?" Naomi said. Her thick French accent sounded exotic and special.

I just stared at her.

Jessica tossed her long blonde hair to the side. "Come on, you should join us. It'll be so much fun!"

"No thanks," said Liesl. "We have other plans."

I turned to stare at her.

We did?

She gave me a significant look.

"Oh, yes. Um, we have other plans," I said.

"What other plans?" Naomi asked, an innocent expression on her face.

I thought for a second, unable to come up with something to say.

"We're meeting our friend Chance. He's an upperclassman," Liesl said, sounding casual.

I raised my eyebrows and looked at Liesl again.

She studiously ignored my gaze, and instead focused on Naomi.

"Well, that's too bad. If you change your mind, we'll be on the west lawn, near the lake," Jessica said as she walked away. "Oh, it'll be at 8 p.m., by the way. You should really come."

They all walked out.

The door shut behind them.

Liesl swung around. "What do you think that was all about?"

"No idea," I said.

Chapter Fifteen
Bonfire

Liesl and I spent the rest of the weekend wandering about the school, familiarizing ourselves where all our classes were.

We didn't have any more encounters with Chance; he seemed to have gone off on some errands, or at least that's what Sarah told us when we asked her.

At one point, Sunday afternoon, Liesl and I were hiking along the northern boundary of the school when she tripped and tumbled over a ledge. It was about an eight-foot drop, and she rolled all the way down.

She wasn't hurt, except for some bruises and scrapes, but by the time she came to a stop at the bottom, her ermine familiar had appeared: It hopped onto her shoulder, and was licking her cheek.

I jumped down beside her. "Hey, are you okay?"

"Yeah, I think so," she laughed, pushing the sleek white creature away. "Stop! You're tickling me!"

"Liesl, you've got a scrape on your forehead," I said. "It's bleeding."

"Oh!" Liesl touched her head, and her fingers came away bloody. "Oh, man."

"Want to go to the nurse?" I asked.

"No, I just want to go back to the dorm room. I can wash up there."

I reached out a hand and helped her up.

Her ermine familiar rode on her shoulder as we walked up to the school.

Halfway there, I could hear voices and laughter.

"I wonder what that is?" I asked.

"Let's go see!" Liesl said.

"But you're bleeding!"

"It's stopped," said Liesl. "Look." she held out the napkin she'd been pressing against her forehead.

The bleeding had indeed stopped.

I shrugged. "It's your decision."

"I vote we go peek, at the very least." She grinned.

I was discovering just how curious my new friend was.

We crept across the lawn, crossing in front of the stairs and over to the bushes. The sound was coming from the north lawn.

"Right here, come on," Liesl whispered.

We crouched against the bushes and looked around the stone wall of the school.

It was another of Jessica's bonfires. The five girls and a number of boys were milling about a large fire, talking and laughing.

"They look like they're having fun," I mumbled.

"Didn't they have one yesterday, too?" Liesl whispered.

"Yeah, I think so."

"Do you want to join them?"

I made a face. "No. Not at all."

Liesl seemed torn.

"What?" I asked.

She looked around the stone wall again, watching them for a minute.

I finally looked, too.

"What?" I repeated.

Liesl sighed. "What if Chance is there?"

I peeked again. "Do you see him?"

"No."

"Then he's probably not there."

"But he could be. I can't see some of their faces."

"Liesl, Chance is in second year. He's probably not interested in them, they're first years," I said. "Haven't you noticed the upperclassmen seem to stick together?"

Liesl looked at me, stricken.

Her face crumpled up and she rose and walked toward the front steps of the school.

"Liesl, wait," I called, hurrying after her. "I didn't mean ..."

Nice going, Holly.

I ran to catch up to her.

"Liesl! Liesl wait up!" I called.

She reached the top of the stairs and stopped, waiting but not turning around.

I caught up to her.

"Listen, I didn't mean he wouldn't be interested in *you.*"

Liesl shrugged. "Doesn't matter. You're right. And I should just concentrate on my classes, instead of worrying about ..." She sniffed.

"Come on, let's get you washed up." I put my arm around her, and we went inside.

Up in our room, Liesl washed her face and arms.

I sat with her on her bed, examining her face in the room's bright lights.

"Hmmm. Well, you've got the scrape on your forehead. That one's not too bad," I said. "Not sure why it even bled."

She turned her arms up, and I looked them over.

"Eh, you've got a few bruises, and this elbow's scratched a bit, but nothing too bad at all."

Liesl looked down at her elbow.

"I'd say it was a brave tumble, and an honest fall. You came out well, all things considered." I grinned.

"And my familiar appeared." Liesl kissed the top of the ermine's head and snuggle him. He began to purr.

"What a sweetie," I murmured, running my finger down the creature's silky back. "Maybe this is a good time for you to practice the spell to send him back to the forest?"

Liesl nodded. "Good idea." She sniffled and blew her nose in a tissue, then turned to me. "Holly, you know him better than I do: Do you think Chance is interested in me at all?"

"Oh, I have no idea," I put my hands up, palms up. "I really have no idea. Don't forget, until just a few days ago, I was living on the streets. I have no idea how any of that is supposed to happen."

Just then, Jessica, Naomi, and the others came into the room.

"What a fun bonfire! WOOP!" Jessica said.

"You were totally flirting with that guy. Ha ha ha!" Naomi said.

"Oh! Sorry, we didn't see you there," said Jessica. "I have to go wash up anyway," she skipped out of the room with enthusiasm.

Naomi turned to us. "You two missed another great party."

I shrugged.

"Maybe next time," Liesl said.

"Definitely next time," Naomi said with a grin.

We all sat in our bunks reading until bedtime.

I caught Liesl doodling. It looked like her and Chance holding hands.

179

"Nice drawing," I said.

Liesl flipped the notebook up to her, hiding the doodle.

I smiled.

"Liesl," I whispered. "You awake?"

We had been in bed, and the lights had been shut off for a while.

"Yeah, I'm awake," came Liesl's voice. "What's up?"

"I'm thinking of going to the next bonfire," I whispered. "Do you want to go?"

"I don't know. Maybe." Liesl whispered.

"Maybe we could even get Chance to go with us."

"Then definitely count me in!"

I chuckled.

The next day was Monday. We were ridiculously busy all day, learning things I had no idea existed.

"Have you done okay?" I asked Liesl as she came into the lunch room.

"I guess." she rubbed her forehead. "I had no idea it would be so hard."

"Yeah, my classes are tough, too." I saw Chance approaching. "Hey. Here he is," I whispered to Liesl.

She swung her head around, nearly bumping into Chance.

"Oh, um. Hi," Liesl said, blushing.

"Busy day, huh ladies?" Chance said.

"Beyond busy," I said.

We all sat down to eat.

It was fried fish and corn muffins, and I ate so fast I got the hiccoughs.

"Easy, easy," Chance chuckled, patting me on the back.

"Um, Chance?" Liesl said. "Uh, there's a bonfire the girls in our dorm are having."

"Oh?" he said.

"Yeah, um, it looks really fun," said Liesl. "Can you come?"

"Oh, um, Friday night?"

"Yeah."

"I think I can come," said Chance. "Are both of you going to be there?"

Liesl and I exchanged a look: YAY!

"Yes, we'll both be there," said Liesl. "It's on the north lawn, just at the edge of the woods, at 8 p.m."

"It's starting at 8 p.m.? An hour before lights out?" Chance asked.

"Yes, apparently the girls in our dorm room are throwing it," I said. "Maybe they got special permission? I'm not sure. But they've already had two others, so it must be okay."

Chance looked troubled.

I mentally shrugged it off.

Midweek, we named our familiars in the Magical Beasts and Familiars class.

"Now that you've mastered the spell to send your familiars away, and the spell to call them forth, we will teach you how to name them," the professor said.

"First you must summon your familiar. Please do so at this time."

"Good, that's it. Excellent. Now. Think of your familiar. Close your eyes and picture them in your head. Now that you've got them firmly in your mind, I want you to asked them what their name is. In your head, not out loud, Mr. Tumley. Yes, like that."

"Now, when you hear its name in your head, you must repeat it five times, out loud, so it will be fixed in your mind."

The class lasted a long time.

Liesl learned her ermine's name was Snowbear.

It took me a while, as I had two to discover, but in the end, I learned my familiars' names were Aspen and Tundra. I also learned to tell them apart. Aspen had one blue eye and one blue eye with a tinge of beige in one corner. Tundra had two blue eyes.

I learned they were indeed sisters, and were magical and intelligent.

It was a fantastic class.

Later that week, Liesl and I felt as if our brains were going to drip out.

"I can't believe how hard this week has been!" Liesl said.

"At least we have the bonfire to look forward to," I said.

"That's tonight, isn't it?"

"Yes."

We walked back up to the room.

"It's seven thirty, we should get ready," I said.

We got out of our school uniforms and into casual clothes.

"Liesl, that sweater looks fabulous!" I said.

"Thanks!" She twirled in a circle. "I knitted it myself."

"Oh, wow!"

Jessica, Naomi, and the others filed into the room.

They looked at us brightly. "Are you two coming tonight?" Naomi asked.

"Yes, we are, actually," I said.

"That's great! We'll see you there!" Jessica said.

They left.

"Do you think they're acting a little weird?" Liesl quietly asked.

"Maybe a little," I said. "It's like they're way too enthusiastic about this."

"I know, right? So weird."

We finished getting ready and walked downstairs.

The school was quiet and mostly deserted.

"Looks like everyone's either in their rooms, or outside at the bonfire," I said.

"Yeah," said Liesl. "It's a little unnerving. Hey, do you think Chance will show up?"

"I don't see why not." I said.

We walked outdoors and around the corner to the north lawn.

It was twilight, and clouds were scuttling across the moon as it rose.

It was very pretty.

"Huh, Holly, wasn't the other bonfire last week somewhere over there?" asked Liesl.

I looked to the spot where the Sunday bonfire had been. Tonight, there was no fire. But Naomi and Jessica stood there, waiting.

"I wonder what's going on?" Liesl said. "Hey, do you think my hair looks okay?"

I looked her over. "I think it looks fine, Liesl. Come on."

I walked up to the two girls. They turned to face me. The light had all but faded, and their faces were mostly in shadow.

"Hi," I said.

"Hey!" Liesl said.

"So," I said, my hands in the pockets of my jacket. "Where is everyone? Where's the bonfire?"

"Oh, hi! We actually moved it to a better spot," Jessica said.

"Yeah, it's a super cute clearing," said Naomi. "Come on, we'll show you."

Without waiting for us, the two turned and walked into the forest.

"Do you think we should go?" I whispered in Liesl's ear.

"Oh course!" said Liesl. "Heck, Chance might already be there. Let's go!"

Liesl walked after Jessica and Naomi, and I followed.

We walked along a path that was very dark. I tripped several times over tree roots and flotsam.

"Over here," said Jessica. "It's just this way."

"Come on, it's not far ahead," Naomi said.

"Coming!" Liesl said, hurrying behind.

Jessica and Naomi were walking fast. Far faster than we could keep up.

They were soon out of sight.

I heard a distant voice call out. It sounded like Chance.

"Was that him?" asked Liesl.

"Sounded a bit like him," I said. "We need to catch up or well get turned around."

"They said it was just up ahead," Liesl said.

"JESSICA! NAOMI?" I called, cupping my hands around my mouth.

I heard a faint voice again.

"Is that just up ahead?" I asked Liesl.

"I'm not sure. Can you tell where we're going?" Liesl said.

I stopped, pulling on Liesl's sleeve. "Liesl, I'm worried we're going to get lost."

I called out again. Then Liesl called out.

The faint voices up ahead called back.

"Where are they?" Liesl asked in frustration.

"Liesl, we should be able to see the bonfire from here, if it's up ahead."

"I agree."

"And we should have brought flashlights," I said.

"I double agree," said Liesl. "I can't even see my face in front of my hand."

"Hey, I don't see anyone up ahead," I said. "I think they ditched us."

"It looks that way," said Liesl, sounding extremely disappointed.

"Let's go back," I suggested.

"Okay," Liesl answered.

I turned around and began to walk back the way I thought we'd come.

The treetops overhead completely obliterated the sky; I could not see one star.

At first, I felt confused.

Could there have been some sort of mistake?

But why would they ditch us?

And where is the bonfire?

Realization flooded through me.

"They never meant to be friendly," I said out loud.

"What?" Liesl asked.

"Those girls. Jessica and Naomi, and the other three," I said. "They've been playing us. They never meant to be friendly. It was all a trick."

A sinking feeling in the pit of my stomach raised alarm bells in me.

"Holly, I don't see the lights of the school."

"We've come too far to see lights," I said. "I think I'm walking back the way we came."

"Are you sure?"

"No," I said, feeling tears well in my eyes, and glad of the darkness of the forest so Liesl didn't see them. "I'm not sure of anything."

Liesl stopped, holding my arm. "Holly, I think we're lost."

We stood there, looking around. Our eyes had adjusted to the darkness, and we could see dimly through the forest.

There was no sign of the school, no sign of any bonfire, and no sign of anyone else in the forest besides us.

"Now what do we do?" asked Liesl.

"We keep walking. We'll eventually get out of the woods," I said.

"Are you sure? I remember riding a long time coming through the forest to the Academy. More than a dozen miles. Possibly two or three times that far," Liesl said.

Well, what do you think we should do, then?" I asked.

"I'm not sure," Liesl said.

"We can't just stay here," I said. "It's getting cold. And I heard it was close to freezing last night."

Okay, let's keep walking," said Liesl. "But let's go this way. I think I remember we came through that thicket."

I shrugged.

We walked on through the forest, and I tripped and conked my head twice. Liesl tripped and went down three times, and scraped her hand. It was brutal.

"Hey," said Liesl. "I think I see something ahead. Some sort of clearing, I think."

She was right. We stumbled through more trees and reached it.

I stopped in my tracks.

We'd been hoping the clearing would be the school lawn.

But it wasn't.

It was a cemetery. A huge, mist-covered cemetery.

Chapter Sixteen

Lost

"Ohhh, no. No way I am going in there," Liesl said, shaking, from cold or fear. Or both.

I looked out onto the vast hillside.

It was covered in shadowy tombstones, so many gravemarkers I could not have counted them if I tried.

The hillside, which rose slightly from the surrounding woods, was covered in a thick, low mist that clung to the ground, which was bare save for the gloomy gravestones.

I stared at the collection of tombstones, and tried to get a sense of the place.

"Wow, that's a lot of headstones," I murmured.

Liesl pulled at my arm. "Come on, Holly, let's go back."

"Did you see this place on the map of the school grounds we were given?" I asked.

Liesl shook her head no, she had not.

"Did anyone ever mention this to you?" I asked.

"No, nooo. Holly, let's gooooo." Liesl's whispered turned to a moan.

"Helloooo?" I called out.

My voice echoed across the cemetery, and was gone.

I'm not sure why, but I was filled with an intense curiosity.

"Let's go exploring!" I said eagerly.

"Are you nuts?" Liesl said in a strangled whisper. "That's a cemetery. Those are gravestones. Under them are rotting corpses."

"I know, I know," I said. "That's what makes it so intriguing."

"Oh, Holly no, please no. No no no no no no," Liesl begged.

"Have you ever seen a cemetery up close like this?" I asked.

Liesl shook her head vigorously.

"Have you ever seen a dead body?" I asked quietly, looking at her.

Liesl's eyes went wide, and she shook her head.

"I have," I said, looking back out across the cemetery. "Just before I came here, less than a month ago, my Aunt Clare died."

I heard Liesl gasp softly.

I went on.

"We were living in an underground cubby off an abandoned subway line," I said. "I woke up one day, and she was there right in front of me, just like the night before. But she didn't move, didn't react to my touch, didn't do anything. She was cold."

Liesl put her hand over her mouth, trying not to make any sounds.

"She had been alive and warm the day before. We'd gone to sleep, and I guess she passed away the evening before, because like I said, in the morning she was cold and still, and would not move. So I sewed her up in a blanket, and dragged her to another part of the tunnel."

I heard Liesl moan softly.

"I carefully wrapped her in her blanket, and sewed up the ends with needle and thread, until she was snug. Then I pulled her to a private little place, and wedged the door shut." I fell silent, remembering.

"Holly, do ... do you ... do you think we could go back to the dorm room now? I want to go to bed," Liesl said in a low, scared voice.

It was kind of odd, if you think about it. Liesl was terrified, and I didn't feel any fear at all.

Well, that's not entirely accurate.

A low moaning cry drifted over the gravestones. It started off so quiet I thought it must be the wind. But then it grew to such a volume there could be no question: It was not the wind; it was a voice.

A voice calling out over the cemetery.

A voice calling out to us?

I had to find out.

"I'm going in," I said, probably a little too eagerly.

"Oh, no, please no, Holly, don't, just don't ..." Liesl grabbed my arm and tried to pull me back into the woods.

My feet did not move. It was as if they were glued to the ground.

"Come on," I whispered.

Liesl moaned in fear.

I took a step out, onto the scrubby land, out onto the mist-covered cemetery.

My foot sank about an inch into the moist ground. I took another step, and when I pulled up the first foot, it made a sucking-squelchy sound that echoed across the quiet cemetery.

"Weird that there's no fence or wall around this, don't you think?" Liesl asked.

I jumped a foot in fright.

"I thought you said you didn't want to come," I said.

"I know, but I didn't want to be left alone even more," said Liesl. "Besides, I'm not sure why, but I'm not that scared anymore."

"Really?" I said.

"I'm serious," said Liesl. "The moment I stepped into the cemetery, I felt my fear of it drain out of me. Replaced by a kind of quiet friendliness."

"You feel a friendliness walking through the cemetery?" I asked, surprised. I felt no different now than before. I hadn't been afraid then, and I felt the same curiosity now.

"Liesl, come on," I whispered.

"Right behind you," Liesl said.

We tiptoed between the gravestones, taking care not to step directly on anyone's graves. We walked in between the graves, and zigzagged across the hillside until we were pretty much smack dab in the middle.

Liesl was holding on to me and shaking like a leaf.

I guess the fear has come back.

I sat down in the dirt and weeds, and wrapped my arms around my knees.

This was a surreal experience.

The low moaning voice cried out again.

"I think that's a wight," mumbled Liesl.

"Give me a break," I said.

"No, really," Liesl said.

I took a deep breath. Whatever was making the moaning noise, I was willing to bet it was a wild animal.

Not a wight.

"It's getting cold," I said. "Let's get back to the school."

"Okay," said Liesl. "Do you know which was to go?"

"No, but I'm going to just walk. It has to take us somewhere," I said.

"Do you think Chance came out to join us at the non-existent bonfire?" Liesl asked.

"No idea," I said. "But when I get back to our dorm room, I'm going to really break Jessica's nose this time."

We walked out of the cemetery and into the woods again, and onward for at least a mile.

We should've come to the school by now, if we were going in the right direction.

Wait.

I saw something up ahead.

I burst through the trees and onto ...

"Oh, no!" exclaimed Liesl.

It was the cemetery again.

"I was sure we weren't going in circles," I said. "I know I was walking in a straight line."

I couldn't figure it out.

Could there be two cemeteries?

I peered out at the collection of gravestones.

Looks like the same one to me.

"Okay," I said. "It's got to be closing on midnight. We've got to get back to the school."

Think, Holly. Think.

"I have an idea," I said.

"What?"

"Let's call for help. If anyone hears us, they'll come rescue us."

"Okay."

I took a deep breath. "HELP! HELP! HELP! ANYONE!"

"HELP! HELP US!"

We continued calling out for several minutes, until we were both out of breath.

"Do you think anyone heard us?" Holly said hopefully.

"No idea. Maybe. Let's wait," I said.

We paused to listen. We practically held our breaths.

Nothing.

Not even the moaning cry.

In fact, we'd probably scared off whatever had made that noise.

I sighed.

I had no idea what to do, and it was growing colder.

Wait a minute.

I stood up, put my arms out, palms facing downward.

Then I recited the spell in ancient Gaelic to summon my familiars to me. While I recited the spell, I thought, "*Aspen, Tundra both of you come to me, come to me right now!*"

Suddenly, they were there.

"Oh, well done, Holly! Brava!"

I knelt and buried my fingers in each of their thick coats. I raised my face to them.

"Aspen? Tundra? We're in trouble and we need your help." The wolves both looked directly into my eyes with deep intelligence.

"We are lost. Some girls played a mean trick on us."

The wolves raised their heads and looked around the cemetery, then returned their eyes to me.

"We need your help, my beauties. Can you carry us home?"

I held my breath. I know I was asking a lot. Wolves don't normally carry riders.

But my wolves were huge, much bigger than any normal wolves. I had high hopes for them.

They both looked at me unblinkingly and sneezed, then panted, their pink noses lolling out the sides of their mouths.

The message was clear: *Get on.*

I stood and put my arms around the nearest wolf, jumping up and pulling myself on.

She didn't even blink at the added weight.

I sat astride my wolf familiar and held on to a tuft of her fur at the base of her neck.

"Climb on, Liesl," I said unnecessarily. Liesl was already climbing onto the other wolf, her long legs hanging halfway to the ground.

I bent my head low. "You know the way back to the school?"

The wolf pawed at the ground.

"Ho ... Holly ..." Liesl said in a strangled voice. "Lo ... look ..."

I turned my head to see where she was pointing.

Out of the mist, a ghostly figure was coming, gliding across the ground straight toward us.

Its arms were outstretched, its mouth open, and a moan issuing forth from it.

"*aaaaooooooooooommmmmm!*"

That was all the encouragement I needed.

I squeezed my legs, urging the wolf forward, and she took off with a long-striding trot. She ran, leaving the cemetery and the ghostly moaning figure behind, and weaving through the trees as if pulled toward the school grounds.

I glanced back and saw the second wolf, with Liesl astride her, running fast on our heels.

It took about twenty-five minutes of trotting to get back to the school lawn.

We must've been really far away.

We were finally walking (trudging?) up the steps and through the front doors. The wolves followed us, staying close behind me.

In the main hallway of the school, we encountered the headmistress, Sarah the dorm supervisor, and Chance, all talking.

"There they are!" Sarah cried, rushing toward us.

"What happened? You look all scratched up and filthy!" asked the headmistress.

Chance opened his arms, and I fell into them. Then I grabbed Liesl and brought her into our hug.

The story came out one fragment at a time.

"Jessica, Naomi, and the other girls in our dorm ..."

"Tricked us and led us into the woods ..."

"Told us there was a bonfire party at eight in the evening ..."

"Led us into the woods for miles, and then abandoned us ..."

"We walked for hours through the wood ..."

"We found a cemetery with a wight trying to get us ..."

"The only reason we made it back home was because of Holly's wolf familiars ..."

"Could have died of exposure ..."

"Getting freezing outside ..."

"We called for help, but nobody answered ..."

We both fell silent, breathing hard.

The headmistress spoke then. "Do you mean to tell me you walked all the way to the cemetery?"

We nodded our heads.

"But that's over five miles away!" the head mistress exclaimed.

We just stared at her.

After a minute Chance spoke, "Headmistress, this has gone beyond the pale. Those girls need to be punished. Holly and Liesl need to be in a separate dorm room than them. Those girls' prank could have left Holly and Liesl in serious danger."

The headmistress nodded.

"There's a vacant dorm room on the second year's floor. Take that one. We'll have your things moved." She thought a minute. "Now go get cleaned up. Baths for both of you. Are you sure you don't need the nurse? No? Very well, then. Sarah will escort you to your new dormitory. Bathe and get comfortable. And I promise you, those girls will be punished."

We all nodded. Chance and Sarah led us back to the central room of the dorm, but then turned us down a different corridor and up an entirely new set of stairs.

"Okay, when you get there, I want you to take long baths, both of you. Wash yourselves thoroughly."

"I'll take my leave now, ladies. I'll see you at breakfast tomorrow, okay?" Chance said.

"Okay," I said.

"Okay," Liesl said begrudgingly.

"Thanks for everything, Chance," Sarah said, smiling.

Chance left, shutting the door behind him quietly.

It was nearly two in the morning.

Well, thank goodness we don't have classes tomorrow, I guess.

Sarah led us to the second year's dorm hallway. She led us to the end, and used her keys to open the last door on the right.

"This is a small room, but there's just the two of you," she glanced down at the two arctic wolves following behind me. "There's plenty of room for you two, and the wolves." She pointed to the door next to the dorm room door. "The bathroom is right there. There's several bathtubs. I'll get your belongings transferred over right away."

She looked at each of us seriously.

"I am really unhappy at what happened tonight, girls. I want you to know that. What those girls did was unforgivable. I will make sure they are punished."

She nodded and left.

Liesl and I walked into the new dorm room.

"It's even nicer than the other one," I said.

Chapter Seventeen
Interrogations

The next morning, we woke up to a knock at the door. I opened my eyes and saw that our belongings had been stacked just inside our new dorm room sometime during the night.

Sarah poked her head into our room.

"You both awake?" she asked.

"Not hardly," I yawned.

"I'm sorry to disturb you, especially after what happened last night," said Sarah. "But the headmistress wants to talk to you."

I sat up in bed.

"Now?" Liesl said, yawning.

"Well, it's nearly breakfast time, and she wonders if you could come to her office to give your account of what happened directly after your meal," Sarah said.

I nodded. "Yes, we can do that." I thought for a minute. "Wait, Sarah. Will Jessica and Naomi and the others be there too?"

"At breakfast? No, they've been confined to their dorm room until the headmistress can do a proper investigation. They're taking their meals and being questioned there as well." Sarah closed the door.

"Huh, I'm still not awake," Liesl fell back down on the pillow, yawning.

"We've only had a few hours of sleep. The headmistress must really want to hear what happened," I said.

"The least they could do was let us sleep in," said Liesl. "Can we even think clearly when we're sleepy?"

I got up and decided to take a shower. "Maybe she wants to talk to us while we have everything fresh in our minds."

"True."

A half hour later, we walked down to the dining hall and met Chance for breakfast.

"Hey, how are you two doing?" said Chance. "You only got a few hours' sleep. I'm amazed you're up so early."

"The headmistress wants to talk to us," I yawned. "And I cannot stop yawning."

"I'm getting some espresso," said Liesl. Chance and I followed her.

We were all soon seated with the coffee and some steaming hot eggs.

"So you went to the cemetery last night?" Chance asked.

"Not on purpose," I said. "Trust me, that place is not the ideal vacation spot."

"It was spooky, to say the least," Liesl said.

"I'll bet," said Chance. "Did you come across anything there?"

"Oh, you mean beyond the wight?" I asked.

"You saw a wight?!" asked Chance.

"Just briefly. She wanted us to stay, but we had to go." I grinned.

Chance shook his head.

"I hope those girls get properly punished." Liesl yawned and took a sip of her espresso.

"Oh, believe me, they will be," said Chance. "The forest surrounding the school is extremely dangerous at night. This is by design, to discourage any interlopers."

"Well, seriously, I wonder if maybe the school shouldn't put out some kind of beacon, to help lost students find their way home," Liesl said.

"They expressly don't, though," Chance explained. "If an interloper were to find their way into the forest, trying to get to the school, it would be nearly impossible. There are some pretty strong enchantments at work, and anyone entering the forest is almost guaranteed to get lost."

That explained why we wound up going around in circles when it felt like we were walking in a straight line.

"Those low-down creeps," I fumed. "I'll bet they knew this when they lured us down there."

"We've got to tell all this to the headmistress," Liesl said.

"Eat up, then I'll walk with you up to her office." Chance wiped his mouth with a napkin. "Oh, and she already knows all the enchantments placed on the forest. What she needs to be told are exactly what your experiences were."

We finished and went up to Professor Ó Baoghill's office.

Chance knocked on the heavy wooden door.

"Enter," came a voice from inside the office.

We filed in one at a time. Sarah Goodheart was already there, as well as a transcriptionist and a secretary.

"Please take a seat," the headmistress said, gesturing to the chairs in front of her desk. "Now, before we begin, I want to ask: How are you feeling?"

"Sleepy," I said.

Liesl nodded, yawning.

"And how are your wounds?" The headmistress asked.

I looked at Liesl. She was all scratched up, on her face and her arms. The wounds looked bright and pink against her pale skin.

I imagined I looked much the same, after our ordeal last night.

I reached up to touch my face and felt several scrapes that stung when my fingers brushed against them.

Liesl shrugged. "The scrapes and bruises hurt."

I nodded, my face stinging. *Ow.*

The headmistress folded her hands. "I want to get to the bottom of this. If you will forgive the process, I wish to question each of you separately, so we can obtain accurate testimonies."

Something was off.

"Professor, you already know what happened to us, don't you?" I said. "We told you last night. Why are you questioning us again?"

"Miss Ó Cuilinn, I want to get much more detail," the headmistress said. "I want to make sure of both your experiences. I want to compare what you testify happened with a few other accounts."

I stood up, my chair scraping the floor. "What do you mean, 'a few other accounts'? We were alone, there was no one else there."

"Please calm down, Miss Ó Cuilinn. You are not on trial here. We realize you and Miss Becker are the victims of the prank in this instance." The headmistress nodded.

I sat back down.

"Miss Ó Cuilinn, please go with Mr. Mac Craith to the next room. We will call you when we're ready to question you," the headmistress said.

I followed Chance to the next room, scowling. "It's as if they don't believe us, Chance."

"I don't think it's that at all, Holly," said Chance. "I think they just want a lot more details, and they want pure testimony, with nothing colored by what one of you may say in front of the other."

"But ..."

"I know, I know. But it happens," said Chance. "Oh, and also: They're trying to decide what to do about this. The punishment could range from detention for the other girls, to expulsion from the school."

I raised my eyebrows. "Expulsion?"

He nodded.

Wow.

We were called back to the office a short time later.

I sat down in the chair while Chance led Liesl away. I caught the look on Liesl's face as it changed from worry to elation at the prospect of being alone with Chance in the other room.

I rolled my eyes, and looked up, and caught the keen eye of the headmistress watching me like a hawk.

"No, no, it's just that," I waved my hand, trying to think of the right words. I bent forward to the headmistress, and she bent forward a bit toward me. "Liesl has a crush on Chance."

"Ah." She sat back, smiling. "Well, let us get started, shall we?"

I nodded.

The headmistress folded her hands and looked at me. "Tell me everything."

I took a deep breath and started at the very beginning: my arrival at the Academy and the mocking looks I noticed right away.

And the scene the first day in the dorm room.

And my suspicion when Jessica and Naomi acted friendly the short time later.

And their mention of the bonfire.

And the sight of the bonfire that Liesl and I had seen the weekend before.

And the repeated invitation.

"I think they were inviting us so they could play the prank on us, and when we didn't join them the first time, they had a real bonfire, to show us that they were on the up-and-up. But," I leaned forward, "I don't think they were. I think it was all a ruse to get us to go down there."

"What happened last night when you and Miss Becker walked down to the north lawn?" the headmistress asked.

"We saw no bonfire, and no group or people. We just saw Jessica and Naomi standing at the edge of the lawn, up by the woods," I said.

"They were both there?" the headmistress asked sharply.

"Yes," I replied. "Both Jessica and Naomi were there, standing idle, as if they were waiting for someone. For us. It was weird, because it was only them. No wood to burn, no other supplies. Just them."

"Go on," she said.

"Well, they said they had moved the location of the bonfire to a new 'super cute' clearing. Then they both walked off, without giving any other details, without waiting for us. They just walked off into the woods."

"So, we tried to follow them. We walked a long time. Every now and then, we thought we heard their voices, but far off, so we couldn't make out what they were saying. We walked for a long time. Several hours, I think. Then we came upon the cemetery."

"It was spooky and misty, and we heard a moaning cry several times. Liesl was very afraid at first, then she seemed to become unafraid, but then her fear returned." I thought for a minute. "I think her fear coincided with the moaning voice we heard, but I can't be sure. Then we walked into the middle of the cemetery, kind of, I don't know, exploring.

"I remember talking to Liesl about my Aunt Clare, how she died recently and what had happened with that. Liesl got scared again, so we walked back to the edge of the cemetery, then we left the cemetery, turning completely around and trying to hurry back the other way."

"I could've sworn we were hiking away from the cemetery, but after a while, we walked into it again. I remember wondering if there were two cemeteries. Only I thought it was the same one, because it looked exactly the same. It was surreal. Then we decided to call out loud for help. We yelled really loudly, trying to call for anyone to help us. But no one answered. And it got really quiet."

"Then I thought of calling forth my familiars. I remembered what Chance had said, that they were for protecting me, and other things. Companionship and stuff. So I called them with the spell we'd learned earlier in the week, in class. I did the spell and they came, and everything got better."

"How so?" the headmistress asked.

"Well, the wolves appeared. They're huge. I know I felt immediately better. Liesl seemed to, as well. By the way, headmistress, why did I get two familiars?"

"Oh, ah, well, that sometimes happens, Miss Ó Cuilinn," she said.

"But why? Why does it happen? From what I gather, it is rare, and also, I have been getting the feeling that you all know more about me than I know myself."

"Well, Miss Ó Cuilinn, we can address that later. First: can you finish telling us what happened last night?" the headmistress asked.

"Oh, yeah, last night. Well, I asked the wolves if they could carry us, and if they knew the way back to the school. They said yes to both questions, so Liesl and I climbed on top of them. Just then, the moaning started again and we saw a misty looking figure, looked like a ghost from a TV show, it was gliding toward us, sort of ... reaching out for us. Like I said before, I think it might have been a wight.

"Well, that was the last straw. We rode the wolves back through the forest, and I think they went in a straight line, and, well, you saw they rest. We arrived, we went in, talked to you all, and then got assigned to a new dorm room."

I took a deep breath and sat back. I had never talked so much in my life.

The headmistress seemed to be thinking. She sat with her fingers folded together. Then she consulted with her secretary and sent her off on some task, then turned back to me.

"Miss Ó Cuilinn. You are to be commended on your courage in the face of great danger. I want to express my admiration. For a first-year student to perform the spell to call your familiar so soon after learning it, well, that is impressive.

"Now, as to the forest and why you got lost so easily, there are spells and glyphs placed on the forest land to confound the wanderer. They are there to protect the school from intruders. But they are not perfect, and work to confound any person that walks in the wood at night. Apparently, Miss Penner and Miss Page, the girls who led you and Miss Becker into the woods, got lost themselves. We found them quite far away, just before dawn. Our guards were searching all night for them."

I leaned forward. "We didn't hear them cry out for help. Were they found near the cemetery?"

"No, they were not. Miles away, in fact. They were in a very sorry state and told us that it was *you* and Miss Becker who'd lured *them* into the forest under false pretenses. This is why I wanted to question everyone by themselves. It was most ... enlightening.

"Now, I do want to mention, that should you ever find yourself in the cemetery again, and there is only the one, by the way, that you leave at once. The creature you saw there was not a wight, as you thought, but a banshee. Far, far more dangerous. And wights are not to be trifled with, either."

I sat, stunned.

A banshee?

"Miss Ó Cuilinn, I am finished with your interview. Would you like to join Miss Becker in your new dorm room for a recess?" The headmistress said, getting to her feet.

"Wait. Please." I held my hand up.

She stopped and sat back down.

"I would like some answers. Please," I said.

She waited, watching me expectantly.

I took a deep breath.

"Well, I'm kind of tired beating around the bush. Please tell me: Why are most of the students treating me badly? Without even having met me?" I asked.

It was a minute before the headmistress answered.

"Miss Ó Cuilinn, I understand Mr. Mac Craith has told you the significance of your hair and eye color?"

"Yes, yes, he told me the white colors shows I'm descended from a royal line. He said the black rims on my eyes show I was misborn. Born out of wedlock. That doesn't really answer why over eighty percent of the student body is mocking me," I said. I swallowed hard. I sounded whiney even to my own ears.

"Miss Ó Cuilinn, being misborn is much more significant in the faerie world than it is in the human world, I'm sorry to say. This is no fault of your own, and yet you are being punished for it, and that is wrong and a shame. But it is what it is. This has happened before, albeit rarely. You're just going to have to win them over."

" 'Win them over'?" I asked, incredulous. "Two girls just almost got me killed last night."

"I understand that. But I have no other options. I cannot force the students to like you."

I took a deep breath, increasingly frustrated by the conversation.

Sarah spoke then. "Headmistress, we could put forth a decree against any kind of bullying."

"We could, although I'm not sure it would stop the truly dedicated," the headmistress said.

"It wouldn't hurt," I said.

She nodded. "Very well, I shall have a decree drawn up."

I stood up. "I have one more question, please."

She looked at me expectantly.

"I'd like to know who my father was. Who my 'royal ancestors' were. I'd like to know the reason I'm being treated this way by the students."

The headmistress nodded slowly. "I will get to work on an answer for you, Miss Ó Cuilinn." She got to her feet and took off her eyeglasses.

The meeting was over.

Chapter Eighteen
Enough is Enough

The rest of our Saturday was crazy. I swear, word spreads at a school faster than lightning. Our first clue was when we were walking back up to the new dorm room.

We weren't even halfway across the main hallway when we heard them.

The commotion was unreal.

"Hey."

"Hey you two."

"Stop right there."

"Stop!"

"Hey!

"Hey there!"

"Who do you think you are?"

"Oh look, it's the special kid."

"The new kid we're supposed to tiptoe around."

"Hey, your royal highness, where's your crown?"

"Why did you hurt Jessica? She's my cousin!"

"Holly, wolly, you suck!"

"Yeah: you suck!"

"Creepy girl, creepy hair!"

"Why'd you attack Jessica??"

"Hey, why'd you lead Naomi into the woods?"

"Why are you so strange?"

"Why are you so different?"

A group of about a dozen upper classmen surrounded us. One girl stepped forward.

"You're Holly, aren't you?" She said in an accusatory tone.

I just stared at her.

"I'm Renée. I'm a third year. Naomi's my sister."

"Okay," I said in a quiet voice.

"What did you do to her and Jessica?"

"Yeah, what'd you do?"

"What do you have against them?"

"What's your problem, Misborn?"

"What happened? Are you jealous?"

"Yeah, jealous of Naomi and Jessica 'cause their parents are married?"

"Were you the product of a rape, sweetheart?"

Oh my God.

This last remark made me swing around and walk away fast. I pushed through the throng and ran, my face blazing red.

"Holly, wait up," Liesl's voice called after me.

No.

I had had enough with this school and these girls.

I ran, not paying any attention to where I was going. I came to a stairway and ran up it as fast as I could.

I could hear them jeering behind me, and it only made me run faster.

I ran until I was out of breath and had found a small, dark place to hide. I had gone up, away from everyone, and I didn't care anymore.

I didn't care about the Academy.

I didn't care about the other students.

I didn't care about being heard.

I didn't care about the headmistress Professor Ó Baoghill or the dorm supervisor Sarah Goodheart.

I didn't care about homework, or good grades, or learning anything.

I just wanted to go home.

I huddled in the cabinet I'd found in a dark room, at the end of a deserted corridor, and I fumed.

I hated those girls.

HATED THEM.

They didn't even know me. They didn't know one thing about me.

I hate this school.

Why had I even come here? I should have stayed with Aunt Clare.

Aunt Clare is dead.

I sobbed, tears flowing fast and hot.

I couldn't believe how bad things were in this school. Granted it was my first school, the first I'd ever attended, but ...

And it's the last. I want to leave and never come back!

This was so hard. So hard.

I missed Aunt Clare so much. She'd been the only family I'd known.

And she'd been gone for less than a month.

So much had happened.

My life felt like it'd been turned upside down.

Turned on its head.

I was used to a life of anonymity, a life where I was basically invisible.

I was small and thin, and with my dark hoodie on, walking the streets of New York City, no one had ever paid any attention to me.

Even when I stole an apple or a loaf of bread, and had run, I was so fast and little that I got away, every single time.

No one could follow me, not when I scampered and slid between fences or ran down dark alleyways.

I was invisible.

Here, I stood out like a sore thumb, as if there was a spotlight on me at all times.

And for some unknown reason, everyone hated me.

It was like my worst nightmare.

This was the opposite of what I was used to. The opposite of how my life had always been.

I hated it.

I put my face in my hands and cried silent tears. I felt a deep mourning in my chest. Not just for Aunt Clare, but for my life.

I felt my life had ended, my life as I knew it, had always known it.

This new life was so painful. So awful.

My shoulders shook with silent sobs.

I stayed like that for a long time.

Then ...

A noise.

Huh?

I heard someone call out a long way away. I turned my head away from the cabinet door, and closed my eyes.

Then I heard it.

A howl.

AWOOOOOOOO!

It was close by. I think it was in the corridor I'd run down.

AWOOOOOOOO!

Or maybe in the room I was in.

"Down here, I hear them," the voice sounded like it was down at the end of the corridor. Far away but close enough that I could make out the words.

I thought the voice sounded like Chance's.

Then I heard the click-click of wolf paws on the shiny classroom floor.

Then a hot and wet pant, a wolf breathing against the crack in the cabinet.

"Go away," I sobbed.

A scrabbling of paws, the shuffling of a furry body pushing against the cabinet doors.

Then.

A wet nose.

Pushing against my neck.

A wet tongue, licking my ear.

I couldn't help it. I started to smile.

"Come here, you furry thing." I reached out and hugged the wolf's neck.

It was either Aspen or Tundra, one of the two.

The other wolf was beside her sister, and getting jealous. She pushed her nose up into the crook of my arm.

I plopped down on a chair and grabbed both arctic wolves and buried my face in their fur.

A few minutes passed.

Then –

"Holly," Chance whispered. "Oh, Holly." He put his arm around my shoulders and hugged me.

"Holly, don't listen to those idiots," Liesl said.

"Idnttcre," my voice was muffled, my face still buried in white fur.

I lifted my head just enough to repeat myself, "I don't care. I want to go home."

"Awww, Holly. Don't say that," said Chance. "Listen, things are going to get better. I know it. I just know it."

"Holly, you're my best friend," said Liesl. "You can't leave, you just can't."

I sat up.

No one had ever said they were my best friend. No one, not in my entire life. I looked at Liesl and Chance.

Liesl smiled at me, and I could see tears in her eyes.

Chance winked at me.

Oh, lord, Liesl was right, he was cute.

Really cute.

I took a deep breath.

"I don't know how to deal with a crowd of people attacking me," I said.

"You want to know how to deal with that?" Chance asked.

I nodded my head. I really did want to know.

"You pick the biggest, meanest, nastiest bully out of the crowd and you deal with them, as hard and tough as you can," said Chance. "Just like you did with Jessica. She insulted you, and hurt Liesl, so you punched her in the nose, you made her bleed. You made her flee."

Hmmm.

"Now, I really think we need to go tell the headmistress what happened," said Chance. "This is worse than she realizes." He got to his feet, and reached his hand out. "Come on."

I took a deep breath and then took his hand, and he pulled me to my feet.

Liesl hugged me, then took my other hand.

We all walked back, holding hands.

All the way out of the classroom, all the way down the corridor, all the way down the three staircases I'd run up.

All the way down to the first floor. To where the mob had been.

My wolves followed me the whole way.

Chance glanced around as we walked through the main hallway, and to the headmistress's office.

"Let me do the talking," Chance whispered as he knocked on the door.

"Enter."

He pushed the door open, and we all walked in.

The headmistress was not alone.

The third-year, Renée, was there. *Naomi's sister.*

"You three, take a seat on the side, I'm almost done," the headmistress said, then she turned back to Renée.

"So, Miss Page, do we understand each other?"

Renée nodded.

"And what a fortuitous turn of events. We have Miss Ó Cuilinn right here," said the headmistress. "You may commence, Miss Page."

Renée slowly rose from her seat in front of the headmistress's desk and turn toward me.

With a start, I realized she'd been crying.

She slowly stepped toward me, until she was a few feet away, then she knelt, putting her face in her hands.

"Please forgive me, Holly."

Chapter Nineteen
A Secret Kept

I stared at Renée, not believing my eyes.

What was going on here?

"Renée?" I whispered.

She raised her head and looked at me, her eyes stricken. I could not believe the difference in her from what she had been a few hours ago.

I could not think of anything to say.

"Miss Ó Cuilinn," the headmistress said softly.

I looked up.

"Perhaps I need to do a bit of explaining. You see, when you and Mr. Mac Craith left my office, I waited a few seconds, and then followed you. I witnessed the students; I saw what happened. I was aghast when I heard their words, and I was not surprised when you ran off. I immediately called Miss Page into my office and demanded an explanation for her words."

I took a deep breath. I did not know what was coming, but I knew the other students, or most of them, hated me for some reason.

I was curious as well as hurt.

The headmistress continued. "I owe you an apology, child. I had not realized the bullying was so bad."

I couldn't help myself, although I tried. I'd been able to keep a straight face for most of the conversation, but now tears, hot and angry, spilled out of my eyes and ran down my face.

The room remained silent.

To my horror, my nose started running.

The headmistress handed me a tissue.

I took it gratefully and blew my nose.

She handed me another.

Chance took the liberty of lifting the box from the headmistress's desk and placing it beside me on a small table.

It was a while before I could get hold of myself. I think I went through a half dozen tissues before I could look up at her again.

She smiled sympathetically.

"I was very upset at what's been happening to you, especially because of your ... extended circumstances," the headmistress said. "I made a decision I would not normally make, but I could in this instance because Miss Page is a singularly odd member of the fae."

She glanced at the girl, who was now sitting on the floor at my feet, looking sodden and miserable.

"Miss Ó Cuilinn, Miss Page is a member of a rare strain of woodland fae who are receptive to an ancient form of faeborn magic. Because of this, I was able to lay a secrecy spell on her. This was all with her consent, I assure you."

I was puzzled.

"What is a secrecy spell?" I asked, unable to stop myself.

The headmistress looked pleased, and I remembered that she was, in essence, a professor, and so would be happy in teaching.

"A secrecy spell is a magic, performed by the secret speaker, that binds the person to an oath. In effect, they are told a secret, and they cannot expose that secret in any way, on pain of death."

I felt an immediate shock. I stared down at Renée.

"I don't want anyone to die," I said quietly.

Renée looked up at me and smiled gratefully.

"Miss Ó Cuilinn, she is not going to die. She agreed to accept this magic, in exchange for knowing what your secret is," the headmistress explained.

I looked up at her sharply.

"You told her a secret about me? How could you do that without my consent?"

This is not good.

"I realize I was making a decision that you might be angry with, and if you are, I don't blame you. But I needed to get to the bottom of this hazing, Miss Ó Cuilinn. Your safety is at stake."

I wiped my tears away hastily; they burned hot against my face. "My safety has now been put in more danger because you told Renée a secret about me, and now ..."

The headmistress held up her hand. "You were not put in danger, Miss Ó Cuilinn. Remember: the magic of the secrecy spell. I performed the spell before I revealed the secret."

From the floor, I heard Renée sob.

I tried to calm myself down.

Breathe, Holly. Just breathe.

I looked at the headmistress Professor Ó Baoghill and tried to not get more upset. I needed to be calm.

"Headmistress," I asked.

She leaned and looked at me, all her attention on me.

"What information did you get from her, that you found so valuable that you had to reveal secrets about *me* to her, without getting my permission?"

The headmistress took a deep breath. "I learned because of your lineage," here she nodded toward my hair and gestured toward my eyes, "the students can tell you are descended from a royal line, and they can tell you were conceived outside of marriage."

Couldn't she have figured this out by simple deduction?

There is was again.

"Conceived outside of marriage? Why on earth was this such a big deal?" I said. "I know Chance had said the fae world was much more traditional, but, I mean, life happens. Everything is not always how we want it to be. An it's not always our fault."

"I agree with you on this, Miss Ó Cuilinn, said the headmistress. "But I cannot change how our fae society is, although I can push back against dangerous tendencies whenever I have the opportunity."

She sat back.

"One more thing," she said, steepling her fingers and speaking slowly, choosing her words carefully. "Most of the student body understands you appear of human and magical royal fae heritage; that is a large part of the anger they feel. Miss Page explained to me the combination of royal fae lineage and human lineage makes them angry."

"Most of the students here at Titania Academy are descended from not only the common lines of fae heritage, but from the poorer lines as well. The badger, the rabbit, the faun ..."

I noticed Chance shuffling his feet.

The headmistress went on: "Now, that does not mean they are any less worthy, but it denotes something less, however incorrectly, in our fae culture." She looked at me. "Something similar occurred back one hundred, to one hundred and fifty years ago, in the city you grew up in." She looked at her papers, then back up at me. "New York City. In the late 1800s, with regard to the Irish immigrants. Do you know about that?"

I shook my head.

"Irish immigrants were treated very poorly back then." She consulted another paper. "And apparently, back then and more recently, Africans."

I took a deep breath. I'd had enough of the history lesson.

"I understand, headmistress. That doesn't make it right. These people have been vicious toward me. It began as I pulled up to the school on that very first day."

The headmistress looked sad and bowed her head. "I understand, and I apologize that I did not realize how bad it had gotten. I am taking steps to make things better for you."

I shook my head. "I am not even sure I want to stay in this school, to tell you the truth."

The headmistress's face went white.

"Oh, please, Miss Ó Cuilinn, please give us another chance. I am working hard to make things better, and now we have Miss Page to help us," she gestured to Renée sitting on the floor.

The third-year girl was tall, and her long legs splayed out sideways as she sat at my feet.

She looked up at us when the headmistress mentioned her name, and nodded.

"Holly," said Renée. "I promise I am going to do everything I can to help you, to make things better, to help you in your situation."

The headmistress held up her hand. "Miss Page, I think it will be vitally important *not* to make things worse. I do not think we should be hinting that there is anything special or out of the ordinary with Miss Ó Cuilinn. That could make her more of a target. Remember, we must not only keep her secrets, we must make it seem as if she doesn't even *have* any secrets. She is an ordinary, intelligent, wonderful young lady who deserves to be treated well. That is how we should approach things."

Renée nodded. "Yes, headmistress. That's a good idea."

"I am curious about this secrecy spell, Renée. I think it would make me feel better if I knew what it entailed," I said. "It would make me feel safer." I fixed the headmistress with a pointed look.

"Renée, why don't you tell Miss Ó Cuilinn, in your own words, everything that occurred with you and I, before she and Mr. Mac Craith entered the room," the headmistress said quietly, then folded her hands.

I stared at Renée expectantly. I did not feel she was an ally nor a friend.

"Well," said Renée. "The headmistress grabbed me out of the crowd and pulled me into her office."

I glanced at the headmistress.

She nodded. "I did exactly that. I took her by the arm and pulled her into this office. She did not want to come at all. She fought me, but I am stronger than I look."

Renée took a deep breath. "So, then she pushed me into the chair and slammed the door behind me. The headmistress spoke in a raised, angry voice. She asked, 'WHY WOULD YOU SPEAK THAT WAY TO ANOTHER STUDENT? ARE YOU OUT OF YOUR MIND?' and I got angry. I told the headmistress all the reasons we hated Holly." Renée glanced at me apologetically.

I nodded for her to continue.

"It was for all the reasons the headmistress said, plus I was angry that Holly had fought with Jessica and my sister Naomi. Angry that Jessica had gotten her nose hurt. Holly," Renée glanced at me, "I know Jessica and Naomi hurt you much worse, and that they were picking on Liesl, and that Jessica deserved to have her nose punched. I understand all that, but I was still angry." Renée looked down at her fingers, which were entwined together.

"I guess I just pushed aside these reasons you had for fighting with Jessica. Although now I think I would have down the same." She smiled and balled her hand into a fist, then mimicked punching someone.

"Keep to the narrative, Miss Page," the headmistress reminded her.

"Oh, yes. Um," said Renée. "Then the headmistress was quiet for a few minutes, and I just sat in the chair. Then the headmistress said, 'You're of the Woodland Pixie Fae, aren't you,' and I told her I was. Although the last pixie in my line was my great grandmother. Then the headmistress asked if she could perform the Revealing Glyph over me, and I consented."

"So then, the headmistress stood and walked around her desk and made the glyph over my head, and I glowed blue, so she knew the pixie woodland strain was still binding." Renée took a deep breath.

"Then the headmistress asked me if I would allow her to perform the secrecy spell on me, so that I might better understand you, Holly." Renée glanced at me again and smiled what looked like a genuine smile.

I could not believe it.

Her smile was so bright and beautiful I couldn't help myself, I smiled back.

This is the girl who seemed like she hated me just a few hours ago.

"So, I gave permission for the headmistress to perform the secrecy spell on me. So, she did. It took a few minutes. I don't remember any of the words." She looked up at the headmistress.

"Some spells are forgotten after they've been overheard because they have extra protection placed on them when they're first created," said the headmistress. "Much like the spell to summon your familiars."

I put my hand down and buried it in the coarse fur of my familiar wolf on my right. The other leaned against my leg. Her meaning was plain: *I love you.*

Renée was talking again.

"After the secrecy spell was performed, the headmistress sat back down and divulged the secrets about you, Holly. And my eyes were opened."

I blinked. "What do you mean?"

The headmistress held up her finger. "Miss Page, remember that Miss Ó Cuilinn is not aware of most of the secrets I told you. She knows where she grew up, but little else. She knows that she is descended of a royal fae line, but she knows no specifics. She knows her mother's name, but not her father's. Remember."

Renée nodded. "I remember. There's little else to say except, you and Chance and Liesl knocked and entered the room just a few minutes after your secrets were revealed to me."

Renée looked down, then up at me. "Holly, please forgive me for what I said. It was cruel and wrong to say that to you, to anyone, really. I want to help you with the struggles you've been having. I will fight by your side." Tears were forming in her eyes again.

"I don't want any fighting," I said. "Can we just stop with the fighting?" I pleaded.

"We will try," said the headmistress.

"Okay, well, thank you for telling me what happened, Renée. I will admit to being very curious. And I *really* hope that you are being sincere."

"I am," Renée said solemnly. "I swear on my life I am."

I turned to the headmistress. "I have one question."

The headmistress raised her eyebrows

"What," I asked, "secrets about *me* did you disclose to Renée?"

Chapter Twenty
Secrets Suck

I stomped away from the headmistress's office, a huge scowl on my face.

"Holly, wait up," called Liesl.

Chance and Renée hurried after me, too.

They all trailed after me, but gave me a wide berth. They stayed about ten paces behind, but did not let me out of their sight.

I stomped out the main front doors of the school, fuming.

How dare she?!!

I stopped in my tracks, remembering.

I thought back to the headmistress's face when I'd asked what secrets she'd told Renée about me.

It had been a look of resignation, but right before that, right at the very beginning, I remember a look ...

A fleeting look ...

Of fear.

The headmistress was afraid.

I replayed the scene in my mind

"What secrets about me did you disclose to Renée?"

"Miss Ó Cuilinn, I cannot tell you that," the headmistress replied.

"EXCUSE ME?" I raised my voice despite myself.

The headmistress's face remained calm.

I stood and began to pace.

My two familiars began to walk back and forth after me, their paws faintly click-clacking on the polished stone.

I stopped, bending to pet them and hug them, whispering love in their ears, asking them to sit and stay.

They obeyed me.

I loved how intelligent they were, how responsive and protective they were. They were fast becoming quite precious to me.

I felt tears spring to my eyes as I hugged them, the white wolf fur brushing against my cheek.

Get a hold of yourself, Holly.

I rose and turned back to the headmistress, sitting there behind her desk looking just as pleased as she could with herself.

I struggled to keep my voice calm.

"You mean to tell me that, secrets, personal secrets, about me, my parents, and my heritage, are known to Renée and you and to goodness knows how many other people here, but I am not allowed to know these secrets?"

The headmistress nodded.

I took a deep breath.

"Those are my secrets. They are mine. MINE."

The headmistress remained silent, hands folded together in front of her, fingers intertwined. I was fast learning what this meant: It was as though she were bolting the gates of a fortress. She would tell me nothing.

A slow boil was occurring in my mind, like a volcano, a hot bubbling of emotion.

ARRGGGHHHH! I wanted to scream.

But outwardly, I remained calm.

Calm and cool.

"Why not?" I asked. "Why can't you tell me? I am not about to blab my own secrets to the world, and the world already seems to know them! In fact, everyone seems to know more about me than I know myself!"

"I sympathize, Miss Ó Cuilinn, believe me. I really do," the headmistress said. "And no, the whole fae world doesn't know more about you than you do yourself. In fact, there are very few individuals who know your secrets."

I tapped my foot impatiently.

Cool, Holly. Stay cool ...

I knew from growing up the way I had that it helped if those around me did not know I was upset.

I took a deep breath.

"Okay then," I said. "I'm curious. *Who* knows my secrets?"

The headmistress remained silent. Then: "I think that it would be best if I not tell you that."

"But you've already revealed that Renée knows!"

Calm, cool, be cool ...

She pursed her lips.

"All right. First off, the education board knows. The fae counsel knows. I know. Miss Page knows. Mr. Mac Craith knows. Your professors all know. The ..."

I heard a soft groan come from Chance.

I held up my hand. "Excuse me? Chance knows?"

"I ..." the headmistress looked troubled. "Miss Ó Cuilinn, Mr. Mac Craith is given thorough dossiers on every student he is sent to collect. That is normal operating procedure. He cannot do his job without this knowledge."

"And what, exactly, is Chance's job? I asked, my voice coming out steelier than I would have liked.

The headmistress took a deep breath. "Mr. Mac Craith is tasked as a Collector, Miss Ó Cuilinn."

My head tipped to the side. "What?"

"He is employed by the school to collect fae children who have ... gone missing," the headmistress said.

"I'm sorry. 'Gone missing'? Missing from where?" I asked.

"Missing from the fae world," said the headmistress. "Children, though it happens rarely, sometimes go missing from our world and are lost in human society. For different reasons, this does happen. Mr. Mac Craith is ... very good ... at finding these children. At connecting with them. At bringing them back home to the FaeFolk."

OH, HOLY HELL.

"He sounds like a gangster," I said.

"No, not a ... Miss Ó Cuilinn, he is especially skilled at making a personal connection so that the children are most likely to return with him, but they ... you ... are never obligated. Never forced. Mr. Mac Craith is especially gifted in this regard."

I started pacing again.

"Miss Ó Cuilinn, try to understand. Children of the FaeFolk have magical gifts, and these gifts often manifest themselves in the human world at ... inconvenient times. This puts the fae children in danger. We tried different types of fae as Collectors, but none have been as adept as FaunFolk at this particular task; that is why we use them almost exclusively now. They know how to gain a child's trust in a way most strangers who speak of the magical realm cannot. It can be ... a lot to take in, even for the older recruits."

I shook my head, trying to take it all in.

"Chance is ... what did you call him? FaunFolk?" I asked.

"That is correct," the headmistress replied.

I looked over at Chance, who grinned at me sheepishly and waved his fingers.

First-years were just learning all about the different kinds of FaeFolk. There were so many kinds it was hard to keep them all straight.

And each type had its own attributes and gifts.

I tried to remember back to the class last week, we had just been learning about ...

I looked up.

"FaunFolk. Lineage from the fauns. Is that right?" I asked.

Chance nodded.

"Attributes include," I said slowly, remembering, ticking off the attributes on my fingers one by one. "Sympathetic magic, companionship, ease of the mind, friendship, ..."

I tried to think. *What were the other ones?*

"Musically inclined, easy-going. ..." I shrugged. "I don't remember the rest. I'll have to study up on them more from my textbook."

Chance grinned.

The headmistress nodded. "The point is, he needs a complete dossier on each child to be able to do his job properly. Do you understand?"

I sighed.

"I guess so. But it doesn't feel right that he knows secrets about me that I don't. I mean, what could it hurt to tell me? I'm fae, I was lost, but now I'm back, and I am a part of the fae world, right?"

The headmistress, Chance, and Renée all nodded.

"Well, then, why not tell me?" I pleaded. "I know it would make things easier for me."

It was the headmistress's turn to sigh.

"Miss Ó Cuilinn, I know you think that knowing these secrets about yourself would make things easier for you," she said. "But it would not. It definitely would not."

I stared at her. I had never felt more frustrated in my entire life, and this included the time I was stuck in one of the downtown butcher's back cupboards for hours, having gotten stuck there while attempting to liberate a fully cooked honey-baked ham for a holiday dinner with Aunt Clare three years back.

"Try to understand, Miss Ó Cuilinn," said the headmistress. "If I revealed ... if *anyone* revealed the secrets to you, it would be placing you in grave danger."

I caught movement out of the corner of my eye, and turned to see Renée nodding vigorously.

"Really?" I said to her.

"I don't mean to upset you further, Holly, but she's right. When she told me the secrets, it sent my heart racing."

"You're not making things easier, you know," I said in exasperation.

"Sorry."

"Miss Ó Cuilinn, I am withholding this information for your own protection. Until you know more, perhaps after a few more years in the Academy classes ..." the headmistress said.

I whipped my head around. "HUH? More classwork? How will that ...?"

She held up her hand. "Let me continue. The decision not to tell you the secrets was not made by me."

I blinked.

I felt stunned.

It's like there's a whole committee that's deciding my life for me.

I shook my head slowly.

She continued. "The decision has been made by the Regent himself. And he has made it known that when you have learned all about fae society, magic, rules, and all the rest – all about protecting yourself, then, and only then, possibly, he will allow you to know."

I sputtered.

"It is for your own protection, Miss Ó Cuilinn," said the headmistress. "Try to understand, your heritage can make you a target. I have already said too much as it is."

I thought for a minute.

"And Chance," I gestured toward him. "Has he been sworn to secrecy as well?"

"Chance is not like Miss Page. He has had other restraints placed on him," the headmistress said.

I took a deep breath, hoping to calm down and understand more.

"And it's my royal lineage that's the danger? Then am I not already in danger, just from my hair and eye color?" I asked, lifting a lock of my platinum hair up.

"This is a good example of what I'm talking about, Miss Ó Cuilinn," said the headmistress. "They see your hair and eyes, and treat you the way they have been. But they have no idea what line you're descended from. It could be some moldy old distant duke that you're related to. That's all it would take to give you that coloring, and the duke's line could have died out centuries before and be of absolutely no consequence."

AHA.

"Are you implying I'm from a much more recent or esteemed royal line?" I asked.

The headmistress looked incredibly uncomfortable.

"Well," she said, rising from her desk, "I think I've said enough, uh, Miss Ó Cuilinn. I think we will end this conversation here, and ... uh ... I will be counting on Mr. Mac Craith and, uh ... Miss Page to ... uh ... greatly aid in your protection. Isn't that correct?" She nodded at Chance and Renée as she herded us all out the door.

Chance nodded, "I will protect her with my life."

"Absolutely, headmistress, said Renée. "I will do everything in my power to help and protect Holly, I swear it.

"But ...," I protested as I was rushed out of the headmistress's office. "I want to know more ..."

The door clicked behind us.

I turned and pounded on the massive wooden expanse.

"YOU CAN'T DO THIS!"

"Holly," Chance put his hand on my shoulder, "It's no use. She's not going to budge ..."

I whirled on him, my fists balled, an angry glower on my face.

His concerned expression held my tongue.

I turned and stomped away from the headmistress's office, a huge scowl on my face.

Chapter Twenty-One
A Shooting Star

"Miss Ó Cuilinn."

I stopped in my tracks. I had stomped away from the office and made it to the front doors of the school, and out.

The headmistress's voice stopped me halfway down the stairs.

I turned and waited for her to walked down to meet me.

"Miss Ó Cuilinn. I forgot to tell you," said the headmistress. "The children who took part in the bullying earlier today will all receive black marks on their academic records, which seriously damages their prospects for entry into dozens of coveted programs. And also, they have been warned that a second incident will result in immediate expulsion."

She glanced at Renée. "Miss Page already knows this, and understands. The other students have already been informed. Miss Page will impress upon them all the seriousness of this issue."

She looked at me, her face grave. "Titania Academy takes such things extremely seriously. Despite your unhappiness at me not being able to disclose your ..." she glanced around. We were outside now, and in public. "... your history, we are still here to protect you and teach you, all the knowledge we can concerning our world."

I nodded. I was calming down.

"Professor Ó Baoghill, I appreciate all you and the school have done for me. I'm still not sure I want to stay," I said.

The headmistress looked deeply distressed.

"Miss Ó Cuilinn, please stay at our Academy," she said.

I shook my head. "I probably won't, to be honest."

"I am begging you, Miss Ó Cuilinn," she whispered. "Holly."

I raised my eyebrows. This was the first time the headmistress had used my first name. It meant something, because this was me. I hadn't even known my last name until Chance told me.

The headmistress looked into my eyes. "Please."

I frowned.

"Headmistress, I will think about it. But from what you've implied, I'm probably someone of importance. And as such, I would really like honesty from you, from now on," I said.

"I will give you all the honesty I am allowed to give, I promise," the headmistress whispered.

The sun was shining down on us, and the stone steps we were halfway down, having this important exchange, were bright in the daylight.

Everything seemed just a little bit better when the sun was shining.

"Thank you," I said. "For everything. I will do my very best as well, to fit in and thrive."

She nodded, taking my hand and squeezing it gently; then turned and slowly ascended the stairs and walked back into the school.

"Well, this was a heavy day," Chance said, a long sprout of grass in his mouth.

We were all relaxing in the grass, enjoying the sunshine.

He was right: The day had been so serious and tense, after such a hurtful morning, that spending the day in the sunshine felt like a physical healing.

I leaned back in the grass, my eyes closed, the sun warm on my face.

Liesl lay next to me, her hand holding mine. She hadn't said anything, but had squeezed my hand and held it, and I felt her support and friendship through it.

Chance lay in the grass on my other side, his hand behind his head, one knee flexed, with the other lying across it.

Renée sat at my feet, busy making a flower necklace our of clover buds. She seemed determined to stay near me, as much as possible. She'd taken a particular liking to sitting at my feet.

Weirdo.

I was slowly beginning to like Renée.

"I could fall asleep here," Liesl yawned.

"I could, too," I said. "We only got a few hours of sleep, and last night was unreal." I lifted my shoulders onto my elbows. "Did you hear the headmistress say that thing in the cemetery was *a banshee*?"

"You know," said Liesl, "when she told us that? It did not make me feel any better."

I laughed. "Ha ha ha! Liesl, didn't we think it had been a wight? Which is worse?"

"Wights." Chance spoke with absolute certainty.

"I looked over at him. "Really? But I thought a banshee's cry could kill?"

"Nope. I think that tale comes from America; the old legends have been altered. A banshee's cry heralds a death in the family she protects."

"You're kidding." I said.

"No, he's right," piped up Renée. "My great grandmother came from Ireland, and when she moved to France as a child with her parents, they brought the family banshee with them. I'm not sure what's going on with it, but my mother told me all about it."

"Told ya," Chance winked.

I laughed "Ha ha ha!"

"Now, a wight is a bit scarier," Chance said. "They don't help anyone. In fact, they are quite dangerous, especially to humans who don't have any protection against them."

"When do we learn this protection you speak of?" Liesl said.

"Second year. I'm learning all about the different forms right now," Chance said.

I turned to Renée, "You're third-year, right?"

"That's right. Third-year. Two down, six to go," Renée said.

"So, we go from age fourteen ..." I said.

"Sometimes kids start at thirteen," said Chance. "It depends on when your birthday is."

"... and we go for eight years?" I asked.

"Yep. And when we leave, we are thoroughly ..." Chance said.

"Burned out," interjected Renée.

"Ha ha ha!" I laughed.

"... ready for the fae world," Chance finished.

"That's a lot of schooling," I said.

"It's all good. We need to learn this stuff," Renée said.

"This must be why the headmistress wants to nip all bullying in the bud," Liesl said.

"Yeah, imagine what a place it would be if it was that out of control?" I said. "It'd be like a gangland."

"Tell me about it," Chance said.

I turned on my side. "Chance," I said softly.

He turned his head toward me.

"You really know all my secrets?" I asked quietly.

"Every last one," said Chance bragging. "I even know what your favorite color is!"

"I don't have a favorite color!" I said.

"That you know of," he said.

"Ha ha ha ha ha!" I laughed.

Chance grinned.

"No, but ... seriously. You know the secrets? The secrets about my past? The secrets the headmistress is not allowed to tell me?" I asked.

He looked into my eyes. "I know them, yes."

I didn't know what to feel. Chance was my friend. The Fae Council was not allowing anyone to tell me. These people were trying to do what they thought best, and what they thought best was to keep this knowledge from me.

My knowledge.

A zillion emotions swirled in my head.

"Holly," Chance said.

I looked at him.

"I'm not keeping this from you because of the Fae Council, I'm doing it because I care about you."

I nodded.

"It's just so frustrating," I said. "I don't know anything about my heritage. And every single person I had – my mother, my Aunt Clare, everyone – is gone. I feel like I'm adrift in a very small boat, on a very large sea. Probably everyone else at this school knows their family history. Everyone but me." I shifted on the grass. "Did you know that, before you told me, I'd had no idea when my birthday was?"

Liesl rubbed my back.

"Holly, you can come home with me for the holiday break," said Liesl. "My family will love you."

I smiled at my new best friend.

"Thank you," I mouthed.

That evening, Chance invited me to walk in the moonlight: "I want to show you something you may not have seen before."

So, after the evening meal, I walked out the front doors and down the steps to meet him.

It was just after sunset, and the sky was a deep, dark blue. The horizon, just over the treetops, still showed a bit of color; I couldn't tell if it was orange-blue, or pink-blue.

I turned my back to the sunset and looked out over the darkening sky.

Stars were beginning to appear, faint and barely twinkling.

The cool, crisp evening air felt good in my lungs, and a soft breeze ruffled my white locks.

Aunt Clare had always told me to hide my hair: that it made me stand out in a crowd, so it was easier for people to spot me.

When you're sleeping rough, you want to be able to hide, to disappear into the background. Especially if you stole food every day.

Which I had.

I closed my eyes, inhaling, and thinking about the past month.

The hardest thing to get used to had been the regular meals.

They fed you so much at the school!

Breakfast, lunch, dinner, snacks: It was very different than what I'd been used to. Living in New York, I'd felt lucky if I ate once a day.

I patted my middle.

Was I gaining weight?

"Hi," said Chance behind me.

I turned around.

"Hey there," I smiled. "I never got the chance to thank you, for earlier. I'm sorry I ran away, I just ... I couldn't take the jeers ..."

"I understand completely," said Chance. "I think things are going to get better. At least, I hope they are."

He looked up into the sky. "Okay, it's almost time."

"Time for what?" I asked.

"You'll see," he said, smiling. "Come on," he extended his hand.

I stared at it for a moment before taking it slowly.

This is weird.

Chance led me down the front steps and out to the lawn in front of the school. We walked for about ten minutes, up a short slope that led up a hill.

"Wait, I can't, ha ha ha!" I stumbled on a rock. "I need both my hands!"

"Here, I'll pull you up," he said.

"Fine but I'd do better on my own," I said.

"Nonsense," he said as I climbed up to join him.

"Chance," I said. "Why are you so protective over me? It's kinda weird."

"I'm protective over all the kids I bring to the school," he grinned.

"Yeah, right," I said. "How many did you bring this year?"

"Four, counting you."

"And of those four, how many are you being overprotective with?"

"Um ..."

"I thought so," I said. "So why me?" I demanded, facing him, my hands on my hips.

Chance just stared at me.

I scowled.

"Well, there's ..."

"Yeah?" I asked, trying to get an answer from him.

"Um, well, there's your royal background," Chance said, a foolish look on his face.

"Yeah. It's been implied more than once that that probably means I've got a great-great-grand-uncle who died fifty years ago who was once a duke or something. How is that grounds for over-protecting me?" I asked.

"How is that grounds for excessive bullying?" Chance raised an eyebrow.

"Are you saying they are bullying me for some other reason?" I raised my eyebrows.

"I'm not sure exactly why they're bullying you. I just want it to stop," Chance said, exasperated. "Holly, I will admit I'm a little protective over you, but it's not because of what you think."

"Oh, yeah? Then why is it?"

"Look," Chance whispered.

"What?"

"Turn around," he said, gently pulling on my arm.

"Is this another trick? I swear, Chance, if you ..."

His insistent tugging made me turn just to satisfy it.

"Look," he said.

I turned my back to him and looked out over the grass.

"Look up," he whispered.

I glanced upward, at the sky.

And gasped.

The moon was full. And it was huge.

Hundreds of fireflies were milling about in the evening air, all over the front lawn of the school.

I gasped as a shooting star blazed across the sky.

It was so beautiful, I couldn't stop looking at the sky. The cool breeze blew my hair up, the fireflies kept gathering, and the grounds looked like a sparkling festival with all the floating firefly lights, and the comet arcing across the sky. It was all so magical.

A second shooting star flickered across the black inky expanse.

"This is amazing! Do they portend something? An event that's going to happen?" I asked.

"The shooting stars or the fireflies?" asked Chance.

I laughed. "The shooting stars."

"Well, I'm no astronomer, but a poet would tell you, yes," said Chance. "Now as for the fireflies, they are really active on cool, late summer nights. I think they're wonderful."

"They're so beautiful!"

"I thought you'd like them," Chance whispered.

"What?" I said.

"Nothing."

Chapter Twenty-Two
Forest Outing

I woke up the next morning feeling both hopeful and trepidatious. I didn't know what to expect. Yes, I was "special" – but at this point is my short academic career, I would have far preferred being normal and ordinary.

I certainly didn't *feel* special. I'd always been a survivor, but so were most people living rough.

Aunt Clare had been a true survivor; she'd taught me all I knew about how to survive on the streets. She had not, however, taught me how to survive when other people – people who may have wished me ill will – knew more about me than I knew about myself.

It was insane.

Liesl and I made our way downstairs to breakfast. Chance was already there, and Renée soon joined us.

We made quite the group.

"Chance, do you want to go down to the forest?" Liesl asked. "I've heard it's filled with all sorts of magical creatures."

"Maybe," said Chance. "Should we all head down there after breakfast?"

"Sure," I said. Having spent my first fourteen years in the human world, I was itching to see what discoveries the fae world held in store for me.

"Sounds like fun," said Renée. "This time of year, we might even spot some of the spring and summer babies that were born."

"Curious," I said, munching on a slice of half-crispy, half-chewy bacon. "What year do we learn about all the creatures in the fae forest?"

"I think that's in second semester of Year One," said Renée. She glanced at Chance. "Isn't that right?"

Chance nodded.

I picked up another slice of bacon. I was loving all the exotic foods in the lunchroom. I'd never tasted bacon before, living on the streets of New York City, I had missed that experience.

I thought back to my life before meeting Chance.

Back to life with Aunt Clare.

We had always had it rough, but we'd always somehow made do.

The others living on the streets were always there to compete with, but also there to help out.

Central Park had been a refuge to visit nearly every day. It hadn't been that far from the underground tunnels.

My life with Aunt Clare had been hard, that was for sure.

But I missed her so much.

"Come on, daydreamer," said Renée. "Let's go have some forest fun before we start all the hard work next week."

We made our way out of the lunchroom. Chance ducked into the kitchens and emerged ten minutes later with several bags he distributed to each of us.

"Lunch," he explained when I looked at him with a questioning look.

"What about water?" Renée said.

"There's a stream in the woods," said Chance. "It's got clean water. We can drink from it. The water there tastes better than any water I've ever tasted anywhere."

"Okay," Renée smiled.

Down the stairs we went, Chance leading the way. As his foot touched the bottom step, Chance fell forward and dropped to the ground.

"OH!" Liesl rushed forward to help Chance.

He lifted himself into a sitting position, and sat there, holding his head.

A trickle of blood dripped from a small wound on his eyebrow.

"Hey," I said, crouching in front of him, "You okay? Let's get you inside."

Chance shook his head. "No, I'm fine, I'm fine."

He got to his feet and stood there, swaying.

Liesl grasped his upper arm. "Chance, you're feeling kind of warm."

Renée studied the fifteen-year-old boy. "Your face is a bit red. You sure you're okay, Chance?"

"Yes, yes, I am fine." He brushed off Liesl's concerned hand and stretched, arching his back. Then he smiled and winked at us.

"Let's go!" Chance laughed and trotted out onto the grass.

"You sure?" called Renée.

"Absolutely! I feel fine. Let's go. We're burning daylight." He stopped and gestured for us to follow.

"Guess we should go," Renée shrugged, and started walking.

Liesl and I jogged to catch up.

We turned to the right, then headed across the field and into the woods.

The minute we stepped into the trees it got darker.

I looked around.

"Why ...? I asked.

Renée pointed up, and I looked skyward.

The treetop canopy nearly obliterated the sky, and let in very little light.

"Is that normal?" Liesl asked.

"Normal for this wood," said Chance. "It's not like the forest in the human world." He looked around.

"A lot of magical faeborn live in these woods, a lot of creatures interacting together," said Chance, half whispering.

It was like that. I glanced behind me and saw the schoolyard just a few paces away, then turned back to the majesty of the dark woods.

"Let's go this way," Renée suggested.

We followed a faint animal trail about a mile into the forest. Then another mile.

"We should be near the stream by now," Chance said. "Then we can take a breather and eat lunch."

We walked another mile.

No stream.

Chance was still leading us along the animal trail. Liesl was close behind Chance, followed by me, then Renée. We were spreading out quite a bit, and I could barely see Chance ahead of me.

I jogged up to Liesl and tapped her shoulder. "Hey," I said.

She turned her head. "Yeah?"

"Switch places with me?" I asked.

"Okay," Liesl said.

We switched.

I had thought Chance looked funny and I wanted to get a closer look at him hiking.

I studied him as we walked on another half mile.

Yep.

Sure enough, Chance was weaving as he walked down the trail, bracing himself against the trees every now and then.

"Hey, Chance," I called. "Hold up a minute?"

He stopped in the middle of the trail, and stood, swaying unsteadily.

I walked up to him. Liesl and Renée joined me.

Chance stood still, facing away from us, holding on to the oak tree next to him.

He looked like he could fall over any minute.

I put my hand out. "Chance?"

He turned his head to glance at us, then promptly teetered over, falling into me.

Renée, Liesl, and I all caught him as he fell.

He was burning up.

"Let's lower him to the ground," Renée murmured.

We sat Chance down in the middle of the trail in some ferns.

"I'm fine," he said faintly.

I looked into his unfocused eyes. Then glanced at his soaked shirt and red color.

"He's practically delirious," I said. "And burning up with a fever. This is not good."

"Okay, okay," Renée said, glancing around. "I actually don't think we're anywhere near the stream. We should have come upon it already."

Liesl looked worried. "We're miles from the school. Is there any way we can get a message back to them?"

"Chance got ill awfully fast." I looked down at him, puzzled.

"I think he was already sick," said Renée. "Then he hiked for a few miles through uneven forest."

"And this made him sicker," I whispered.

Oh, no.

"Everyone? Let's sit down. Liesl, can you break out the lunch?" said Renée. "Holly, we need to get a message to the school. I'm going to call my familiar." She spoke the spell, and a large jackrabbit appeared by her side.

She bent down and nuzzled the creature's ears.

It took Liesl and I several tries to summon our familiars; we were nervous, being out here in the forest. But finally, Liesl's snowy ermine and my two wolves appeared.

I patted the ground next to me and Aspen and Tundra lay down beside me.

"Should we lay Chance on the ground?" Liesl asked.

"No, I think he's fine propped up against the tree," said Renée. "His familiar should appear soon, though. He may not be feeling fright, but he's in danger, all the same."

"We all are, aren't we?" I asked in a quiet voice.

"Not as much as you'd think," Renée answered.

"Here's your sandwich." Liesl handed out the food Chance had brought.

I took a bite of the thick crusty bread, tasting the sweet turkey inside. The chef had added tomatoes, and the juice ran down my chin. I tried to lick it away.

I took another bite.

I was beginning to feel better.

Things are always brighter with food in your stomach," Aunt *Clare used to always say.*

I turned to my wolves.

"Aspen?" I whispered. The closer wolf turned her head to stare at me.

I swear, the best thing about having a familiar is that they understand what you're saying.

"Can you find the stream? Find the water?" Aspen got to her feet, still staring at me.

"Here," said Renée, handing me her bag. "It's water-tight. Oiled it myself last year, when I went on a summer trip to Sweden."

I took the bag from her and carefully put the handles into Aspen's mouth, making sure the top was gaping open. Then I held the wolf's face between my palms and touched my forehead to hers.

"Find the stream. Fill this with water. Bring it back to me," I whispered. "Go."

Aspen turned and began running through the woods.

"See now, I would've though the stream was back there," Renée pointed in a different direction than the wolf had gone.

"I think she'll find it," I said.

"Oh, she'll find it, all right," said Renée. "I think that's one of the reasons you were given two familiars, and two such powerful ones."

"How do you mean?" I asked, curious.

"Because of your heritage, you're ... drat it all, I can't say," Renée looked frustrated. "Suffice it to say, not even the headmistress of the school had such a powerful familiar, not to mention two of them."

"I wondered why Holly has two," said Liesl. She cuddled with her snowy ermine, kissing the crown of the beautiful animal's face.

"I don't think anyone's got as cute a familiar as you, Liesl," I said. "Snowbear is adorable!"

"Okay," said Renée, brushing the sandwich crumbs from her hands. "I'm sending Jade to get help."

"Jade?" Liesl said.

Renée picked up her rabbit familiar, cuddled her for a minute, kissed her forehead, then set her down on the forest floor. The rabbit turned and looked at Renée, unblinking.

Renée said, "Maintenant, va à l'Académie et dis-leur que nous sommes perdus dans la forêt."

The rabbit dipped her head and turned and ran back the way we'd come.

"Look at her go!" Liesl smiled.

"Yeah, Jade can run very fast," Renée said, pride in her voice. "Now we just wait."

I glanced over at Chance. His eyes were closed. "Maybe we should lay him down now. He seems to have gone to sleep," I said.

Renée looked closer at Chance, then leaned over and lifted one of the young man's eyelids.

Chance didn't react, which was really weird.

"Uh oh," Renée murmured, pulling Chance from the tree and gently lowering him to the forest floor, with Liesl's help. "He's not asleep, he passed out." Renée looked around the forest. "This is not good."

Chapter Twenty-Three
Nightfall

Night was falling.

"Okay, Holly, Liesl? This is not good. Really not good," said

It had been at least six hours since we'd sent off our familiars, Aspen to find water, and Jade to get word to the school.

"They should've been back by now," said Liesl.

"Holly, Liesl, help me," said Renée, getting to her feet. "We've got to build some kind of temporary shelter."

"Renée, don't you think we should just walk back the way we came?" I asked. I remembered when Liesl and I were lost in the other part of the forest, by the cemetery, my wolves had led us back to the school.

"No," said Renée. "I was testing that with Jade. She is very fast. We've only come four miles or so. She should have been there and back again within an hour. Certainly, within two. I'm really worried she's not back. It wouldn't help to move from our spot and get even more lost in the forest, trust me."

I frowned. "And Aspen should've been back with the water, too."

Renée nodded. "Something's wrong." She glanced about. "Here, let's drag some of those larger branches over here. Help me?"

We gathered maybe a dozen long branches that had fallen from the evergreens overhead.

"It's weird," said Renée. "It should be getting colder now, but it feels warm and cozy."

"Oh, I should have explained," I said.

The other two looked at me.

"Explained what?" Renée finally said.

I shrugged. "Well, for some reason, it never gets too cold around me. I'm like a hot water bottle."

Liesl just stared at me.

Renée blinked. "You're kidding?"

I shook my head. "Is that something weird? I thought maybe other faefolk could do it, too."

"Uhhh, a few can, but it's very rare," said Renée. "Rare like, one in a million."

Now it was my turn to blink.

Huh. Weird.

Renée shook her head. "Well, it'll come in handy tonight, that's for sure."

I grinned, and she smiled back.

Renée was able to use some rope we found in Chance's pocket, and string up a line across two trees.

"There," said Renée. "These two are pretty close together, now let's lay the branches against the rope, like so." She rested a branch against the line. The smaller branches and twigs growing outward from the main branch spread out and acted like a windbreak.

Liesl and I brought two more large branches, and then we all got the rest.

By the time we were finished, we had a respectable lean-to built against the two main trees.

"Now we gather smaller bits and make a fire," said Renée. "Let's try to get enough to last until at least tomorrow."

"We'd better hurry, it's almost dark," said Liesl. "Does anyone have flint and steel?"

"No, but I've got a lighter," I said, grinning. "Aunt Clare always said to keep one on hand, because you never know when you might need one."

"Oh, thank goodness for Aunt Clare," Renée smiled.

Ten minutes later, we'd gathered a substantial pile of dried branches, each several feet long.

"I'm going to go get one more handful," said Renée. "Holly, you know how to start a fire?"

I nodded.

I sure did.

Renée grinned. "Excellent. While you make a fire, I'm taking Liesl." She glanced at the girl and gestured *'Come on.'*

They hiked off, Snowbear the snowy ermine riding on Liesl's shoulder.

I turned to the space I'd already cleared.

"I'd better hurry, it's nearly dark," I said to Tundra, who had stayed by my side the whole afternoon.

I glanced at Chance. He'd been unconscious the entire time.

As I busied myself arranging branches for the fire, I wondered about Chance. Was this illness normal for a faun? He'd told me fauns came from the woods, so I would've hoped he'd be more resilient.

It's almost like he's been drugged. Except he's burning up with fever. He's definitely sick.

The wood was laid; now I needed kindling. I glanced around in the dying light.

"Tundra, can you pick up some small twigs and bark for me?" I asked the wolf. "To use to start the fire? But, listen: do not go out of sight of me. It's important."

The wolf bowed her head, then started walking around the forest, staying within ten feet of me.

Thank goodness.

I was really starting to worry about Aspen. Taking this long to find the stream very likely meant she'd met with some kind of problem.

Where could she be?

I looked out into the forest. An owl hooted.

Tundra trotted up to me, her mouth full of dried forest flotsam, and dropped it at my feet.

"Good girl. Just a bit more?" I said.

She trotted off.

I arranged the moss and twigs under the larger branches, then applied my lighter.

The fire caught immediately, and was soon blazing merrily.

Tundra walked up and dropped more twigs next to me.

I put my arm around her and gave her a hug, then patted the ground next to me. I didn't want her to get lost; I wanted her right by my side.

It was another ten minutes before Renée, Liesl, and Snowbear returned, their arms laden with a huge amount of firewood.

"Hope we didn't worry you," said Renée, dropped her wood on the growing pile. She stood, hands on hips, surveying the fire.

I watched her, waiting for a reaction.

She nodded and smiled. "Good job, Holly."

My back straightened in pride.

"Look what I found, Holly," said Liesl. She held out several handfuls of dark berries.

"Ohhh!" I glanced up at Renée. "Blackberries?"

Renée nodded, then she and Liesl joined me on the ground.

Liesl glanced at Chance. "Do you think we should do anything for him?"

Renée looked over. "In the morning, we'll try to wake him again. I'm just not sure what to do. I've never seen anyone get sick with a fever and pass out."

I shook my head.

Me neither. It's very weird.

An hour later, we'd eaten another sandwich each, and were licking our fingers.

"We should leave the rest for tomorrow," Renée said. "Thank goodness Chef is so generous."

We'd each brought a bag of food, enough for days.

"Generous? I think he overfeeds the entire school," I chuckled.

I heard a whine in the distance.

Tundra's ears perked forward, and she turned her head to the noise.

Another whine sounded, a bit closer.

"That's Aspen. I'll bet my lighter on it," I said.

"You'd better not, we need that," laughed Liesl.

Tundra stood up, and I followed her.

I whistled into the dark. "Aspen! Here girl!" I took a few steps toward the direction of the noise.

The whine sounded again, even closer.

I was about to walk a short distance into the woods, thinking Aspen might have hurt herself, when Tundra stopped me cold.

A low growl emanated from my wolf, and the hackles down the top of her back rose.

Just the sight of that sent a streak of fear through my heart.

"Holly," Renée said quietly, "Back up to the fire again. Now."

I felt an icy trickle of sweat drip down my temple.

I reached out and grabbed Tundra's ruff, pulling her as I took several steps backward, keeping my eyes on the dark forest ahead.

I felt a hand grasp the waistband of my skirt and pull me from behind, guiding me backward.

"Come on," whispered Liesl.

Tundra and I backed up and stood alongside the fire with Renée and Liesl.

Renée tossed another few branches on the fire, and they caught immediately, blazing up high and lighting up the woods further.

Tundra continued to growl, her head down. She was an impressive sight, and whatever was out there in the dark would think twice about approaching further, I hoped.

We stood there for at least ten minutes, waiting, but the whining did not happen again. Eventually, we all sat back down.

"Good thing you guys got more wood, I said, trying to calm down.

"Renée, what would do that? Whine like a wolf like that?" Liesl said.

"I am sure that was not Aspen," I said, petting Tundra next to me. "Her sister would not have growled that way."

"Besides," said Renée. "If it had been Aspen, she'd have come right into camp and straight to you, instead of staying twenty feet out and whining, trying to get us to go out there." She shivered. "Liesl, to answer your question, there aren't many creatures that can mimic a wolf's whine like that. But there are a few. And we wouldn't want to tangle with any of them."

It was a long time waiting as we calmed down.

About two hours later, Tundra suddenly jumped up and barked, and Aspen came trotting into camp.

"Oh my gosh!" I said as the white wolf ran straight up to me and dropped the bag she was holding at my feet.

I caught it as it fell, and grinned. I held the dripping bag up for the others to see. "Water!"

We all drank our fill, faefolk and familiars alike. About two inches of water were left at the bottom of the bag.

"Let's leave this till morning," said Renée. "Good Aspen, good wolf!"

I laughed and patted the wolf's head.

She'd returned to camp with all kinds of brambles stuck in her fur, as if she'd run twenty miles through the underbrush to get to the stream.

"Very weird," said Liesl. "Wasn't the stream supposed to be close to the edge of the school?"

Renée nodded. "Within a mile, I think."

"It's like we're dozens of miles from the school, but how could that have happened?" I asked out loud.

"I don't know, but if that's the case, we're in more danger than I realized," Renée said.

"What do you mean?" Liesl asked in a small voice.

"The forest surrounding the school is protected," said Renée, "But the protection has boundaries. It keeps out dangerous animals, from the expanse near the school. Farther out? No protection."

I swallowed in nervous fear.

I hugged my wolves close, extremely glad they were back with me.

Renée tossed another branch onto the fire.

"Gerghuik, klasdcvgh ...," Chance mumbled.

Renée rose and walked to where he lay, crouching next to him.

Wow, he's even hotter," she said, her hand against Chance's forehead. "Here, hand me the water sack?"

Liesl passed the large bag over.

Renée dribbled some water against Chance's face.

"He's delirious," Renée dribbled water into his mouth, and he swallowed automatically.

"Do you think he'll be all right?" asked Liesl.

"I hope so," murmured Renée.

I looked at Chance, worried.

"Well, listen, I think maybe we'd better try to get some sleep," said Renée. "It's well past midnight, and if we don't sleep, we'll be zombies in the morning."

"Ohhhh, why did you have to say 'zombies'?" moaned Liesl.

"Ha ha ha!" laughed Renée.

And suddenly, the dark night wasn't so spooky anymore.

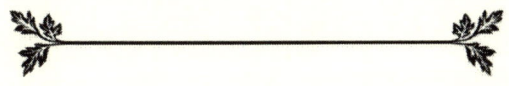

Chapter Twenty-Four
Attacked

An hour later, it happened.

We'd lain down next to Chance and the fire, the lean-to of branches over our heads, and tried to get some shuteye.

I fell asleep between Aspen and Tundra; they acted like a white furry blanket around me.

And all was still and quiet.

An hour later, it couldn't have been more than that, I was awakened by the sound of low growling.

I opened my eyes and saw Tundra and Aspen on either side of me. Their hackles were raised straight up, making them look almost twice their normal size, which was considerable to begin with.

The sound of two wolves growling and the sight of them staring into the darkness, their eyes fixated on some unseen threat, was enough to make me nearly pee my pants.

My heart began to beat so hard it nearly pounded its way out of my chest.

I glanced at the others and saw they were still fast asleep.

How on earth can they sleep through this?

"Liesl! Renée!" I whispered. "WAKE UP!" I reached out and shook Liesl's shoulder hard.

She did not react.

No one could sleep through that.

I sat up, now more alarmed with my unmoving companions than the mysterious threat in the dark woods.

I could barely see their faces.

It's as if the darkness is a physical thing.

Tundra and Aspen shifted as I moved, momentarily distracted by what was happening in camp.

I reached for the half-empty water sack, and splashed water onto Liesl's face.

No reaction.

It's like she's drugged.

I splashed some onto Renée's face, and got the same result. After a moment's thought I flicked water onto Chance's face.

No response.

Well this is weird.

I had no idea what had drugged my companions, but I realized that, since there was an obvious close danger, I was thankful I was awake.

And I was grateful for my two wolf familiars.

Aspen and Tundra shifted against me, unwilling to move from my side. They licked my hand and glanced at Renée, Liesl, and Chance, but then their attention returned to whatever was out there in the dark.

They no longer growled, but stared into the darkness, their ears pricked forward, their hackles half raised.

They didn't even blink.

I held my breath, staring into the darkness, trying to pierce it to see what was there.

Chance had shown me the fireflies on the school lawn by the previous night's full moon, so I knew the moon should be nearly full again tonight. There should have been enough light to see by, even with the thick forest canopy.

Yet my eyes couldn't penetrate the darkness beyond camp.

I glanced at the fire, which had been reduced to glowing coals. I threw on a new branch, then another, and soon the flames returned.

I pulled on my shoes. The academy uniform footwear was a cross between a shoe and a low boot, the leather rising past my ankle, with the latch on the outside of each foot.

I needed to be ready.

My heartbeat thundered in my chest so loud I was sure it was audible to what lurked beyond the camp.

Whatever was out there, I hoped it was afraid of fire.

Or at least wary.

Firelight flickered and jumped, illuminating the trees around us momentarily.

I kept trying to peer out and see what had Aspen and Tundra's attention.

What is that?

Suddenly, the wind kicked up, tossing the tree branches overhead to and fro in an unexpected gale.

The bushes just beyond the firelight suddenly moved.

Aspen and Tundra began growling again.

I felt so alarmed that I hastily got to my feet, nearly teetering over in my haste.

I heard a sudden, loud HUFF behind the bush to my left. The thing had moved.

The wolves growled even louder, shifting their gaze several feet toward the new location.

I'd had enough.

I kicked at Liesl and Renée hard, the leather toe of my shoe hitting their bodies midsection. I felt my shoe hit Renée's hipbone.

The blows probably made a bruise. They should have awakened.

But they remained asleep.

What the hell is going on?

Suddenly, there was a crashing sound, and the bushes seemed to part.

At the same time, a dark shadow descended on the camp, foot by foot, and I could see the line of dark, of blackness, of the absence of light, moving swiftly, inch by inch, creeping toward us.

It was the weirdest, the most frightening thing I'd ever seen.

I looked wildly around but could see nothing moving above that would have cast such a deep shadow.

I looked back at the large bush.

Something was coming. Something big.

The wolves were going crazy, growling and spitting, their coats standing straight up on their backs, so high the hair wavered with their movement.

No longer worried about the source of the shadow, or even if it *was* a shadow, I fixed my eyes on the dark form emerging from the bush not a dozen feet from me.

The line of darkness advanced until it was right next to me. Then it crept closer and touched me. Then it inched its way past me.

And I was in shadow.

I could see out, to the fire and my companions, but when I looked down at my hands and feet, a dark, filmy shroud seemed to cover my eyes.

"WAKE UP!" I shrieked at my companions, who seemed a million miles away beyond the shroud of shadow.

The wolves snarled and barked and raged at the thing as it advanced.

It was nearly as tall as I was, and as wide as I was tall.

It HUFFED as it came, step by step, slowly, almost hesitatingly, only I did not get the sense it was hesitating at all.

I got the sense that this was how it hunted. The shadow, then the creature.

Maybe it has to wait for the darkness to cover its prey before it can come closer.

It was so close now that I could smell the stink of its breath.

Waitaminute.

If its breath was hot and this smelly, then it stood to reason it was not a specter, like the banshee, but an animal, like the other animals in the fae forest.

And if it was an animal then it had vulnerabilities.

I took a step back and grabbed a branch out of the fire, and brought it to the forefront, brandishing it like a sword.

The thing stopped advancing.

It HUFFED in seeming frustration.

I held my breath for a heartbeat. Then a second heartbeat.

It took another step.

Aspen let out a deafening snarl and leaped at it, her sister less than a second behind her.

The wolves were on it, whatever it was, and my heart skipped a beat as they snarled and growled and bit at it.

I could hear their jaws snapping.

I took a step forward, thrusting my branch forward, the flames flickering out into the almost palpable darkness that surrounded the thing.

I was rewarded by a YELP! that I knew did not come from either Aspen or Tundra.

The darkness faded about ten percent. Just enough for me to realize it was manifested by the animal we fought.

I jumped forward, pushing my flame farther out.

I could see the faint image of a large brown expanse of fur.

Suddenly, the thing roared loudly, and its hot, rank breath blew forward into my face.

Then it grew larger in front of my eyes, and it was no longer shorter than me, it towered above me.

It was huge.

Aspen and Tundra still fought it, jaws snapping as they lunged and pulled back, again and again and again.

I quickly darted back to the fire and grabbed a second flaming branch from the edge, and pulled it back to the fray.

I noticed the thick darkness had blanketed almost the entire camp.

I pushed both the flaming branches out and nearly touched the beast, and it screamed again.

I lunged forward again, daring to tap the thing with my blazing boughs.

The light of the fire I wielded only reached out a few inches before being enveloped by what I now guessed was a spell of darkness.

As they touched the beast that towered above me, behind the shadow, I saw brown fur again.

Coarse, brown fur.

Holy crap, this looks like a bear.

I was no longer afraid.

The second I felt my fear dissolve, the second I felt I understood the situation better, Aspen and Tundra became ten times as furious.

They leaped and lunged at the bear, throwing themselves against it, biting at it, ferocious in their intent.

I rushed forward again and held my makeshift torches to the beast's fur long enough for them to light the thing on fire.

The flames caught and began to spread upward.

They illuminated a massive bear face; a wide, snarling snout, small, glowing red eyes, and a fat, furry face.

The flames licked up its chest, spreading slowly to encompass its head.

It cried out and dropped to all fours.

Aspen and Tundra followed it down, biting it viciously, their mouths rimmed with the bear's blood.

As soon as it began to crumple, the darkness fell away as if washed off by rain, and my companions woke up.

"OH MY GOD!" Liesl yelled, struggling to stand in all the commotion.

"HOLLY! THAT'S A BUGBEAR!" Renée called out.

"Yeah, I figured that out, thanks," I cried.

It would have been comical if not for what happened next.

The bear was on the ground, but seemed to rally, and lunged at the nearest wolf.

It grabbed Tundra in its jaws and bit down.

My wolf familiar yelped loudly.

"TUNDRA!" I cried out, rushing forward. I slammed one of the flaming branches down on the bear's head.

It let go of my wolf, who limped back to my side.

"HEY!" I heard Chance cry out.

"Here, let me," Renée was there, lifting her arms, muttering an intricate sentence that was forgotten as soon as my ears heard it.

The bear cried out as a bolt of lightning lashed out from the third-year and arced across at it, scorching it across its length.

More spell casting and Renée unleashed a second bolt of lightning at the bear.

The lightning opened up a slash of bloody red surrounded by scorched fur across its back, and had left one of its ears on fire.

It dropped and lay unmoving.

Chapter Twenty-Five
Confusion

We sat around the campfire, which we'd built up to flame several feet high, and discussed what had just happened.

Tundra in my lap. Her legs had been crushed by the bugbear's jaws.

"You've got to send her back, Holly," said Renée. "She will heal almost instantly in the fae realm forest."

I nodded through my tears. I needed to get a hold of my emotions if I was going to perform the spell correctly.

"Here," Chance handed me a handkerchief from his pocket.

I smiled gratefully and blew my nose.

It was amazing how much one nose could run when one was trying to hold back one's tears.

I blew it a second time, then tried to perform the spell.

It worked on the second try. Both wolves disappeared.

I hoped I wouldn't need them for a while.

"They can come back anytime, she's already healed," Renée assured me.

"What happened while I was out?" Chance asked. He hadn't been too happy when we told him he'd been unconscious for half the day and night.

We filled him in. He glowered.

"Not how the picnic was supposed to go," Chance murmured.

"I'm surprised the school hasn't sent out a search party," said Liesl. "What about your rabbit familiar, and my ermine familiar?"

"We aren't even sure they ever reached the school," said Renée. "It's clear from the bugbear attack that we somehow traveled past the school grounds and boundaries."

"Isn't there some kind of barrier?" I asked. "Wouldn't we have seen it when we passed through it?"

"Not if it had been tampered with," Renée grimaced. "Something foul is going on here, and I'd like to know what it is."

"How are you feeling, Chance?" Liesl asked.

"I'm still feeling dizzy and hot, but no longer enchanted," Chance grimaced.

"Something is definitely going on here," said Renée. "And the first thing we need to do is get back to the school.

"I think we should all call our familiars back," said Chance. "They obviously got waylaid on their tasks to find the school."

"It took Aspen a ridiculous amount of time to return from the stream with the water," Renée said.

Chance sat up. "This is more than just some prank or mischievous enchantment. It smacks of an attack on the school."

"The school ... and possibly us, specifically," Renée said grimly.

"Well, I don't think anyone is going to get much more sleep," Chance said. "Plus, the sun will be up in less than an hour. I think we should pack up and get going."

"But how?" Liesl asked. "We seemed to be lost yesterday; that's why we stopped and camped. Well, that plus you basically passed out."

Chance grimaced. "I'm not sure why. I'm guessing whatever has worked magic on the school grounds, did this to me."

"Or you just might be really ill," I said. "You said you were still dizzy and pretty warm with fever, Chance."

"Well, let's hope he's not too ill to travel," said Renée. "We really need to get back today. Now, everyone: let's eat breakfast. At dawn, we ride!"

Huh?

Renée grinned at us and bit into the last sandwich in her bag.

We all tried to remain calm and eat our last food.

"You sure it's okay to eat everything?"

"Shouldn't we make it last? What if we're here another day?"

"Yeah, I'm not sure about this."

Renée just smiled mysteriously and winked.

We all performed the spell to bring our familiars back. Aspen and Tundra returned to me whole, happy, and well.

Liesl's snowy ermine Snowbear returned, happy to see her.

Chance's hawk returned, too, and so did Renée's rabbit Jade.

As dawn pinked the forest, bestowing a rosy glow on the forest, we all stood up with our familiars.

Renée glanced at everyone, nodding. "Ready?"

We were ready.

"This way," Renée said, turning and walking off in a seemingly random direction.

We spent the next twenty minutes hiking up a slope, until we were on a small ridge, looking down on the deep forest.

"Okay," Renée said, pointing. "See the sky? We don't want to go that high. We just want to clear the treetops. Now, everyone hold hands. Grip your neighbor's hand tightly. Do not let go, no matter what happens. Don't worry about the familiars; they will follow."

I glanced at Liesl with a questioning look, but she just shrugged and took my hand, clutching it tightly.

I took Renée's hand, and she took Chance's; he held Liesl on his other side, as we formed a small circle.

Renée nodded at each of us, then closed her eyes and began uttering an intricate spell.

"Ohhh," whispered Chance. "I've heard of this: It's a third-year spell that ..."

"Shhhhh," Renée said, smiling, her eyes still closed.

"Sorry," Chance whispered.

Renée began uttering the spell again.

She spoke quietly but fervently in Welsh, her eyes tightly closed, her chin dipped almost to her chest.

"Bwrw ni i fyny, O frenin celyn. Dewch â ni i gopaon y coed, helpwch ni, cadwch ni'n ddiogel, nes i ni gyrraedd adref."

which translated to:

~

"Cast us up, O Holly King. Bring us to the tops of the trees, help us, keep us safe, until we get home."

~

Renée chanted the spell over and over, in a long rhythm that ran together, her voice gathering strength and becoming stronger each time.

And we began to rise in the air.

Our feet left the ground, and we rose slowly, foot by foot, until we were at least a hundred feet up. And we rose more, we kept slowly levitating skyward, Renée chanting the whole time.

We finally slowed our ascent when we reached the top of the trees.

We must've been at least two hundred feet off the ground.

As we came to a stop and hovered there, Renée opened her eyes. She turned her head until she saw a white column of light rising from the ground. It looked nearly fifteen miles away.

A dark fog shrouded the forest around us, and came to a stop about two-thirds of the way to the column of white light.

Renée fixed her eyes on that column, and our small circle slowly swung around and then we began drifting toward the column. Slowly at first, then faster after a few minutes.

I looked back and saw Aspen and Tundra were floating in the air, following my path, as was Snowbear the snowy ermine, Jade the rabbit, and Chance's hawk.

I must ask him what he named the hawk, sometime soon.

We drifted across the treetops, our dangling feet barely clearing the leaves, carried by the magic of Renée's spell.

I felt stress and worry drop away as the source of the light came into view.

It was the Academy. The column of white light rose from the spire atop the astronomy tower, disappearing into the blue sky.

Renée uttered a few more words and we descended onto the front lawn of the school, where the Headmistress stood, among many others, to meet us.

As our feet touched down, she walked up to greet us.

"Well done, Miss Page! Very well done."

Renée finally nodded, and we released our hands; then she turned to the headmistress. "Professor Ó Baoghill, Chance is ill," Renée said, a worried look on her face.

As I watched, the headmistress waved her hand and uttered a spell, at which the column of light winked out.

She saw me staring and smiled. "The column is lit whenever a student goes missing, to help them find their way back," she said. "It is especially useful when the missing student is a third-year or above, who has already learned the levitation spell."

Liesl and I were astonished.

Renée was helping Chance up to the school doors, while he protested.

"I'm fine, I'm fine! I swear, Renée stop being such a mother hen ..." said Chance.

"You're burning up with a fever; you need to go to the hospital wing," Renée replied, ignoring his protestations.

The rest of the day was lost in chaos.

Apparently, the whole school had been in an uproar when we hadn't returned from the forest. Upperclassmen had been searching for us the whole night.

"Come with me, you two," the headmistress called.

We all followed Chance and Renée up to the hospital wing.

Once he was settled into a bed, and dosed with the first of two medicines, we gathered in a semicircle around the end of his bed, including the headmistress and several guards.

"I can't tell you how happy we were that Miss Page was able to return you all," the headmistress was saying.

Liesl and I were each eating a bowl of porridge, because no matter how much we told the nurse, she insisted that we must be half starved and weak from hunger.

The porridge was creamy and delicious. It also served to mildly glue our mouths shut while we ate, so we tucked in and stayed busy eating and listening.

And the headmistress had some revelations that were astonishing.

If I hadn't been sat in a deeply cushioned chair already, I might've fallen out of it in surprise.

"We are besieged once more," the headmistress began. "This happened many years ago, and the history is taught beginning of second year, just after the autumn harvest holidays."

She looked over at Liesl and I. "You two won't learn the full history until next fall. But I'll teach you some of it now, out of necessity. "As I was saying, the Academy is beset. And I think they are watching us, as well. There is no other reason we can determine for the timing of this attack."

"Headmistress," asked Liesl, "did you say we are under attack?"

The elder woman raised her hand in a settling gesture. "Do not be alarmed. This is an attack with magic, not human weapons. As I said, you will learn the school's history next fall. For now, you only need to know that, while we are weathering this, no students are to go off grounds, and that means the school grounds. Do not venture into the forest, nor anywhere near the edge of the wood."

I raised my hand tentatively, and she nodded for me to speak. "Please, ma'am, I was wondering," I said. "Who is attacking us?"

The headmistress blinked and her eyes went vague, then she seemed to focus again.

"That is not important. Suffice to say, your professors, your fellow students, and all the school employees, are on your side. They are the people you've always known them to be. But if a strange gnome emerges from the forest and beckons to you, do not follow him." The headmistress smiled at us all.

This is ridiculous. I need more information.

"Is there any reason the school is under attack?" I asked.

The headmistress sighed, looking at me. "Holly, I cannot tell you that. It's ..."

"Wait," I interrupted. "We need to know all the facts, so we can protect ourselves. I mean, really! We're first-years. What if Renée hadn't been with us?"

"I understand, trust me. And I think, in time, more will be revealed. But for now ..."

"I have a question," said Liesl. "Why didn't Renée go back to the school yesterday?"

Renée spoke then, "Because Chance was unconscious. I couldn't perform the spell and lift him at the same time."

Wait.

"Then why not return to the school and bring back help?" I asked.

Renée scowled at me.

I stared back at her, astonished.

Then I glanced at Chance in the hospital bed, and he was scowling too.

What is going on?

A mist began to rise up from under the hospital bed, and everything around me dissolved into nothing.

I woke up with a start and sat up. It was night, and the campfire flames were a few inches high.

"What is going on?" I said out loud.

The others were asleep.

How much time had passed?

I looked around, utterly confused. My head spun. Could that have been a dream?

I spotted the dead bugbear off to the side and stared at it as my brain oriented itself into day and night and time. I felt dazed.

Aspen whined beside me, raising her head and looking at me questioningly.

I took a deep breath and patted the wolf, and glanced at her sister on my other side.

It must have been a dream.

I lay back down, still feeling confused. I stared at the dying flames of the campfire for a long time before my eyes fell shut again.

Chapter Twenty-Six
The Faerie Ring

"Holly. HOLLY! WAKE UP!" Liesl was shaking me awake. Violently. I opened my eyes, feeling so groggy it was as if a shroud lay over my mind.

A shroud?

I sat up "I'm awake. I'm awake."

"Holly, you wouldn't wake up. We've been trying to get you up for fifteen minutes," Liesl said.

I looked around and saw it was well past dawn.

Renée was packing everything and kicking dirt over the fire. Chance was standing up, his backpack on his back, staring at me. He still looked pale. I wondered how he was feeling.

Why is he staring at me?

"What?" I asked.

He shook his head. "I had a really weird dream."

Renée swung around, "Oh my God, me too. We were back at the school. I had performed some weird levitating spell ..."

I jumped to my feet, stumbling in the process. "I had the same dream! How could we all have the same dream?"

"I had it, too!" Liesl said. She turned to Renée. "Is there such a thing as a levitation spell?"

Renée looked amused and shook her head. "No, not at all. There's nothing like that. If there were, I'd have been back at the school the first hour we were lost."

"That's what I thought! In the dream!" I said.

"I remember," Liesl said.

"This smacks of dark magic," Chance said. "If we all had the same dream, it's likely it wasn't a dream so much as a mass hallucination."

"What could work dark magic on us?" Liesl asked.

"Unfortunately," said Renée. "It's not unknown magic, it's just generally frowned upon."

I turned to her. "What do you mean?"

"I mean that the spells are not unknown, nor hard to perform. The school runs on an honor system, which is why the headmistress was so worried about the bullying against you, Holly."

"Do you think it's your sister doing this?" Chance asked in a quiet tone.

Renée looked worried. "I honestly don't know. First-years wouldn't know such magic, but the higher years would."

"Chance," asked Liesl. "How are you feeling today?"

"Still sick, but not dizzy anymore," he replied.

"So, what are we doing? Are we going to try to hike back?" I said. I was worried about the dark magic and had a burning desire to get back to safety. "I think we should."

"Yes, that's probably a good idea," said Renée. "Let's try to get back to the school. But if there's a spell on us, or on the forest, it may be tricky. It may be nearly impossible."

"I think we need to stick close together," said Chance. "Verify all experiences. If you see something or hear or smell something: ask the rest of us if we do, too."

Liesl and I glanced at each other and took deep breaths. I nodded.

"Okay, I have an idea," I said. "My wolves were able to lead Liesl and me back to the school once before, when we were lost in the forest. I don't know if any dark magic was at work, but there was the cemetery banshee after us."

"Not a bad idea, Holly," said Renée. She glanced around camp. The fire had been put out and dirt tossed on it. All wrappers had been picked up. There was no trace of our having spent the night there. "Everyone ready to move out?"

We all nodded.

"Let's go, then."

Aspen led the way, Tundra beside her.

We followed the wolves in a line. I had to make sure my steps didn't touch Tundra's feet and trip her. That's how close we followed.

We hiked about an hour, nonstop.

Then the wolves stopped. They had found something.

"What is it, girl?" I murmured, walking up to Aspen's head.

She whined, then put her nose to the ground.

I glanced up ahead and froze.

On the ground was a thick, wide ring of mushrooms. They were all of different sizes and shapes, and different colors ranging from light brown to yellow, to moss.

I felt an icy fear creep down my spine, and I slowly took a step back.

"Hey!" Liesl protested behind me.

"Shhh," I said, pointing.

They all crowded around me, staring.

"What are we staring at?" whispered Renée.

"It's a faerie ring," I murmured.

"It sure is!" Renée said.

"I was conceived in one of these, or so I was told by my Aunt Clare," I whispered.

"Okayyy," said Renée. "That's not unheard of in the fae world, Holly."

I took a deep breath.

Then why was I so affected?

I stared down at the ring of mushrooms, feeling less scared, beginning to feel mesmerized.

"Holly," said Chance. "There's an old wives' tale: that if you stand in the faerie ring and speak your troubles, that the woodland Oak King will give you aid."

"That's for spring and summer," said Renée. "It's nearly October, so it's fall."

"Oh, that's right," murmured Chance. "Okay then, it would be the Holly King that would answer your plea."

"An old wives' tale?" I asked.

"Old wives' tales often have a basis in fact," said Renée, smiling. "My grandmother would tell you a tale of the Oak King granting a request she made over fifty years ago. She'd swears up and down it's the absolute truth."

"You've got a better chance of being heard than the rest of us, Holly. You're from the royal line," said Chance. "The royal line can trace it's lineage all the way back to the first of the fae."

I glanced at him, smiling. "Do you really think I should?"

He nodded. "I do."

I took a deep breath.

I looked around the area. I could hear birdsong, and the trees rustled in the breeze. It was a sunny day, and the forest seemed friendly all of a sudden.

"Do it," whispered Liesl, nudging me.

I took a step forward, then another.

Then a few more.

I was in.

I slowly turned around, looking down at the mushrooms. They were really beautiful, if I thought about it. Sunshine dappled the ground, and the whole effect was very magical.

As it should be.

I closed my eyes.

"Now, concentrate," said Renée. "Think about your problem. Then say it out loud and ask for help."

I considered for a minute, then thought: *We're trapped here. We want to get back to the school.*

A feeling came over me, a buzzing sounded in my head. I thought of my mother.

I murmured as I slowly turned,

"Holly King, Holly King, hear my plea,
Help me to be happy and free.
Trapped here in this forest we roam,
Help us to continue on home."

I felt a warmth in my heart, and my closed eyes saw light and dark glittering across the inside of my eyelids.

I murmured my spur-of-the-moment poem twice more, then slowed and stopped turning in the faerie ring, and opened my eyes.

I was facing my friends, who stood with their jaws open, staring at me.

After a minute, Renée found her voice. "Okay, that really might work."

"Holly, light came down on you while you were turning and speaking," Liesl said in a quiet, awed voice.

Chance just looked stunned, then stepped forward and took my hand, and helped me step out of the mushroom circle.

"Come on," he whispered. "Let's go."

We hiked for another hour, and I felt dazed and happy the whole time. It was as if the time spent in faerie ring had injected joy inside my mind.

311

We didn't want to stop for lunch, so we nibbled on what little food we had left and kept hiking.

It was slow going, making our way through virgin forest.

I began to feel worried. If the undergrowth was this undisturbed and overgrown, we were likely far from the school.

And getting farther by the hour?

It was only midday, but the forest suddenly grew much darker.

I looked up but couldn't see the sky clearly. It must've been overcast.

As if on cue, it began to rain.

Oh, that's why.

"Let's shelter under this thick bush," said Chance. "We can wait it out."

We crouched under a large bush; the rain still dripped through onto our heads, but we weren't getting soaked the way we would have out in the open.

As we squatted under the thickly growing leaves, a few drops came down on my face, dripping down my nose, but out from under the bush the rain fell harder, in a downpour.

"Oh my God!" whispered Liesl.

"What?" I said, turning to look.

Renée and Chance stared at what Liesl had seen. I looked, trying to see past the heavy rain.

Then I saw it.

My God ...

The man had green skin, and was clothed in ivy, which wrapped around his body from head to toe, and reached up to wind itself around his head like a crown.

His beard and hair were a darker green, the same color of the moss covering much of his wooden walking stick.

He walked slowly through the forest, ignoring the rain, and seemed to be looking for something.

There were several deer beside him, and several more following behind.

We could see him through the trees, he was maybe fifty feet away.

I heard a whine and put my hand on the wolf lying beside me. I didn't know which wolf it was, because I did not want to take my eyes off the man in the woods.

The wolf I was touching crawled forward a few inches, then hopped up and ran to the man, her sister in hot pursuit.

I didn't call after them.

It was like a spell that I didn't want to disturb.

My familiar wolves ran to the man we were watching.

The fae creature? It was clear he was of the faefolk.

The wolves sat before the man. I thought I saw a slight shake of his head, and his mouth utter a command.

Then Aspen and Tundra turned and ran back to me, crawling under the large bush we were taking refuge beneath, turning around, and lying down on either side of me. They were back in the same position they'd been in before.

We watched the fae man pause a moment, his silhouette facing us, and he seemed to be contemplating something. Then he lifted his walking stick and brought it down hard.

I felt a tremor run through me, and swore I felt the trees shiver, and the ground dip. The man then nodded to himself and then walked off.

I stretched my head to follow him, for as long as I could.

My eyes stung from not blinking.

A minute after he left, I let out the breath I hadn't realized I was holding.

No one said a thing. It was as if the scene we'd just watched had been something so special and holy it would be sullied with the commonness of mere speech.

Five minutes later, it stopped raining, and the forest became bright again.

We crawled silently out from under the bush and stood up to brush ourselves off. A minute later, we were back on our way, hiking.

I knew I would never forget the incredible experience we'd just had. It had been beyond belief. And yet, I'd seen it with my own eyes.

Chapter Twenty-Seven

Specter

The deep, soaking rain had drenched the forest, and the undergrowth made a squelching sound as we hiked. As the sun warmed the cool woods, a thick mist rose from the bracken that had been wetted so thoroughly by the prolonged cloudburst.

We were soon hiking in a thick fog.

We'd been on the move for about an hour, with no school in sight, when the fog became too thick to walk through spread out. We stayed close to each other, walking single-file, each person's hands on the school tunic of the person just ahead.

Renée was in the lead, followed by Liesl, then me, then Chance.

My attention was split between those in front of me and Chance behind me. He'd said he felt better, and indeed, he was not weaving as he walked, but he remained pale and warm. The pink flare of fever dotted his cheeks.

If we'd been back at the school, I was sure he'd be in the infirmary.

We walked through the forest in a single line, facing mostly down to make sure our feet did not get tripped up by the brambles underfoot.

I couldn't keep quiet any longer.

"Chance," I whispered, glancing back.

"What," he whispered back.

"That ... that man," I said. "Who was he? Why didn't we ask him for help? Where did he go? Why did my wolves obey him? Why ..."

"Shhhh," said Chance. "We don't speak of such things."

I stopped and, in doing so, pulled on the back of Liesl's top to stop her. She, in turn, stopped, pulling on the back of Renée's tunic.

We all stopped and faced one another, unconsciously drawing close together because of the fog.

It had grown thicker and thicker, until it formed a white wall of mist all around us.

Aspen whined at my side, unhappy at stopping.

Tundra snuffled her sister's fuzzy ear, then sneezed.

I looked at the faces of my companions.

"Well?" I asked in a hushed tone. It was that kind of afternoon.

Chance just looked down and shook his head.

Liesl shrugged.

I huffed in frustration. I realized I was probably getting a reputation of impatience at my new school, but I wanted to know what was happening. What was happening everywhere.

That was important if you wanted to survive growing up on the streets, and it was ingrained in me.

I tapped my toe silently on the forest floor.

Renée finally sighed, leaned her head in, and whispered. "To speak of things, magical things, that have just happened is to jinx them. To break the spell. To bring misfortune down upon one's head," she said. "I will just say that what appears to have happened is what happened."

I sighed again.

Maybe I was thick.

Chance suddenly brought his palm up and cupped it at my ear, leaning over. In a tone so quiet I could barely hear him, even though his lips were speaking so close they brushed my ears, he whispered, "The wish you made in the mushroom circle is coming true."

He pulled back and met my eyes with a significant look.

I suddenly understood and was filled with even more questions. My mouth formed an "o" of surprise.

Renée put her finger to her lips in a silent 'shhhh' gesture.

It was maddening, but I understood. And we needed to get back to the Academy before night fell.

Renée nodded to me and pointed onward.

I nodded slowly, agreeing. We needed to go now.

She walked back to her place at the head of the line, and we continued to hike.

A million questions ran through my head as we walked.

Who was the man?

Why was his skin green?

Was he a faerie?

Was he a friend?

Was he going to help us?

The others seemed to think that if we remained silent and just hiked, the man would help us, and we'd get out of this.

But how? He's not even here. He's not leading us, Renée is.

I glanced up and over Liesl's shoulder at Renée, wondering if she was somehow acting with the green man's guidance.

Green Man!

Well, he had been a man, and he had been green. I wonder if he was the Green Man.

I almost instantly dismissed this idea. We'd been studying the different fae in class, and the Green Man had been one of the first lessons. He was supposed to be made of leaves, and he was part tree, literally. The man we'd seen was definitely a man *wearing* ivy leaves.

And he'd been muscular. Very muscular. Something told me the Green Man was not like that.

A picture in our schoolbook had shown a depiction of Green Man, and it had looked nothing like the man we'd seen. There'd also been a grainy, half-blurry photograph of the Green Man, and he had looked far more tree than human.

I remember asking the professor if the photograph had been of a person dressed up as the Green Man, like at a Halloween party, or if it was the Green Man himself. Because the lessons on the fae creature had been vague in that respect.

Was he real or just legend?

I remember the teacher had just smiled at me mysteriously and winked.

It was frustrating.

But I was beginning to just go with the flow at Titania Academy.

I was learning that many of the lessons we were taught were excruciatingly detailed in some respects, and exasperatingly vague in others.

It is the nature of faefolk legends.

Hmmm ...

I was thinking as I hiked, holding on to the back of Liesl's tunic, and not paying much attention to my surroundings.

Everyone was stopping and crouching to hide.

What?

I dropped to the ground and knelt there, going along with the herd mentality.

Well, it had helped keep me alive before, when Aunt Clare and I traveled had through the city. So logic dictates it should keep helping now, in my new life at the Academy.

Liesl was ducking down far. Ahead of her, Renée was on all fours, her head almost to the ground.

"What is it?" I said in a nearly inaudible whisper.

Renée swung her head around and stared at me with stricken eyes, her finger to her lips.

I decided to just lay down on the ground, on my side, curled in a ball.

I closed my eyes and waited.

It's probably a good thing I didn't see whatever spooked the others.

A minute passed. Then another.

I could hear the forest trees creaking and sighing in the fog. It was a peculiar sound people probably didn't often notice in a foggy forest.

Birdsong and small animal chatter are often muted when it's this misty. And certainly, there is no breeze in a foggy wood, if there were, it would blow the fog away and clear the air a bit.

But no, in a misty wood, the forest sounds are muted, so if you hear some sound, it is usually because it is localized. Because it is near you.

So all I heard was the creaking and sighing of the trees next to me.

That was it.

Except ...

A quiet sound, if that makes sense, sounded in the stillness.

We didn't make a sound, not a peep.

It wasn't us.

But ...

We heard ...

Something.

"A-WOOOOoooooo ..."

A cold knot of fear bloomed in my stomach.

WHAT WAS THAT?

It sounded close by.

It sounded like it, whatever it was, was nearly on top of us.

"A-WOOOOoooooo ..."

It was a ghostly call, sounding both faint and metallic, as if it were far away, and whisper-close, as if a ghost stood next to me, whispering its call into my ear.

The chill of fear was like an icy spear in my chest now, and I was beginning to feel something else ...

Something very familiar.

What?

"A-WOOOOoooooo ..."

I realized my new feeling was a keen and desperate curiosity. The kind of intense desire to KNOW that invades the mind and will not let you go, forcing you to LOOK, even though you know it may lead to your death ...

My eyes popped open. I looked up.

The banshee from the cemetery was directly next to me.

Her grey ghostly shroud floated under her, and the bottom hem fluttered lightly in the air, though there was no breeze.

Her hands were almost skeletal at first glance, but then I realized they were just very bony and wrinkled, like the hands of an old, old woman.

She was barefoot, her feet hovering an inch off the forest floor.

Her hair was long and messy, like your hair right after you've woken up, before you've had a chance to brush it. It floated halfheartedly in the air around her face.

The banshee seemed sad.

She was looking down at me.

She was gesticulating.

Well hell.

I got to my feet. Halfway up, Chance grabbed my top and tried desperately to pull me back down.

Without taking my eyes off the banshee, I grabbed my top and yanked it out of his hands.

I stood there and stared into the banshee's face.

It was something in her eyes that had banished all fear from me the moment we made eye contact.

She looked at me with an expression of beseeching. An expression of longing. An expression of earnest desire.

She was trying to connect with me.

"What do you want?" I murmured, staring into her face.

I barely blinked, not want this moment to end.

"Ahhhhhhhh ..." the banshee whispered.

I strained to hear. I labored to understand.

"What?" I said quietly.

"Oohhhhhhh ..." the banshee's mouth formed into an "o" and a blast of air whooshed out of it, then she began to whisper.

Liesl had taken her cue from me and was standing up, too. She stood beside me, staring at the banshee.

After a minute, Liesl whispered in my ear. "What's she saying?"

"You can't hear her?" I was surprised.

Liesl shook her head, her eyes on the banshee.

It's amazing how fear can flee when the friend next to you isn't at all afraid.

The banshee was whispering to me.

As I listened, my eyes grew wide with surprise.

I could hear the others, but all my attention was on the banshee.

The ghostly apparition paused in her whispering, and I could hear a glimpse of the conversation going on outside of ours.

"Well, what do you expect me to do, Renée?" Chance was saying.

"Try to pull her away, Chance! The thing's got her in some kind of magical grip."

I felt a hand on my arm, and then a pulling.

Well, I want to keep staring at the banshee, but I don't have to.

I swung around and looked at Chance and Renée.

"Cut it out, you two! I'm not in any kind of 'magical grip,' for Pete's sake. I'm just listening to what she's saying."

Renée and Chance stared at me in surprise.

Liesl giggled.

I turned back to the banshee. She began to whisper again.

I listened intently, nodding at the instructions she was giving me.

Five minutes later, she was done.

"Can I hug you?" I whispered.

The banshee smiled and leaned toward me.

I extended my arms and reached around her to embrace her.

I was like hugging a Popsicle.

I grinned and nuzzled her cheek, and my nose got frosty from the contact.

We finally pulled away, and she bowed, then was gone.

I felt a keen sense of loss but drew comfort from the fact that I could visit the spirit any time I wanted to.

She had told me so outright.

She had told me a great many things.

I turned to my companions. "I know how to get back to the school. The banshee told me many things, and one of them was how to get back," I said. "But we have to hurry if we're to get back by nightfall."

I turned and gestured to them. "Come on!"

I turned in a different direction than we'd been walking and began to trot.

"But Holly! What did she tell you?" Chance said.

"Later. We have to hurry." I glanced back. Renée was trotting to catch up to Chance. Liesl was already next to him. "Liesl, help him, he's sick."

Liesl nodded and grabbed Chance's hand, pulling him along.

Renée grabbed his other hand and helped.

I noted how much easier Liesl took direction from me.

We trust each other.

We ran through the forest, zigzagging through the trees.

At one point, Renée, puffing as she ran, asked out loud, "How does she know where she's going?"

"I don't know. Just follow," Liesl answered.

We ran on, for more than an hour. Jogging through the trees and around bushes and in a few cases, jumping over fallen logs and splashing through a stream.

After a long time, I spied a break in the trees.

"Come on!" I sped up.

"Keep up, don't lose sight of her," Renée cried.

I glanced back, and they were both dragging Chance along; he was stumbling slightly.

I slowed until they caught up, then turned and trotted the last few hundred feet.

As we ran out of the forest and onto the Academy lawn, I heard a few shrieks of surprise.

We were home.

Chapter Twenty-Eight
Cursed

As we walked into the school, several students waved to us, but nobody was shocked.

We've been gone an entire day! Or was it two? I could no longer remember.

Chance and Renée headed to the headmistress's office.

"Guess we'll just wait here?" Liesl said.

We sat on the bench nearby.

After a minute, I remarked, "Chance was pretty ill. I wonder why he didn't just go to the infirmary?"

"Yeah, that is weird," said Liesl. "Guess he rallied at the end, in our rush running." She glanced at me. "You're going to have to tell me everything the banshee whispered to you. That was amazing. I don't think the rest of us could hear her."

I shrugged. "I don't know why she was talking to me, or why I was the only one who could hear her."

"We could all hear her calling, at first."

"Was she calling? I thought she'd been moaning."

"You know, now I'm not sure."

We could hear voices faintly on the other side of the door. All of a sudden, we heard the headmistress's voice, louder than the others: "WHAT??!"

Then a bit more conversation, less than a minute later: "WHERE IS SHE? GET THEM IN HERE!"

I glanced at Liesl. She had an 'uh oh' expression on her face.

I gulped. I hoped we weren't in trouble. And I was starving and thirsty. We really needed to go find food.

The door swung open a foot, and Renée's head appeared in the crack.

"Hey," she said in a stage whisper. "You two: get in here. You are never going to believe this."

"What?" I said as I got to my feet.

We approached the door. Renée waited till we were right next to her face. This time she really did whisper. "Holly, Liesl: it's still the day before."

WHAT?

"What do you mean?" asked Liesl.

"Just get in here," Renée said, opening the door farther.

We walked into the office and also into the greatest mystery I've ever heard of.

"Sit down, please," said the headmistress. "We have a lot to talk about."

I was so tired and hungry, all intimidation was lost on me. "Can we please get some dinner? We're all hungry and thirsty." I glanced at Chance and Renée, and they nodded.

Chance looked bad. His face was still red, and he looked like he was swaying slightly in his chair.

"Headmistress," said Liesl, "Chance isn't doing well. He needs the doctor."

"Yes, yes, Miss Becker," said the headmistress. "I have called the nurse to come down and help Mr. Mac Craith while you all debrief us. However, I cannot release you yet. You have information that is vital, which we must hear now. It cannot wait."

I sighed. Adults were always thinking their issues were so vitally important.

"Miss Ó Cuilinn, Miss Becker, I would like to fill you in on what Mr. Mac Craith and Miss Page and I were discussing before you joined us," said the headmistress. "First of all, I understand you went on a picnic? And the chef tells me you stopped into the kitchens for sandwiches to bring along with you on this picnic?"

Liesl and I nodded.

The headmistress nodded as well. "And how long has it been for you since you left the school grounds?"

I glanced at Liesl.

This is weird.

"About thirty-two hours," said Liesl. "We left right after breakfast yesterday morning. And we've just arrived at sunset, and I'm guessing it's about six o'clock?"

"Well," said the headmistress, "What's actually happened is that, while you four were gone into the forest for over thirty-two hours, here on the school grounds, you left only this morning. It has been only about eight hours since witnesses saw you enter the forest."

I sat up in my chair.

"And," the headmistress continued, "I was told you had met and fought a bugbear with your familiars, Miss Ó Cuilinn?"

I nodded.

"Bugbears have been extinct in the forest for over a thousand years."

I blinked.

"Also, Miss Page informed me that you encountered a faerie ring?"

I nodded.

"Those are extremely rare," the headmistress explained. "Let me elaborate. They are never seen unless the fae of the forest, the faun and Kings and the sort, are reaching out to you and want you to step into one. And they are very selective."

"My mother stepped into a faerie ring when she was just eighteen. She was on vacation in Ireland, I mean, over here," I said, remembering the school was *in* Ireland. "She was on Christmas vacation and visited and found the mushroom circle and stepped inside and fell asleep. She had a fantastic dream about kissing a man with horns and green skin."

I'd been wanting to tell that story to someone for a long, long time. Aunt Clare had told it to me every Christmas since I could remember. I loved that story. It sounded so romantic.

I looked at the others and saw they were exchanging looks.

"What?"

The headmistress sighed. "I'll continue. Mr. Mac Craith and Miss Page then told me you all saw a man in the forest?"

Liesl and I nodded.

"And he'd been one of the fae? Green? Clothed in plants?" The headmistress asked.

"Ivy," Liesl said.

"Pardon, Miss Becker?" the headmistress's eyebrows rose.

"Ivy," said Liesl. "He was clothed in ivy. You know: like, the plant?"

"I know," the headmistress said with a faint smile. "Okay, that brings us up to date on your adventures, at least what Mr. Mac Craith and Miss Page told me." She looked at Liesl and me. "Can you please relate what happened next?"

Liesl and I filled her in on what happened after we noticed the man, until we returned to the school grounds, including what motions the man seemed to make, and the part about the banshee.

The headmistress sat back.

There was a knock at the door.

"Come," the headmistress called out.

The nurse entered and began examining Chance.

The headmistress turned back to us while the nurse ministered to Chance, taking his temperature, drawing blood, looking in his mouth, ears, and eyes.

"All of you, I will explain what I know and what we believe caused this to happen," the headmistress said. "Of course, we will have everything confirmed by the doctor in the infirmary. But what I think has happened is that someone has laid a curse on not only the forest, but on Mr. Mac Craith.

On Chance?!

I glanced over. Chance looked feverish.

"Was it Jessica and Naomi?" Liesl asked in a loud tone, jumping up as she spoke.

The headmistress put her hand out. "No, no, no. Such a curse, affecting an entire forest, would have to be cast by a very powerful being. Certainly not by anyone with just the first-year abilities of either the younger Miss Page or Miss Penner. No, this was not the work of schoolyard bullies."

"Also," the headmistress continued, "I believe that your actions in the faerie ring, Miss Ó Cuilinn, actually worked to save you and the others. When you spoke your poem, by the way, why did you recite those words, Miss Ó Cuilinn?"

"Oh," I said, "we've been learning in class how putting our wishes into our own words, and making them rhyme, gives them more meaning. Makes the spells stronger."

"Well, you're absolutely correct. Although how you managed such a rhyme on the spur of the moment, I will never ..."

"Well," I said, interrupting the headmistress in my rush to explain, "I've always liked to rhyme. My Aunt Clare encouraged it when we said prayers every night."

"Well, you have a real gift, Miss Ó Cuilinn," said the headmistress. "As I was saying, the words you spoke in the faerie ring? They summoned ... help. The man you saw placed a charm on the forest, to direct you closer to the cemetery. And he also directed the banshee to you."

"That was so weird," said Liesl. "And a bit scary."

The headmistress leaned forward. "You are both in the First Mysteries class, are you not?"

Liesl and I nodded.

"And have you learned about the faefolk of the families?" she asked.

I thought back to my classes. *The faefolk of the families* ...

"Ohhhhhh my god ..." I murmured.

The headmistress looked pleased.

I stared at her.

She nodded her head. "Continue, Miss Ó Cuilinn."

"It was right after classes started," I said slowly. "The class taught about faefolk ... who were attached, or belonged, to certain families ... oh my God, the banshee comes to those of her family ..." I stared at the headmistress. "Is that banshee from the cemetery of my family?"

She nodded, though it seemed she did so reluctantly.

"The banshee lives in the cemetery near the school, and the cemetery is on school grounds, as is much of the forest. It belongs to the line of the family you are descended from, Miss Ó Cuilinn," the headmistress explained. "That was why she came to you."

"The others," I said slowly, "they said they could hear her calling, at first. But then she came near, and I saw her face, and something told me she did not mean any harm ..."

"You are correct," said the headmistress. "She didn't. She was there, it would seem, to give you aid."

"... And then she started whispering instructions to me, how to get back to the school the fastest. And ... and warning me, too. She told me it was important to get back fast, because the sun was going to set soon, and we'd be trapped another night.

"And we had run out of food. And Chance was getting worse. Or, actually," I said, remembering, "she warned that he *would* be getting worse very soon. It was as if the banshee knew the future ... oh."

The headmistress nodded. "That is an aspect of their magic. They can indeed see the future, especially the near future. That is why they warn their family of an impending death. Many times, it's actually a caution, that an accident is about to take a life ..."

The nurse stood up then and spoke into the air in a whisper, then turned to headmistress. "He needs to go to the hospital wing. He is ill because the curse is worsening, and he needs the counter curse performed. It should take just a few hours for him to recover after it's uttered. I've called for aid."

As if on cue, there was another knock at the door, and two other nurses entered without waiting for an answer.

Chance was hustled out the door and onto the waiting stretcher the nurses had brought.

"He should be recovered by the morning, headmistress," said the nurse.

The headmistress nodded.

As he disappeared up the stairs, I asked, "Will he be okay?"

The headmistress nodded, "I believe so, Miss Ó Cuilinn. But it's vitally important he be treated immediately." She turned to us. "Now, I will look into the curse, which made Mr. Mac Craith so ill, and forced the forest to lose you from the school and misdirect you, and also flip time into a hasten spell. I will keep you all posted on my progress. But for now, I think you should go down to the dining hall and eat dinner. Then perhaps an early bedtime would be in order."

Normally, I would have protested such a sacrilege, but I felt so exhausted that bed sounded wonderful. In fact ...

"Headmistress, would it be possible to take our dinner in our rooms?" I asked. "It's been an awful day and a half, even if we were only gone from the school for half a day,"

She nodded immediately. "That is a sound plan. Miss Ó Cuilinn, Miss Page, Miss Becker; I will have your dinners brought up to you. Please return to your dorm rooms so you may rest and recuperate."

Relief washed over me as Liesl and I walked toward our staircase.

"I'll talk to you soon, Holly, Liesl," said Renée. "I've already talked to my sister; she should give you no more trouble. If she does, she knows she'll have to answer to me." Renée had a grave look on her face as she waved goodbye and turned to go up the staircase to her dorm room.

I slowly ascended our own stairs, lost in thought. I could not stop thinking about the banshee, and how she was connected to my family in some way. I *needed* to learn more about her.

What an enormous mystery.

Chapter Twenty-Nine
Assembly

The next morning Liesl and I overslept, by about a half hour.

"Oh, God," said Liesl throwing me my shoe. "Hurry, Holly!"

"Thanks," I said, catching it. I had been half under my bunk looking for the errant footwear. "We still have time."

"Classes start in less than an hour," said Liesl. "We still need to meet Chance and Renée down at breakfast. We've got less than ten minutes to get down there!"

I slipped my shoes on and rose to my feet, stomping them to secure them. "You worry too much," I said, smiling and walking to the door. "You coming?"

Liesl grabbed her bookbag and ran out the door, and I followed in hot pursuit.

"God, I didn't finish my T and S homework," she mumbled to me as we hurried down the spiral stairs. "I really thought I'd have the evening to finish it."

"It'll be fine."

We hit the ground floor at a run and sprinted to the dining hall.

"No running!" called a voice.

We slowed to a speed walk and scooted in the door and hurried over to Chance and Renée, who were already seated with food.

"Sorry," Liesl panted, grabbing eggs and sausages.

"Glad you're feeling better, Chance," I said.

He grinned and gave me a thumbs up.

Renée leaned forward. "You two are never going to believe what I found out."

I was instantly on the alert.

Liesl froze, her hand, holding a piece of toast with jam, paused midway between her mouth and plate.

Even Chance was riveted to Renée's face.

She leaned over even more to whisper; "I heard the headmistress last night telling one of the other professors: They've discovered who laid the curse." She sat back, folding her arms together.

Oh my God.

We waited for her to continue.

She suddenly leaned forward again, her elbows almost upsetting her plate. We all leaned, too, our heads nearly touching. Quieter than before, Renée whispered, "It's an enemy of the king."

"The king?" whispered Chance.

Renée nodded.

"Wait," said Liesl. "What? You mean ..."

Renée nodded.

"Who laid the curse?" I asked in a whisper.

Renée turned to me, "They aren't sure. But, I mean, it's pretty obvious."

"To you, maybe," I said softly, rolling my eyes.

All three of them looked at me.

"What?" I put my palms up.

Renée grinned and shook her head. "Nothing."

Chance smiled. "Holly, the enemy of the king depends on what time of year it is, because there are two brothers who share the throne. Right now, it is the winter king, The Holly King, who reigns," he said. "So in the spring and summer the Oak King reigns. It's a pretty benign and stable monarchy, but only because the older brother has stronger forces, by far."

Renée nodded. "So, while the Holly King reigns only half the year, he's the most powerful, and the Oak King absolutely resents that. The Holly King is happy to share the kingdom, but his brother would prefer not to share."

"That's a nice way of putting it," Chance chuckled.

"Yeah," smiled Renée. "I thought you'd like that."

"Now," said Chance, "The Holly King is not perfect, trust me, but he's gentler and more laid back than his brother. The Oak King is way more ambitious."

"Of course," said Renée, "I think part of the reason the Holly King is so laid back is because he's got a lot of power. A lot of allies, and he's got the elf warriors."

"Elf warriors?" I asked.

"Yep. Just what is sounds like," said Chance. "He's got a small army of them."

I thought for a minute. "So you think the curse was from ..."

"The Oak King," said Renée. "Yes. That's what I overheard, at least."

"But why would the Oak King want to curse us?" I asked.

"Why would the Oak King want to curse Chance?"" I asked.

"Not sure," said Renée. "Don't know."

Chance raised his hand. We all looked at him. "The doctors told me the curse I caught was random. Set on the first person to enter the forest after the curse had been laid on the ground. It was actually the grounds up to the steps that were cursed."

"Ooooh, so everything in the area except for the school?" asked Liesl.

"Exactly," said Chance. "Remember me falling as soon as I stepped off the from steps of the school?"

Oh my God.

"I remember," I said.

"Yeah, and while we were gone, weird things kept happening on the lawn, all over the place," said Chance. "And the time curse was laid on the trees in the forest, so they didn't notice it on the lawn at first."

"Whoa," said Liesl. "The Oak King did all that?"

"Well, the Oak King's people did it. I doubt he did it himself," said Renée. She leaned forward again and whispered, "The school officials are mad as hell. They think Oak is trying to make an assault on the school."

Chance's eyebrows rose. "Have there been any other attacks on the school?"

"Not yet, but the headmistress is concerned about Oak recruiting agents among the students," said Renée. "Apparently, there are real suspicions."

Chance looked stunned. He sat back, his arms folded in front of him, slowly shaking his head, saying nothing.

Renée gave him a significant look.

A chime sounded in the central hallway.

"Oh, geez, that's us." I grabbed my bag. "Keep us posted?" I whispered.

Renée nodded.

Liesl and I ran out of the dining hall and to our class.

341

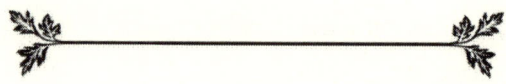

It was three o'clock, and Liesl and I were just entering our last class.

And we were exhausted.

Fourth class, which was at one thirty, had been torture.

It was oral report day, and we'd rushed through ours, both of us, because Jessica and Naomi had sat in the front row making faces at us.

They were masters of it. The professor never saw them. I don't think anyone else ever saw them.

It was as if only we could see them.

Had they put a spell on us?

I dismissed the idea as soon as it surfaced. Jessica and Naomi were first-years, just like us. First-years were barely able to cast simple enchantments, let alone such advanced magic as glamour spells.

Still, they managed to unnerve us, and we both stumbled through the assignment.

We didn't flunk, but the professor looked disappointed.

I felt sick to my stomach.

"Why do they pick on us so much"? Liesl whispered close to my face as she slid into her desk.

I shook my head; I had no idea. They were taking this thing wayyy too far. It had been months since the dorm incident on Firstday.

They're insane, that's why.

Luckily for us, neither nitwit was in our last class, and the professor was off visiting their ailing aunt, so we had a substitute teacher.

We spent the whole class practicing our Seeing skills.

Learning to be a Master Seer was difficult at best, and the class, called "Trickery and Sot" was designed to give us a taste of four different ancient topics that faefolk still practiced as professions.

Although I doubted very many people made a living by divination.

After the class, we wandered over to the dining hall.

"I'm so tired," Liesl said.

"Probably from all the hiking the last two days," I answered.

"Yeah. Phew. I slept so deeply last night," Liesl said.

"Me, too. I think I love sleeping more than eating," I laughed.

Liesl was looking around as we walked. "Do you think Chance will be there?"

"Probably," I said. "You still sweet on him?"

Liesl blushed.

"Well why don't you do something about it?" I asked.

She shrugged. "Half the girls in the school like him. He doesn't seem interested in anyone. Not girls, not boys. There's a fair number of boys who're interested, trust me."

"You been watching for it?" I asked.

"As a matter of fact, I have," Liesl lifted her chin in mock pride. "I haven't seen him take any kind of interest in anyone. In fact, he spends most of his off time with us and Renée."

I lifted my eyebrows, "Maybe he likes Renée?"

Liesl shook her head. "Renée has a year-five boyfriend. Plus, Chance hasn't shown interest in her at all."

Hmmm.

"Is there such a thing as keeping an infatuation secret?" I asked.

"Ha ha ha! Good one!" she laughed.

We entered the dining hall.

Renée was seated in a corner, head over a book, her fork idly winding the spaghetti on her plate.

"Hey, Renée," I said as we walked up to her.

"Hey guys, how were classes today?" she said, lifting her head and yawning.

"Pretty good," said Liesl. "Except for Transfiguration."

"Oh?" Renée sat up more, looking concerned.

We sat down at the table and spooned spaghetti onto our plates, all the while telling her what had happened.

"Hmmm," Renée looked concerned. "I'm going to report this to the headmistress. You're absolutely right, first-years should not be able to do such advanced magic.

Hmmm.

"Now I'm worried," Liesl said.

"I talked to my little sister last week," said Renée. "I *thought* she'd listened. But then again, it would be more like her to nod and smile and then not let a grudge go, than be honest."

"Ooh, here comes Chance!" Liesl sat up straighter and smiled.

"Liesl, wipe your mouth," I whispered.

She grabbed her napkin and hastily wiped some red sauce off her lip.

"Hi, everyone," Chance say down next to Renée and grabbed a plate. "I'm famished. We had flying practice in the morning, and then I had my swim class just now. We're getting ready for a meet this weekend."

Liesl choked on her garlic bread. "You're on the swim team?"

"Yeah," Chance said, spooning spaghetti onto his plate. "But I'm not sure how much longer."

I stared at his tousled wet head. "Problems in paradise?"

"Eh, I signed up for too much, and I'm falling behind in one or two classes," he said.

"Was it last weekend that put you behind?" Renée asked.

"No, that did nothing to my schedule. We gained a day, remember?" he said. 'Did absolutely nothing bad, except maybe to my sleep," he said, yawning.

I yawned automatically, then Liesl yawned, followed by Renée.

We all chuckled.

"Renée," I asked, "do you know if the headmistress is going to give us any information about the curse on the forest? I mean, we were caught in it, that kind of makes it personal."

"Mmm, oh. Yes, I think she's actually going to address the whole school," Renée said. It's best if all the students know what's going on. It's pretty serious."

"Is anyone going to involve the king?" asked Liesl. "He may be able to help."

Renée took another bite of potatoes and shrugged.

"Holly, how do you like your classes so far?" Chance asked.

I blinked. "Uhhh, the classes? They're fine, I'm learning a lot." I glanced behind me. No one was there, as far as I could see. I leaned forward and said in a low voice. "I had no idea there would be so much happening at the school."

"What do you mean?" Renée asked.

"I mean, there's a lot happening other than the classes," I said. "The interaction with the other students, the 'picnic' that lasted nearly two days, the warping of time, the information about my past that I've been given, and not been given, it's all been a bit overwhelming."

"Best thing so far for me is I've found a best friend," Liesl smiled shyly and leaned her head on my shoulder.

"Awww," I smiled and felt warm.

A summoning bell sounded in the distance.

"What's that?" Liesl asked, bringing her head up.

"That's the call to the student assembly," said Renée. "Remember? I told you about it? Everyone has to attend." She got up from her chair.

We all walked out of the dining hall together and toward the Assembly Hall.

"What do you think this is going to be about?" Liesl whispered in my ear as we walked. "I mean besides the attack on the school."

I shrugged. "Maybe about the upcoming holiday?"

"Halloween? Hmmm," Liesl murmured.

"I'm dressing up as a faun," said Chance.

Renée laughed heartily.

"What?" I asked.

She shook her head, her eyes merry. "You'll see."

Liesl and I exchanged a look: *what could that be about?*

We entered the Assembly Hall and found seats.

The headmistress came out and began to talk.

What followed was the most boring forty-five minutes of my entire life.

Professor Ó Baoghill proceeded to tell the whole school everything we already knew.

And nothing else.

"Maybe she doesn't know more?" I whispered to Liesl.

"I don't think she does," Liesl whispered back.

Oh, brother.

Liesl and I spent nearly the whole time whispering back and forth and thumb wrestling. It was a long forty-five minutes.

Walking out, Renée scowled at us in mock anger.

I spied a bright pink and flaming orange color out the nearest window as we passed it. "The sun is setting. Who wants to go watch it?"

"I've got an essay to write," Renée said.

Liesl yawned. "Where do you get your energy?"

"She's of the royal line," said Chance. "They have boundless energy."

I grinned. At least there was something useful about my heritage.

"Okay, don't wait up for me, Liesl; I also love to stargaze."

She gave me a thumbs up and walked toward our dorm room staircase, still yawning.

"Well, the Evanescence essay won't write itself, so, bye! See you tomorrow," Renée turned and walked in a different direction.

I stood and watched her go.

I glanced back out of the window facing west. The pink was getting darker.

"We'd better go on up; the sunset will fade soon," Chance said behind me in a murmur.

I turned in surprise, smiling. "Oh! I didn't know you were coming."

He grinned. "Is the invitation still open?"

"Of course," I said. I looked around the upper stories. "Do you know the shortest route to the top of the castle?"

"Sure. Follow me." He took my hand, which surprised me a bit, and turned to a smaller staircase I'd never used.

We took the stairs two at a time, racing each other to beat the setting of the sun.

"Ha ha ha!" I laughed as I ran up the steps.

Chance grinned as he followed, always staying a step behind.

Hmmm...

Chapter Thirty
Bombing

We'd gone up several stories when a massive explosion shook the staircase, and I nearly fell. Aspen and Tundra suddenly appeared, whining and sniffing the air.

Chance's hawk also appeared on his shoulders and let out a loud squawk.

"Careful!" Chance's strong hands encircled my waist as I tipped backwards.

"OH!" My heart thundered in my chest and a huge lance of fear pierced my head.

He set me firmly on the upper step, and I put my hand to the iron railing and grasped it tightly.

"You okay now?" he asked, looking into my eyes.

"Y–yes, I think so. What was that?"

"No idea, but …" A second explosion shook the castle, and a few stones fell from the upper staircases, dropping down the center of the portico.

I hung on the railing and was able to stay upright.

Chance crouched slightly, his balance impressive.

When the rocking from the blast subsided, he leaned over the banister and called down, "Everyone okay?"

A few voices drifted up from below, including a scream.

He turned to me, "Come on. We'd better get down there and see if we can help."

As we descended the stairs, my two wolves following, I wondered out loud, "What made those explosions?"

"No idea," he answered. "But it can't be good."

When we reached the main floor, we saw rubble was everywhere.

Various familiars cuddled beside their people, licking cheeks and making sounds of distress as each one's person moaned on the ground. In a few cases where victims lay still and unconscious, the familiar hovered over them, trying to shield them from further harm.

Stone and dust and other objects had fallen from the upper levels and hit several students, and in one case, a professor. They lay on the floor, groaning.

Liesl came running. "Is everyone okay? I felt a … oh!" she saw the injured and ran to the nearest one: a boy bleeding from his temple.

"Come on," Chance murmured, and we raced help others.

The headmistress hurried out of a hallway, her hair in curlers, several nurses in tow. They rushed to aid the injured.

Chance had been helping the professor hit by falling rubble, and beside him, I helped a girl whose shoulder had been hit.

"I think it's broken," I whispered to her. She stared into my eyes, her face covered in dust, two tears running down her cheeks making wet trails in the dusty grime that covered her.

One boy was unconscious, his hand still grasping Liesl's tightly. She ran beside the gurney that bore him, and her charge was first to be taken to the hospital wing.

"He's in my morning class," murmured the girl I was helping. "I ate dinner near him just an hour ago." Fresh tears ran down her cheeks.

"I ... I'm sure he'll be okay. The doctors are wonderful, and the nurses, too. I'm sure ..." I choked and could not continue.

A new gurney came for her, and I busied myself helping load her on.

She clutched at my hand. "Don't let go ..." she whispered as she lay back.

"I won't. I promise."

It was awful. Ten people had been injured, several quite severely. The hospital wing was busy.

We all followed the people we'd been helping on their short journey to the doctor's large room.

Up in the hospital wing, we all worked to assist, whether it was continuing to hold our patient's hands, or holding an I.V. bottle high in the air.

The doctor's triage meant my patient had to wait almost an hour for help, after they hooked her up to fluids.

It was amazing to see the healers all hard at work, rushing to save lives.

I wondered in the back of my head why such mundane methods were used to help faefolk, but after a few minutes of thought it made sense: The magic taught at Titania Academy was mostly elemental and native, and used wild means to accomplish needed tasks.

I glanced over at Chance and smiled. He had crawled up into bed and lay beside the professor he'd helped; he held her hand, her fingers curled around his palm even though she appeared unconscious.

Liesl's patient was at the far end of the room, having come in first. Several doctors worked on him frantically.

Liesl's eyes found me across the long room. She was crying.

Another student, an older girl, came and joined Liesl, and held her hand.

Support for those giving support.

It was a long night. We stayed for hours.

"Faefolk always lend aid," Chance said. "Many of the fae heritages are acutely in need of touch and comfort when they are in deep distress. All of us need it to a degree."

The tears on my cheek had dried a while ago. A nurse had brought us all hot cocoa and hot buttered scones. Chance and I sat eating and drinking the best cocoa I'd ever had in my life.

"I don't think humans know about that kind of magic," I said haltingly.

"That," said Chance, "is a real shame. Many more lives could be saved."

We sat in silence for a long time. On one side, we held the hands of our charges, who slept fitfully, having been bandaged and ministered to. On our other sides, we held the cups of cocoa. Our warm buttered scones sat on small plates on the tables beside us.

It was calm and quiet, and the lighting had been lowered until all that remained was the glow from the lamps on each small bedside table, a warm and cozy yellow light.

Liesl's charge had not made it. The first-year boy had been hit directly in the head. It had taken him hours to finally perish.

He held on a long time.

Liesl lay, finally asleep, curled in a ball, on the fluffy shag rug at our feet. The boy's body had been moved to another room, and his parents had been summoned. Liesl had cried for an hour, and silent but copious tears still stained her face.

It was heartbreaking.

After the first half hour, several guards had rushed in to whisper in the headmistress' ear, and she'd hurried out of the hospital with them, a shocked look on her face.

Another professor was already taking her place when I glanced back at her charge.

The Academy, even the entire fae world, took this responsibility very seriously. No patient was left alone while in the hospital. They all had people beside them, holding their hands, and in some cases, holding their whole body.

They heal faster. That's beautiful.

I glanced at the far wall of the large hospital room. A line of people stood there, watching us all, waiting for a chance to provide healing touch. Their faces showed an eagerness to help.

Don't cry don't cry don't cry.

About midnight, nurses came in with cots and blankets, and we moved into those. They were set alongside each bed, and I saw there was already room for the cots, and room to walk between each cot and bed.

They've already thought this out. Heck, they've probably done this countless times.

The explosions had been terrible. A lot of people had been hurt. One student had died. I kept thinking, *I hope this is rare. I really do.*

When I'd come to the school, at Chance's urging, I'd assumed it was a safe place, a place of learning and refuge.

Rare would be really good.

The next morning, we were roused in time for class, given special breakfasts, and sent on our way. We were assured the patients had healed sufficiently and would be all right. We were invited to return for a visit.

I yawned as I made my way to the first class. It would be a long day.

Later on, I learned that those who'd ministered to patients in this way were considered heroes of the day.

The professors and other students clapped as Liesl and I entered each class that day.

I gave them a teary-eyed smile for the first few classes, 'til I got used to it.

What a culture.

I was growing to really love it. A lot.

That afternoon, another assembly was called. This time I was eager.

"I hope they tell us what happened," I said. "No one I've asked has any clue."

"Mmmm, oh. They have a special security system in place at the school," said Chance, joining us as we walked in to the Assembly Hall. "All the entrances and exits to the school are instantly sealed in times of violence, attack, and most emergencies. For the students' protection."

I was shocked. "Uhhh, okay. What about during a fire?"

"That's usually not going to happen, as the school has a spell on it to shower water when smoke or flames are detected," Renée said, joining us as well. "Also, in case of sudden temperature rise. But if the sprinklers don't work, the doors are not locked in case of fire." She glanced at Chance. "This is the only case they are not force-locked, am I correct, Chance?"

He nodded. "You are indeed correct." He glanced at her. "What happened to you, by the way? We didn't see you after the explosions. I was worried."

"I was actually locked outside," Renée said. "The evening was so lovely, and Holly was right: The sunset was brilliant. So I took my essay paper and went out on the balcony of my room to work on it."

"Oh, no," Chance murmured.

"Oh, yes," said Renée. "The first explosion occurred, and the balcony doors clicked shut, then locked in place. I actually spent half the night out there, before someone came to check on me."

My eyes were wide listening to this.

"You have a balcony?" asked Liesl.

Renée threw her head back and laughed. "Yes, third-years and on up have larger dorm rooms and balconies."

Amazing.

We found seats together. The anticipation in the room was palpable.

We didn't have long to wait.

The headmistress walked out, and a huge murmuring began rippling through the room. She put both her hands out, palms down, motioning for silence, and the murmuring ceased.

"Thank you," she said. "Now, as you all know, our school suffered two explosions yesterday evening. We began investigating at once, and we finally have preliminary results to present to you, our student body."

You could've heard a pin drop, the large room was so quiet. Everyone leaned forward in their seats in expectation.

The headmistress took a deep breath. "The explosions were a result of an attack on the castle, which took the form of several bombs."

The room exploded in chaos. It was a good ten minutes before everyone settled back down and she could continue.

"The two bombs damaged a section of wall on the castle exterior. Luckily, that area of the school is not currently in use, because of the current size of the student body.

"Huh?" I murmured.

Chance leaned in, "Fewer students have been enrolling at Titania Academy these past few years," he whispered.

I nodded in understanding.

The headmistress was speaking again.

"We have determined that the culprit who launched the bombs at our school was an ally of The Oak King faction."

What the ...?

Chance had become tense next to me. I glanced over at Renée and saw she looked very stressed.

"The minister of education is teaming up with the queen. Several dozen investigators and additional school guards are being assigned; they should be here tomorrow morning. And ..." the headmistress paused and took a deep breath, "the king will be visiting us next week."

The students jumped up again, roaring in happiness. Chaos took over again.

The headmistress tried to regain control of the student body, but it was no use. After a good twenty minutes of trying, she finally gave up.

"YOU ARE DISMISSED," she called out, and the students cleared the room, heading to the exits in an orderly yet loud exodus.

Chance and Renée motioned for us to follow them, and we made our way up to the second-year dorm staircase. It was so loud from everyone's excited talking, that it was just easier this way.

"Come," Chance motioned us up to his dorm room.

Liesl and I had never seen the second-year room. They were niccceeeeee!

"Okay," said Chance, closing the door behind us to allow us some privacy. "So, you two may be wondering why everyone is so excited."

Liesl grinned, "I know."

"Well, Holly doesn't, so we should explain," Renée said, smiling at Liesl.

Chance turned to me. "First, you should understand, there are two ... 'branches'... of royalty in the fae world. The first is the queen's line."

"Our school is named for the queen," said Renée. "She's been queen for several thousand years. Queen Titania."

"Okay," I said.

Liesl turned to me, "She's immortal, and she rules the fae world, but benignly, similarly to the queen of England."

"And then," said Chance, "There's the other royal line. And the first thing you must know is that, they aren't parallel. Not in the least."

"Queen Titania rules the fae civilization," explained Renée. "The more mundane parts of the fae culture."

"The two kings rule the enchanted side of the fae world," said Chance. "And they are rarely seen. Very rarely."

"The last time the Holly King came to the school was ..." Renée thought for a minute.

"My grandmother says he visited while she was here," said Liesl. "She's pretty old."

Chance nodded. "It's been more than sixty years."

My eyes grew wide. "So, I assume this king is immortal, too?"

"Yes," said Renée. "And you should know that the Oak King has never visited. Only the Holly King."

"He's the most popular," whispered Liesl, giggling.

Renée put her finger to her lips and smiled at Liesl.

"Anyway," said Chance, "That's why everyone is so excited about him coming for a visit. Most faefolk have never even seen him."

Amazing.

Chapter Thirty-One
Melancholy

That evening in the dining hall, Jessica and Naomi and a handful of their friends walked by as I entered the room ten minutes early. The others weren't there yet, so I stood just inside the doors, scouting out a spot that would fit us all. It had to be roomy enough for all four of us.

"Hi, Holly," Jessica said, winking as she walked past.

Naomi grinned at me with a conspiratorial look on her face, moving her eyebrows up and down, as if we shared a juicy secret.

What are they up to?

Jessica walked a few more feet from me, then turned to face me. "You should ask about your bastard heritage when the king's entourage arrives. I hear there's a bunch of minor royals he travels with," she said, her tone sickly sweet and mocking.

"Yeah, maybe you can find a lower footman to marry who's the third cousin to an out-of-favor Baron," said Naomi. "He could show you the ropes ..." she dissolved in giggles, and Jessica joined her.

Chance strode in then, a glower on his face. "You two were cautioned by the headmistress. Do you want to detained?"

"No matter," said Jessica. "Naomi and I were just chatting with our little ... friend here. Right, Holly?" She stepped closer to me, brazen as a troll.

I turned my back on her without a word, looking at Chance instead.

A much more pleasant sight.

Chance stared at the two girls behind me, his eyes going wide. "Hey. HEY!"

I swung around in time to see Jessica's upraised fist stopped by Chance's arm.

"MISS PENNER!" The headmistress Professor Ó Baoghill came striding over from the front of the dining hall, her robes fluttering behind he she walked so rapidly. "Detention! For the whole month! And you shall miss the king's visit."

Jessica wrenched her forearm from Chance's grasp. "But headmistress! It's the king!"

"We do not strike fellow students, Miss Penner, not for any reason."

"I witnessed the whole thing, headmistress," Chance said. "Holly didn't provoke them at all. They were teasing her unmercifully. Holly never even responded."

"Thank you, Mr. Mac Craith. You and Miss Ó Cuilinn may go to the tables," said the headmistress. She turned to Jessica and Naomi. "As for you two, you will go directly to your quarters and skip dinner. I think you need something to dwell on while your stomachs growl." She raised her arm and pointed back out of the dining hall.

Jessica and Naomi looked extremely put out; they walked out glowering, without saying anything.

Chance and I found a good place to sit at the table.

I glanced at him after we were settled. "Thanks," I whispered.

"No problem," he said. "I cannot believe how sour those girls are."

"I can," I said, piercing a bite of potato halfheartedly.

"Hey," he said softly, putting a hand over mine. "It'll be okay. If they keep this up, they'll eventually get expelled. If they let it go, everything will calm down and blow over."

"I just worry someone's going to get hurt before it's over," I looked up at him. "And it will probably be me." Tears filled my eyes.

"I won't let that happen, Holly." He gently squeezed my hand.

He took his napkin and dabbed at the corners of my eyes, then rubbed my back.

"Hey," said Liesl, walking up and taking a seat beside me. "Everything okay?"

"Yes." I took Chance's napkin he'd been using to dry my tears and blew my nose with it. "Everything's fine."

Liesl looked concerned.

"Just a couple of troublemakers," said Chance. "We took care of them."

Renée took a seat with us. "Oh my God, I'm so famished I can't believe it." She grabbed a plate and some fried chicken. "What a weekend that was. WHAT AN AWFUL WEEKEND!"

I turned to her. "Renée, how was your last class?"

"Brutal." She took a bite of a drumstick and began chewing.

By silent consensus the three of us did not mention the unpleasantness of the past ten minutes.

"I'm so excited the King is coming to the school!" said Liesl.

"Oh my God, me too," said Renée. "The *reason* he's coming is upsetting, though." She glanced at Chance. "Have you heard anything about the actual explosions?"

"The headmistress is being very secretive about what actually happened," said Chance, "but I know a few fourth-years who were up on the north tower when the blasts occurred. They say the impacts were close to the base of tower three and about three stories off ground. I went around the side of the castle today to see if I could spot anything, but the damage is out of sight."

"It's probably on one of the inner tower keeps," said Renée. "Can't see it from the ground. Have you noticed any work on the inside?"

"No, but those hallways have been blocked off. I think most of the damage was on the outer walls. The inner wall repairs wouldn't be seen," Chance said.

The rest of the meal chatter faded into the background as my thoughts turned inward.

Jessica and Naomi's hatred of me had not lessened, as I had hoped it would after the center hallway incident.

Apparently, the warning from the headmistress had done nothing but drive them underground.

Renée had said she'd cautioned her sister as well.

I thought for a minute.

Renée knows my true heritage, but is bound by a Secrecy Spell. She cannot tell Naomi my secret outright, but she probably stressed how important it is to stop bullying me.

But it hadn't made any difference.

WHY?

I wondered how many of the students felt the way Jessica and Naomi do?

This bullying was a new experience for me. I'd always been a loner, together with Aunt Clare. We'd stayed to ourselves. We'd never bothered anyone. We'd tried to be invisible.

You had to be, if you were going to survive on the streets.

I smiled, remembering the first time I had stolen an apple from a street vendor.

"Holly, that's dangerous. They notice you when you do that. Being visible means being vulnerable," Aunt Clare had cautioned. And I had cooled it on the thievery.

For a while.

The dry spell had been broken the fall when Aunt Clare and I'd had a string of bad luck.

The week we went hungry.

I was about eight, and it had been windy and rainy all week. Aunt Clare had found half a discarded sandwich in the subway tunnel. She'd snatched it before anyone else could see, and we'd shared it in a dark corner of the underground. We hadn't eaten in a day and a half, so the thing had been gone in a few minutes.

I remembered licking my fingers of every crumb I could find, and wishing I had more.

I'd looked up and seen Aunt Clare watching me.

I knew she'd given me the lion's share of the meal, and I'd felt so much love for her.

I'd jumped into her lap and given her a hug.

"Come on, kiddo, let's go find some water," she'd said.

We'd gone to a water fountain we frequented when we were in that part of the city.

"Remember, sweetheart, never drink from old water," Aunt Clare had always cautioned me. "This means, no puddles, no large fountains, and no rivers or gutters."

And I never had.

"You can get sick enough to die from the tiny creatures in the old water."

Aunt Clare had taught me so much.

But when we'd spent days looking for food during a storm that kept everyone inside, things had gotten desperate. I remember thinking longingly of the half sandwich we'd shared as I searched every trash can and every nook and cranny of the city for something to eat.

Three days passed.

Aunt Clare had retreated to our cubby underground, and a fourth day had gone by without her emerging.

She'd grown weaker and weaker.

It had been up to me. I'd walked miles down the streets on the fifth day, kicking every piece of trash and debris I'd found, trying to ignore the hunger gnawing at my stomach.

I'd wandered down to the farmers market set up on Union Square, staring hungrily at the tables heavy with every kind of green food imaginable.

There'd been a table set up by a grocer, laden with the biggest, reddest apples I'd ever seen. The grocer was making trip after trip back and forth from the table to the truck parked nearby, getting ready for the day's sales.

A thought had entered my mind. A thought of eating one of those apples, and bringing another back to Aunt Clare.

I'd watched the grocer carry box after box from the truck. I'd seen him empty the crates from the truck until he'd had to climb into the back of his truck to grab the next crate. He did this once, then twice, taking even longer the second time.

By the time he'd walked from his table to get the third load, I had darted forward, hiding in the shadows, not thinking, just acting on instinct.

I'd glanced toward the man, who was just climbing up into the back of his truck again, and I'd acted.

Up went my hand, from where I crouched, half in the shadows.

Four apples. Then I'd scurried away.

It was fast, and no one had seen me.

As I ran back to the underground, my heart had thudded in my chest with the thrill.

I could've been seen.

I could've been CAUGHT.

I'd thought about all these things as I ate my apples in the cubby opposite Aunt Clare, who munched on the two apples I had brought her.

I'd watched her face, noticing how hollow her cheeks were growing, and the dark circles under her eyes.

She'd winked at me between bites.

"Just be careful, Holly," she'd whispered.

She understood.

Sometimes such things were necessary.

My thoughts returned to the present. My friends were still chatting amicably.

I looked down at the feast on my plate. The fried chicken, the mashed potatoes, a large pat of butter melting in the middle of the mound. The green beans and carrots on the side.

Aunt Clare and I had been grateful for four stolen apples.

Now I was living like a king, eating three meals a day, and I realized I hadn't been hungry since Chance found me.

I looked around the room. The dining hall was massive, with ceilings several stories high, and tall windows that let the sunshine in.

I felt an overwhelming sense of gratitude.

"Hey, Daydreamer?"

I looked over at Chance.

"Are you done?" he asked.

I looked down at my plate and saw I had eaten every bite except for half a biscuit. *Never waste food.* I grabbed the piece of bread off my plate and stood to join the others.

"Okay, well, see you tomorrow!" Renée waved and walked out.

Liesl turned to me. "I'm going to the library again, I can't get enough of their rare book collection."

"Have fun!" I smiled as she walked out.

"Well, I guess I'll just turn in ...," I said.

"Wait," Chance said in a quiet voice. "We never got to watch the sunset." He pointed out the window. The sky was just beginning to turn pink. "Join me on the roof?"

I stared out at the horizon. "Are we allowed to go outside? The repairs ..."

"I know how to reach the other side of the castle's parapet," Chance said. "And that turret faces west, so it's a perfect place to watch the approach of twilight."

I gazed at him, my head still a daze.

He grinned back at me easily.

There was something in his expression ...

"Sure," I smiled.

Chapter Thirty-Two

Sunset and a Sighting

We walked out and up the stairs.

It took about ten minutes, but we were fast. Chance took the stairs two at a time, and I joined him, finding new energy.

At the very top, Chance indicated a seldom-used hallway, and at the end of this hallway was an old oak door, darkened with age.

He tried the handle, and it opened on the second try, creaking rustily.

He turned to me and put his finger to his lips in a *shhh* gesture, and then beckoned me through the door.

I emerged on the turret and looked around. I was surrounded by stone, there were lamps every dozen feet, already lit for the evening.

"Come this way?" Chance beckoned me to the right, and we walked down the covered parapet walk until we emerged in the open air. Just a few dozen feet farther, and we turned a corner and I felt the breath leave my lungs.

The sky was on fire.

Bright pink and orange color spanned the sky from end to end. Above this was a darkening rose color that slowly, ever so slowly, was turning into purple.

"I love the sunset," I said softly.

"I'm taking an art class this year, as one of my electives, and I'm trying to work up the courage to paint the sunset," Chance said.

"Oh! You should!" I turned to him. "Then you'll immortalize the moment forever!"

He grinned down at me. He was so tall he nearly towered over me. I felt like I was looking up at an adult, even though we were just over a year apart in age.

"Chance?" I asked, turning back to the sunset. It has subtly changed. It was a moving work of art from mother nature.

"Yes."

"Can I ask you about your past?"

"Sure," said Chance. "Ask me anything."

"Where did you grow up?"

"I was born in East Sussex, England," said Chance. "In the Ashdown Forest, to be exact."

"Ohhh! You were born in a forest?"

"Yes. In a stone cottage on the western edge."

"And, all the faefolk come from various heritages?" I asked.

"Yes. I, for instance, come from Faun heritage."

"Faun heritage?" My eyes were on the sunset.

"Yes," he said.

The flaming pink and orange colors were darkening.

"If you watch the land, as twilight comes upon it, you might see a faun or two," Chance said softly.

I dropped my eyes to the school grounds and searched.

Chance lowered his head to my level and looked with me. After a few minutes, the sky had darkened enough so that the magical sparkle of twilight was soaking the land. "There," he whispered, pointing to a spot on the edge of the school lawn.

I looked. "I can't see anything."

"Wait until he moves again; look for movement," Chance murmured.

I trained my eyes on the area he indicated.

The shadows were growing long, and the lamps around the school grounds made glowing circles of yellow here and there.

A cool breeze ruffled my hair as I held still and waited.

I was not disappointed.

The movement was what caught my eye. The faun was right where Chance was pointing.

He moved hesitantly in the bushes at the edge of the grounds, and seemed to be playing a flute as he walked. I'd never wished to be able to hear something as much as I did in that moment.

The blond faun looked grizzled and wore a short beard. He had hooves and long, pointed ears, and was, for all intents and purposes, naked as a jaybird. Large horns curled around either side of his head. He looked wild and natural. I couldn't take my eyes off him and had to consciously force myself to blink when my eyes began to sting.

We watched him as the sun set into the trees, until he wandered back into the forest and was gone.

I stared at the spot he had disappeared into for a few minutes after he was swallowed by the trees, thinking about fauns and heritage and the true forms of the faefolk.

We'd been learning the different heritages in class, and also about how the fae could shift into glamours and appear human. And about how this shifting into a different form affected not only their physical form, but their mindset.

I turned to Chance.

"I have questions," I said, smiling shyly. I hated to get personal, but I figured it was kind of like continuing my lesson from class.

"I have answers," Chance grinned.

"Okay. We've been learning about the different heritages and the shifting of forms and how it changes both appearance and mindset."

Chance nodded.

"So, you're shifted right now?"

"Yes," Chance said.

"And do you ... 'unshift' when you go to sleep? You know, change back when you're unconscious?" I hadn't noticed any difference in Chance when we were lost in the forest."

Chance ducked his head and smiled. "Er, no. I stay in this form, all the time. I've been in this form for so long that it's changing *back* to fae form that I have to concentrate on."

"Ah," I said, thinking about what he said. I looked back up at him. "Why?"

Chance smiled. "Shifting into form happens naturally, as a defense mechanism, starting when you're very young. At first you do it on accident, then on purpose, and it feels safer, so it becomes second nature."

"So ... does it hurt to shift back?" I asked.

Chance slowly shook his head.

I thought of something.

Can I shift? Have I ever shifted? What would I look like if I shifted into a defensive glamour?

"Shifting in an adult is a rather personal thing," explained Chance. "An intimate thing. That is why you never see it unless the faefolk is very young, or very elderly."

"The faun we saw down there, was he an elder?" I asked.

"Yes. He was grizzled and had a beard and grey in his hair, plus his horns were very large and probably deeply ridged."

I glanced back down on the lawn and forest. The light had dimmed enough so that it was impossible to see details, except ...

Fireflies!

"Oh!" I was enchanted. There were hundreds and hundreds of them, little dots of light floating across the school lawn, dancing in and out of the bushes, winking in and out of sight in the forest.

"Look." Chance pointed again. "Where the faun was, and where he walked. There's a thick line of fireflies there."

The fireflies were everywhere around the lawn and forest, but Chance was right: The path where the faun had been was especially thick with the glowing insects.

You could almost draw a line and follow it to follow the faun.

"The fauns are the spirits of the forest, as close to mother nature as the dryads," Chance murmured. "The fireflies are drawn to them, and, in fact, that is where the magic began, long ago, of the fireflies following the forest magic. The fireflies are not part of the fae, and yet they are drawn to them. Have you ever heard the expression 'drawn like moths to a flame'?"

I nodded.

"That is where the magic of light drawing moths and other twilight insects to it began."

I stared at the fireflies. It was amazing they were not fae, and yet were drawn to the faun.

"So, in this case, the faun is the light the fireflies are drawn to?" I asked.

"Yes. The light of the magic every fae exudes."

Hmmm.

"Okay, that makes sense," I smiled back.

Waitaminute.

I glanced at him. "I've never felt drawn to any insect or faefolk in particular."

He smiled. "That is because *you* are part of the faefolk."

I thought about that for a minute. "So, I could possibly shift into human form? What would that be like? Would I look any different? Would my hair change color?"

Chance chuckled. "Holly, you are already shifted. Right now."

What?

"But, but ... I've never looked any different, as far as I know," I sputtered.

"Like I said, it starts very young, and it a defense mechanism, so the child doesn't really realize they are doing anything different," said Chance. "You said your Aunt Clare raised you?"

I nodded.

"And no one else? Your mother ..."

"My mother died when I was a baby," I said.

"So, your Aunt Clare would have noticed."

"But ... she never mentioned anything," I said, feeling troubled. "Aunt Clare was human, as far as I know. I never noticed her looking like anything other than a human. She was my adopted aunt."

"She probably *was* human, but somehow knew to hide your difference," Chance said. "Or she might have been fae; we have no way of knowing."

"But ..."

"How old was she?"

"Oh, she was old. I think she was already in her fifties," I said. "She looked it. Her hair had streaks of grey."

"Then she was probably human," he said. "Faefolk live for a very long time. If she appeared that old, she would have been hundreds of years old. Possibly thousands, depending on the heritage. What color was her hair?"

"Just brown."

Chance nodded. "Very likely human."

"Aunt Clare told me she'd made friends with my mother in a shelter, when my mother was only twenty years old," I said. "Aunt Clare was lots older. They became close friends, so she took care of me after my mother died. She died just a few days after I was born."

"I'm sorry she died so young," he said. "It sounds like she died before you could even know her."

I took a deep breath. I didn't like feeling sad.

"Um, so. Something you said earlier," I said. "You mentioned I was already shifted?"

He nodded.

"So, what do I looked like when I'm in my true form?" I asked.

"No one knows until you show us," said Chance. "And you're not the only orphan who's first shifted back at the Academy. Don't worry, I know it's a shock. The professors will show you how to do it. Soon, I'm sure."

"Will it hurt?" I asked again.

"No, Holly. It will not hurt."

I felt insanely curious about Chance's natural form, but he'd said it was very personal, so I didn't ask him about it.

Thinking back to the older faun we'd witnessed, I understood why it would be personal. That old man had been in his birthday suit.

I put my hand up to cover my grin.

A gust of cold autumn breeze whooshed over us, and I shivered suddenly.

"We'd best be going inside again," said Chance. "We didn't bring jackets."

"Okay." I turned to walk back. As we got to the door that led into the castle, Chance turned to me.

"Holly, I have something to tell you," he said. "The headmistress had wanted to wait until Christmas, but recent events have forced her to move the date up."

"Oh?" Curiosity bloomed in my mind.

"Can you meet me here at midnight tonight?" Chance asked.

I looked into his eyes, and saw he was very earnest.

I nodded. "Yes, sure. But why not just tell me now?"

"Because it's a special secret. Oh, and bring your birthday necklace," he said.

I stared at him.

He is so mysterious.

"All right," I whispered.

"Good," he smiled. "Now let's get you to your dorm room."

We walked down the stairs and around the hallways until finally we were standing outside Liesl's and my room.

"Goodnight, Holly," Chance said. "It's only seven thirty, so I'll see you in about four hours."

I nodded.

He bowed slightly, turned and was gone.

So mysterious.

I turned and entered the room.

"Hey!" Liesl smiled. "Sooooo, tell me what happened!"

I shook my head. "What happened, what happened ... oh my gosh. Well, the sunset was really beautiful. Much brighter than in New York City."

"Probably because of the smog," Liesl laughed.

I had been telling her about the city. Clean air wasn't one of its charms.

"And ... Oh! We saw a real life faun!" I exclaimed.

"WHAT?" shrieked Liesl.

I nodded, grinning. "It was incredible! Oh! And he was NAKED!"

Liesl threw her head back and laughed. "Was he cute?"

I smiled. "Probably sometime back in the day. He was an old man."

"EWWWWW! Ha ha ha!"

"Ha ha ha!"

"So, what else?" Liesl asked.

"Um, a short lesson in shifting into a glamour," I said. "Did you know I've been shifted nearly all my life?" I shook my head in amazement, plopping down on my bed and flinging my arms wide. "I had no idea. Can you even imagine?"

"I can," Liesl smile. "Plus, all of us are, shifted, I mean. From a very early age."

I sat up. "Oh, right! So, your heritage is, wait, I know you told me when we first met ..."

"Sylph heritage," Liesl finally said, laughing.

"Right! Sylph. The faefolk that inhabit the ... wind?" I guessed.

"The air," Liesl said. "We usually live high up, either on the sides of mountains, or up in tall trees. We can fly."

"YOU CAN FLY!?" I exclaimed with delight.

Liesl nodded, looking proud. "Yes. Fly. It's actually very cool." She grinned broadly.

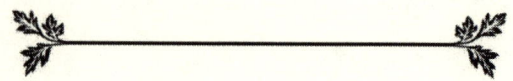

Chapter Thirty-Three
A Secret Revealed

I lay there in bed for a long time, unable to sleep. I'd been worried about oversleeping and missing the secret rendezvous with Chance, but my mind wouldn't allow me to doze off, let alone sleep.

I held the alarm watch in one palm, my fingers twirling the wristband around in nervous agitation, my eyes closed, trying to fall asleep for over an hour, but it was no use.

I glanced over at Liesl. Soft snores came from the mound of blankets on her bed, and her tousled hair was just barely visible in the moonlight.

I shifted my gaze to the window. I could just see the moon if I leaned over a few inches. It was full, and beautiful.

It will light the way tonight.

Clouds drifted slowly across the bright harvest moon, looking very fluffy and fat.

My thoughts turned inward, and I thought about what Chance had said.

I wasn't quite sure what to make of his cryptic words, but I was so excited I could not sleep.

A mysterious and special secret that the headmistress had wanted to save for Christmas.

Something that can't wait.

"...recent events force its disclosure..."

What had happened recently that might force the headmistress to divulge a secret?

The explosions.

My stomach hurt.

The headmistress had said that those responsible were agents of the Oak King. She'd implied the people who'd attacked the school were close to the Oak King.

What if the attackers are distant royals, like me?

What if she decided that I might be associated with the people who bombed the outside of the castle?

WHAT IF I'M BEING EXPELLED?!

All of a sudden, I felt like vomiting. The remnants of dinner rose to the top of my throat, and I scrambled to untangle myself from the blankets and sit up.

Oh God oh God oh God ...

"This can't be happening," I whispered aloud.

"Mmfmrglbb ..." Liesl mumbled and turned over.

My eyes went wide, and I held my breath until she settled back down.

I closed my eyes and bent my head, trying hard to tamp down my nausea.

How could this happen?

Not much had been said about the people behind the bombing. The student body knew next to nothing about what had actually happened.

Or at least the first-years didn't know...

My head started hurting.

I loved it here at Titania Academy. I couldn't go back. I just couldn't. I thought back to the summer and surviving on the streets of New York, and my stomach started hurting even more.

OhGodohGodohGod

I scowled. I had apparently become soft during my months here at the school. *How ridiculous. BUCK UP, HOLLY.* I tried to feel better. *You can survive anywhere.* It wasn't working. I felt sicker than ever.

Maybe some fresh air will help.

I put my shoes on, being as quiet as I could, grabbed my birthday necklace from the nightstand, where I'd placed it earlier, and tiptoed out of the dorm room, shutting the door behind me with care.

I stared at the moon through the hallway window.

Just a short while ago, I had thought it so beautiful; now all I could think about was how it had looked in the New York smog.

Unshed tears in my eyes, I descended the staircase, staying quiet, and walked to the edge of the school's central hallway.

It was deserted this late, and I took a few minutes to look at everything I had grown so fond of.

I took so long that the chime on my alarm watch sounded, making me jump.

I press my finger to shut it off, then looked up.

Had I heard a sound?

I shook my head, trying to clear it.

Sadness and longing filled my head, warring with fear and regret.

"Well," I said out loud, "I'd better get going. Don't want to postpone the inevitable. Chance is waiting."

There is was again.

I strode to the opposite staircase, and quickly ran up the first two flights, then turned around and look down onto the hallway where I'd just been standing.

Nothing.

Wait, a shadow was emerging from the back hall. I held my breath and waited, trying not to blink.

It was the night guard, walking his rounds.

I remembered now: the headmistress had set several guards to roam the school, day and night, since the explosions occurred.

He looked bored as he slowly walked toward the front doors of the school, peaking in side hallways and doors as he went.

I let out my breath as he passed, then turned and walked up the steps a little slower.

I was still very worried. I was sure that this might would bring the most horrible news of all, and I would have to leave the school behind, and return to living on the mean streets of the dingy city I had grown up in.

Or rather, under.

The underground subway cubby Aunt Clare and I had called home had seemed cozy and relatively safe while she was still alive, but the day she'd died, it had turned into the worst nightmare of my life.

Loneliness and misery had filled my head, and I'd cried myself to sleep in a vacant doorway. The cubby no longer felt safe. It felt as if it was filled with ghosts of the past.

I shuddered, blinking back tears.

Stop thinking of such things. Just stop. STOP IT NOW.

I reached the top hallway and looked down on nearly a dozen staircases. The main floor hallway was not visible.

How had I gotten all the way up? I didn't remember. Just walking up steps, over and over, thinking about my past, I guess.

"Okay," I whispered to myself. "Let's get this over with."

I reached out and grabbed the door handle and turned it downward ten degrees. It was not locked. I pushed it open and was greeted by a face full of cold air.

I'd worn a jacket this time, and the wind had died down a bit.

I stepped outside and closed the door behind me.

Wouldn't want the night guard to come looking for the source of the cold midnight breeze wafting down into the school.

I checked my watch. I was a few minutes early, but as I took a few steps around the corner and looked at the spot Chance and I had watched the sun set early, I saw his silhouette framed by the light of the moon.

He was already here.

He turned, as if sensing my presence.

"Holly," he said. It was not a question.

I walked forward slowly, glad for the darkness of night that hid my swollen eyes.

"Hi," I said lightly. "Well, I see the wind died down."

"Yes," he glanced around. "Thank goodness. But I see you wore your jacket. That's good. It's cold up here at midnight, regardless." He led the way to the stone wall edge.

I was beginning to think of it as "our spot."

The moonlight illuminated the entire parapet once we walked out from under the covered area.

We stood there, looking out at the school grounds, now much darker and half in shadow.

I closed my eyes, breathed in the cool night air, and tried to savor the last minutes before Chance dropped his news.

My stomach felt tense, but luckily, the night air helped to tamp down any lingering nausea.

"Holly," Chance said in a quiet voice. "Do you have your birthday necklace?"

I pulled it from under my jacket. The green leaf and red berry holly design twinkled in the moonlight as I held it aloft.

"The headmistress wants you to know who sent this gift for you," Chance murmured.

I looked up at him. THIS is what he was going to tell me? Who'd given me the necklace?

Thoughts raced through my mind.

Should I still be worried?

Was it a bequest from my father's side of the family?

Was it tied to the people who attacked the school?

Was I going to be expelled?

I held my breath and watched his face, waiting.

Chance gazed into my eyes.

"The necklace is from your father," he said.

WHAT?

"Is he still alive? I thought ..." I swallowed, my throat suddenly hurting.

"I cannot answer that, I'm sorry," said Chance. "I am just to tell you the necklace is from your father."

"That's all?"

"Yes."

omgomgomg

Maybe I'm not going to be expelled.

My eyes filled with tears.

Did I dare to let joy enter my heart?

I had to make sure.

"So," I looked at him. "I'm not going to be expelled?"

"What?" Chance looked confused.

Of course you're not going to be expelled. Idiot. You were worried about nothing. NOTHING! It's your birthday necklace, that's the surprise. It's from your father.

Oh my God.

A silly grin spread out on my face.

"Nothing. Nothing." I looked down at my necklace. "My father gave me my birthday present." I looked up at Chance again. "So, he knows about me? He knows I exist?"

My voice was unnaturally high.

Now it was Chance's turn to hold unshed tears in his eyes.

I looked into them and began to drown.

I couldn't blink, couldn't turn away.

I was fully in the moment.

I thought I smelled juniper berries waft over on the night air.

Chance leaned forward, ever so slowly. He eyes held mine.

He bent down, so close I could smell the minty scent of his breath.

He stopped a few inches from me, a look of love in his eyes.

I couldn't help myself.

I leaned forward, closing the last bit of space between us, and kissed him.

I had never kissed a boy before. His lips were warm and soft, and as we kissed, I got a fluttery feeling in my stomach, as if a thousand butterflies were dancing in a circle, celebrating the kiss.

Finally, he pulled his head back, and looked at me, a soft smile on his face.

He stepped back and put his hand over mine and kept looking at me. And that smile didn't leave his face.

I probably have a similar smile on mine.

Then it happened. The loving expression on Chance's face morphed into one of surprise and shock as he was shoved hard from behind, and lifted, and thrown over the edge of the open parapet.

Less than a second after he was thrown, I was tossed over the edge. We fell almost at the same second.

The entire thing seemed to happen in slow motion. I remember feeling the shove and the scoop and being tossed over the edge.

Those few seconds took a million years.

We were nearly two hundred feet high.

One second after the fall, I was facing up to the parapet edge, my body half turned, and I could see faces watching us fall. I could see Jessica and Naomi.

I could see Aspen and Tundra, their paws up on the stone edge, their eyes open wide in utter shock. They must have sensed my surprise and fear at being pushed over the edge.

The next second, I was turning.

The third second, I was facing down, falling in slow motion alongside Chance.

I fell sideways, my head turned to the sky, and slowly turned to face down.

Chance was falling face down, his hands out in front of him as he fell.

The fourth second into the fall I saw something flying up to us. Something small.

It was Chance's hawk familiar.

The fifth second of the fall, I saw the hawk grow, from a normal sized hawk, to a hawk the size of a bus. It was swooping down and under us.

It was catching us.

We fell onto its back. It shuddered, then regained its balance and flew gently ahead.

I thought I was going to have a heart attack, my heartbeat was thundering in my chest so fast.

Chance put his arm around me to steady me on the hawk's feather-covered back.

The giant raptor glided to the ground, landing gently, and folding its wings against its sides. It crouched on the school lawn, and Chance and I slid off. A few seconds later the hawk was its normal size again and flew up to perch on Chance's shoulder and nuzzle his cheek.

I swung around and looked up from where we'd fallen but saw no one there anymore.

A pop! heralded the arrival of Tundra and Aspen, and suddenly the world was filled with warm, rough wolf fur, and wet licks from eager tongues.

We stood there, Chance's arm still around me, and I tried to slow my breathing down to normal again.

"Before we have company," murmured Chance, and he turned and kissed my lips.

I closed my eyes and pressed eagerly against him and flung my arms around his waist.

"Oh my God!" came the faint call. "Mr. Mac Craith! Miss Ó Cuilinn! ARE YOU ALL RIGHT?"

We broke away from each other and turned toward the voice.

The school front doors were thrown wide, and light from the inside hall spilled out onto the front steps, and Professor Ó Baoghill was running down the steps and toward us, as only a middle-aged woman in a warm purple robe, fluffy beige slippers, and a bright yellow nightcap can.

Chapter Thirty-Four

A Surprise

Chance and I sat in the headmistress's office, blankets around both our shoulders, sipping hot mead from large mugs.

The headmistress's nightcap was askew, and her face was flushed.

Aspen and Tundra lay at my feet, refusing to leave, even after I uttered the correct spell.

Chance's hawk perched on his shoulder, also refusing to leave him.

Renée had been called, and stood near us, her expression a mixture of shock and relief.

Several other professors, and a nurse, stood behind us, crowded into the back of the room.

I sipped my hot mead, and amazed at the warm, honey flavor coupled with the verboten taste of alcohol. The headmistress insisted it would help us gather our wits and recover faster.

Liesl was brought into the room and ran to me. "HOLLY! They said you'd fallen off the parapets!"

The headmistress shook her head. "They did not fall, Miss Becker. They were pushed."

I glanced up at the headmistress sharply.

So she knows.

As if reading my mind, the headmistress continued. "Contrary to popular belief, I know *most everything* that happens in my school," she said. "Ever since Miss Ó Cuilinn and the others were lost in the forest, I have had her watched. We cannot afford to let any more mischief befall her. I was alerted to her being out of bed," she glanced at me and nodded. "Not only is your dorm room being guarded and watched, so is your movement in the castle and on the grounds."

I just stared at her, mixed feelings warring in my head.

"I was notified when she proceeded to the parapets, and so I joined the watch assigned to her myself, and we traced her steps," said the headmistress. "We stayed hidden using advanced spellwork, no one would have been able to see us. I observed the culprits at the last minute, they were similarly cloaked. We believe they were given an elixir to produce this effect, as they are not yet at the level for such advanced spellwork." She took a deep breath, clearly upset that such an elixir had been used.

"I observed them just at the moment they pushed Mr. Mac Craith and Miss Ó Cuilinn over the edge of the parapet," the headmistress continued. "I was, sadly, too late to reach them before they fell, but I was able to grab the two offenders before they could flee. The guards I was with took them into custody, and they are now being held in the dungeons."

I glanced at Liesl and mouthed, *'the castle has dungeons?'*?

Liesl's eyebrows rose in surprise.

The headmistress was speaking again. "My heart was in my throat when I realized they had fallen. To be honest, I think Mr. Mac Craith's familiar is to be credited with saving their lives." She looked at the hawk, which began to preen itself proudly.

That hawk knows what the headmistress just said.

Oh, my God, our familiars can understand our speech.

I held my birthday necklace in my fingers, idly turning it over and over, lost in thought.

Then something the headmistress said brought my attention back to the present.

"The two students have been summarily expelled, in fact, they were no longer students of the school the moment they committed the double attempted murder," said the headmistress. "The authorities are on their way to

401

take custody of them." She turned to Renée. "Miss Page, I am sorry to say your sister was involved."

Renée's eyes went wide.

"Miss Penner and your sister are the culprits who committed this act upon Miss Ó Cuilinn and Mr. Mac Craith," the headmistress said. "The two girls are first-year students, so I believe it's safe to say they had help. Help with procuring the Elixir of Invisibility, at the very least."

Renée looked down at her feet. "I am sorry for my sister's actions." She put her finger up. "She's actually my half-sister."

The headmistress nodded. She'd probably already known.

I hadn't and was somehow relieved at the news.

"But," Renée continued, "I am beyond happy that Holly and Chance are okay."

I put my head down and smiled.

My friend.

"Now," the headmistress continued. "As for the two of you," she looked directly at Chance and me. "*Especially* you, Mr. Mac Craith."

Chance sat up in his chair, his attention riveted on the headmistress.

"You are aware, I presume, of the rule that *no student shall be out of bed after hours?*"

Chance went pale and nodded. "Yes, headmistress," he whispered.

The older woman turned her eyes to me. "And you, Miss Ó Cuilinn. You were made aware of all the school rules upon arrival, I presume?"

"Yes, headmistress," I mumbled.

"Beg pardon?" she said.

I sat up and cleared my throat. "Yes, headmistress," I said, louder.

She was silent for a minute, her gaze going from me to Chance and back again.

"You could have died this night," she whispered harshly, somehow managing to project her voice throughout the room.

Chance and I hung our heads.

Another minute of silence filled the room. No one in the room was willing to make a sound.

"I have called your parents to the school," the headmistress said.

My eyes went wide, and my head snapped up.

I stared into the headmistress's eyes and my jaw dropped open.

"Not to be punished, because I think avoiding death and being scared out of one's wits is punishment enough," the older woman said. "But because you both deserve to see them and be comforted by them. And because both of your parents went nearly mad with fear at my first missive."

MY PARENTS?!

I knew my mother was dead, because Aunt Clare had told me, and she'd actually been by my mother's bedside in the hospital room, holding me, when my mother had passed.

So "my parents" must mean ...

I gulped in excitement.

It must mean MY FATHER WAS COMING. HE'S ALIVE AND HE'S COMING TO THE SCHOOL TO SEE ME.

omgomgomgomgomg

I began hyperventilating.

"Okay, here we go," said the nurse, coming forward and examining me. "Slow down your breathing, Holly. You can do it." She patted my shoulder and held my back as I coughed.

"I'm fine. I'M FINE," I said.

"She's fine," said Chance, shooing the nurse away. He glanced at me, "You are fine, right? Slow down your breathing, Holly. You do NOT want to be confined to the hospital wing when he arrives."

I glanced around the room. Only the headmistress, Chance, and Renée knew my father's identity.

And before dawn, I would know it, too.

"Mr. Mac Craith, the next time I put you in charge of guarding a royal student, I expect you not to break any school rules," the headmistress said in a grave tone. She turned to me. "And you, Miss Ó Cuilinn. I would like you to reread the student handbook, paying special attention to the school rules. In fact, I want you to memorize them." She looked down at me, a serious look on her face.

"I will do so by tomorrow," I said. It was after midnight, I had about 22 hours, I guessed.

How hard could it be?

There was a knock at the door, and everybody turned to see who was there.

"Enter," the headmistress called out.

Her secretary poked her head in the door. "Headmistress, their parents have arrived."

"Send them in, please."

The secretary nodded, and the door opened farther.

A couple entered. The man was a middle-aged copy of Chance, with a few wrinkles, and grey hair at his temples. The woman wore her hair coiffed in an updo, a few strands out of place, and had a worried look on her face. She scanned the room upon entering, and as her eyes fell on her son, she rushed forward.

"Chance! Oh, Chance!" She whisked him into a hug as he rose to greet her and pressed his face to her in a tight squeeze, tears in her eyes.

Chance's father stood next to his wife, his arm around his son, his head bent forward until his forehead touched Chance's shoulder.

Both his parents' shoulders shook softly.

They were crying.

The headmistress and I stayed seated, but the rest of the people in the room backed up tightly against the wall, wanting to give the family some privacy.

There wasn't a dry eye in the room.

A minute passed.

Then another figure entered.

He was tall and muscular, and wore a forest green coat trimmed in white against the late-autumn chill. His fluffy beard was tinged with green, and going mostly white. A vine of ivy wound its way from his polished black boots, around one leg, and around his middle once; it curled up to the back of his wavy hair and ended in an ivy crown around his head.

He looked like the old version of Santa Claus I'd seen in the shop windows in New York.

A hush fell over the room, then a murmur started up.

"The Holly King! It's the king! The Holly King!"

I held my breath. I felt my heart flutter.

It couldn't be ...

His eyes scanned the room, and fell on me, and went soft as tears filled them.

He stepped forward and the crowd in the room parted as he came.

I stood up.

"Holly. Oh, Holly," he murmured in a deep, rich voice.

And I knew.

Father.

I rushed forward, not caring if it was appropriate, and ran into the arms of the Holly King.

He hugged me tightly, and my arms circled his huge form, my head turned sideways, my eyes squeezed shut, tears flowing.

His coat smelled of spruce and evergreen, and his arms felt strong as they carefully squeezed me. The top of my head barely came to his chest.

After a minute he began to cry audibly.

He loosened his grip on me and bent over and grasped me around my waist. Up I went. He held me, my feet off the ground, and he leaned backward, holding me tightly in his arms again.

I never want this moment to end.

But we couldn't stay like that forever, and soon, the headmistress came around and pulled a large ornate chair out of the corner and pushed it behind the king.

He seemed to know it was there. He sat down in it, bringing me with him, and I was suddenly in my father's lap.

I lay my head on his shoulders and closed my eyes, and I don't think I've ever been so happy.

I had a faint awareness of my father's deep voice rumbling in conversation with the headmistress, whose own voice had a tone I'd never heard from her: deference.

I didn't care. I wanted to stay in his lap forever and ever.

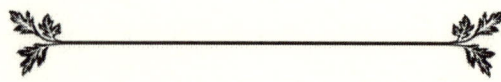

After a while I think I dozed off, because my father was gently nudging me. I kept my eyes shut. I absolutely did not want this to end.

I heard him chuckle.

"I think she's asleep," he said.

His arms continued to hold me. I was never so happy to be a small girl in my whole life.

"She's had such a hard evening," I heard the headmistress murmur.

Then, I heard a voice close to my ear. "Holly, goodnight. I'll see you tomorrow," said Chance. He kissed me on the cheek and was gone.

I blushed. It gave me away.

I felt my father's middle bouncing up and down as he chuckled again. Then I felt him lift me up in his arms.

"Just show us the way, and we'll both go to sleep for a few hours," he said.

"This way, Sir," said a voice. I think it was one of the other professors.

My father walked a short distance to the guest quarters and carried me inside. He lay down with me in a huge sleigh bed, and we both fell asleep, me still in his arms.

Unfortunately, with sleep comes unconsciousness and the relaxing of arms and legs, and when I finally woke up, I was alone in the bed.

"OH!" I cried out in sorrow.

Had it just been a dream?

"I'm right here, Holly."

I turned, and there he was, sitting in a grand ornate chair at the side of the bed.

Sunlight flooded the room and I moved to sit on the edge of the bed next to him.

I studied him. His eyes were blue, and I saw the green tinge to his skin was gone. In its place was a rosy glow and a happy smile.

Merry eyes met mine, and he reached out to grasp my hand in his.

Speaking of his hands, they were huge. My hand looked so small in his.

He'd taken his coat off and sat there looking like what a father should be. Relaxed and happy, love shining from his eyes.

"I expect you have a lot of questions, my dear," he said.

Chapter Thirty-Five
Explanations

"I sure do," I blurted out, louder than I'd meant to.

"Why don't I tell you the story of me and your mother, and then you can ask your questions to fill in the blanks."

I wiggled on the bed in anticipation, nodding eagerly.

He looked up thoughtfully. "Where should I start? Hmmm. Oh, I know!"

He looked down at me and grinned. "I'll start at the very beginning."

"I met your mother Noelle, when she was visiting Ireland, about fifteen years ago. It was mid-December, I believe, and I was walking in the forest near a string of cottages that were rented out by the week. Noelle was eighteen; fresh and beautiful and full of energy. She was there on a vacation with her friends and her grandmother.

She would take frequent walks in the forest, and so would I, so I saw her often. About a half mile into the wood, there was a particular spot she was drawn to. It was a faerie ring, a large circle of mushrooms of every size, shape and color imaginable.

"This faerie ring had been grown deliberately, for it sheltered the faefolk during times of distress, providing not only calm and retreat, but protection and energy. Well, Noelle had been raised in America, and did not know of the customs and tales of her people."

"Wait. 'Her people'?" I asked.

The Holly King nodded. "Noelle must have been adopted by a couple who moved away. It turns out she was raised in America, in a human household. She did not know of her fae nature."

"Mother was one of the faefolk?"

He nodded.

"I had no idea! This must mean I am not half human?" I asked.

"No, you are full-bred fae," said my father. "And what's more? Every person in the school knows it."

I gasped.

"How ...?" I felt amazed.

He smiled. "You would not even be able to see this school if you weren't. I am sorry, Holly. I instructed the school not to tell you much at all. Not because I wanted to be the one to tell you, but because of the war."

"There's a war?" I asked.

He nodded. "But we'll get to that later. I want to tell you about your mother."

I nodded; my brain was eager to find out what he had to say.

"Noelle would frequent the faerie ring, bringing her sketchpad and drawing the different mushrooms that made up its edge. It was quite a beautiful ring."

Something told me he had been the one to plant it.

"Now, one of the times she came to sketch, Noelle fell asleep in the faerie ring. Up until that moment, I had seen her, I had watched her sketching, but I had not revealed myself. But this time she'd fallen asleep, and she was irresistible. I could not help myself. I stepped into the mushroom circle and lay down next to her, and studied her face, memorizing every feature.

"You see, she was a type of fae that was very rare: she was Elfen. I had not seen one of the Elfen for more than three hundred years. So I was drawn to her. I lay down and studied her features up close. And the magic pouring out of her affected me so greatly that I fell asleep."

"Wait, my mother had faerie magic in her?" I asked.

He nodded. "It was very subtle, and no human would've been able to detect it, but I did, and I was very deeply affected by it. It made me drowsy, and almost drunk with happiness. And so I fell asleep. And apparently, while I was still asleep, Noelle woke up. It was getting late and cooler in the forest, and she needed to return to her cottage.

"Now, she told me that when she woke up and saw me, and I was in my fae form, she kissed me. Her type of Elfen fae are very sensual, and her kiss woke me up. I remember it like it was yesterday. I opened my eyes and beheld this lovely creature kissing me and my arms came up and held her and we did not stop kissing, not for a very long time.

"Eventually night fell, but we didn't care. We were completely absorbed in each other's magic. We kissed and kissed and eventually, we fell back to sleep. Well, her friends became worried, and in the morning, they began to search for Noelle. It was very early, and I was awoken by the sounds of the search party. I gave Noelle one last kiss, and left the faerie ring. Now, what I believe happened is that her friends found her, and she returned to America. And I had not known you were conceived until this summer."

I realized I was holding my breath while I listened. The tale of my mother and father was so alluring, so magical, that I hadn't want it to end.

But all stories come to an end.

I took a deep breath. "Okay, I do have questions, but I'll tell you what I know," I said.

He nodded and seemed as eager as I had been to hear the second half of the long story.

"Until this summer, I lived with my Aunt Clare in New York City. We were homeless," I glanced at him, steeling myself for possible judgement, but none came. He looked saddened but continued to listen.

"Mother had returned from her vacation and returned to school. I think Aunt Clare said she was attending New York University on a scholarship. A few months later, Mother realized she was expecting a baby."

"That was you," my father said, his eyes moist.

I nodded.

"When her parents found out, they threw her out of their home. She had nowhere to live. She dropped out of college and became homeless," I said. "Aunt Clare said she met Mother in a shelter in downtown New York. Aunt Clare said mother was already big with me inside her. So, they became friends."

"Ah, so your Aunt Clare was not your blood relative?" he asked.

"No," I smiled. "I guess she was adopted, like me."

He beamed. "Go on. I want to hear more."

"So they lived in the shelter. She was nineteen by this time. It was late summer. A few months later, my mother grew larger and went into labor. Aunt Clare said she took her to the hospital. They had to walk, and this made everything worse for my mother. But Aunt Clare said it was less than a mile, so they eventually got there."

"Aunt Clare told me my mother was in the hospital room and was in labor, and the doctors told her she had something wrong with her. I was born, and then she died a few days later. Aunt Clare said she told the hospital she was my mother's aunt, so they would let her have the baby, which was me."

Father nodded. I continued.

"Then Aunt Clare took me, and some other homeless people helped her find our cubby."

"Cubby?" asked the Holly King.

I nodded. "We went into the subway tunnels, and back behind a fence into the old abandoned part of the subway lines, and Aunt Clare walked a while down the walkway above the dip with the rails and found our cubby. There were several: If you peeled back the grate, there was a small room they used to keep stuff in, I guess. She carried me there."

"She just had a few blankets and some bags of food at first. But she said she made a sling out of part of one of the blankets and would tie me onto her back. She told me she begged in the early days, holding me like that. Then I grew up a little and would help. One time, it was during a bad time, we couldn't get any food. It was days and days. That's when I started stealing." I looked down, suddenly ashamed.

I felt his finger under my chin and slowly lifted my head.

"Hey," he said. "You did the best you could. You survived. That alone was amazing."

"I guess so," I said, still feeling weird about it, but not so bad anymore.

"You know, when you got close to your fourteenth birthday, the magic in you became visible to the Fae Council. They gather fae students from near and far, and invite them to the school. To Titania Academy," Father said. "That's when I got the news that you existed. Before that, I'd had no clue. None of the faefolk knew. You were quite the surprise, Holly," he grinned.

Then he looked thoughtful. "Your mother must've somehow known to name you Holly. I wear holly leaves, growing in a vine, as part of my magical garb. She probably remembered."

"I've always loved my name," I said. "Aunt Clare said it was very special, and that mother had insisted on naming me, even though she was very sick."

Father looked sad. "I was so sorry to learn your mother died, Holly. She was a very special young woman. Pure magic."

"Can you tell me about the Elfen fae?" I asked.

He nodded. "They used to be all over these isles, in Ireland, Scotland, and even Britain. Then one year, over a thousand years ago, most of them just disappeared. No one knows why. But a few are still around. Mostly, they hide. We found evidence that Noelle had been adopted when she was very young. Now, where she came from no one knows. It's a huge mystery we are still researching."

I nodded. "I want to know whenever you have more information," I said.

"Of course," he agreed. "The Elfen's closest relatives are the Elves. They are a more modern fae genetic line, and less wild than the Elfen. But that's a lesson for another day."

"Now can you tell me about this war? When Chance found me and brought me here, I was very happy. I wouldn't be constantly hungry anymore, I'd have a bed, it was a great thing," I explained. "But when the headmistress and Chance wouldn't tell me anything about my fae heritage, except that I was part of a royal line, I felt awful. I want to know everything," I looked up to his face. "Please, tell me everything?"

"You are half my royal line, which is the purest. And half Elfen fae. Your platinum hair is the hair color of my royal line. So are your eyes. The black rings around your platinum eyes mean your mother was Elfen."

"Wait." I put up my hand. "I was told the black ring around my eyes was because my parents were never married."

"Oh, dear. No, that is not accurate at all. That's an old wives' tale. Granted, it happened that most children from Elfen fae were not from married couples, but that is because of the nature of the Elfen. It is a correlation, not a causation."

"Hey, that sounds familiar!" I said.

"You probably heard it in a science class," he smiled.

"The only school I've ever attended was Titania Academy," I said. "Aunt Clare did teach me how to read and write and do numbers, sorry, do math. Maybe I heard it from her."

"Not sure, but let's push on. So, when they told me you existed, I insisted we go find you. And they did, thank God, and I couldn't have been happier. But we had to protect you," he said.

"Because of the war."

"Yes," he said.

"I did not know there was a war going on," I murmured.

"Our wars are not the same as human wars. They happen very infrequently, for one," he explained. "But mostly, they're just a bunch of intrigue and kidnappings, oh, and rarely, they throw bombs."

"Like the ones that went off here, at the school?"

He nodded. "That was incredibly unfortunate. There's an unspoken agreement between the two fae factions, that schools are off limits. We are worried they targeted the school on purpose."

"What is the other faction involved?" I asked.

"The Oak King and I rule the fae world, and we share the year: I rule half the time; he rules the other half. There is a group of the Oak King's followers who want him to rule the whole year. The Oak King insists this group is acting independently, and that he does not wish to rule the whole year, but that's like a starving man denying he wants a hot fudge sundae. The Oak King has always been power-hungry. He's always craved more."

"But why did you order the headmistress not to tell me about my background?" I asked, still puzzled. "What does that have to do with the war?"

"If she had told you, it would very likely have been leaked to the rest of the student body, and that would have made you a target. They are capable of doing great harm, and I was worried you would get hurt," he said in a concerned voice.

"So, everyone knew I was full Faefolk, they just didn't know I was your daughter?" I leaned over and gave him a quick hug.

"That's exactly it. Being the daughter of the Holly King makes you a target," He put his finger on the side of his nose and thought for a moment. "I have an idea of how to protect you, which I will reveal in due course."

I nodded. "I guess I understand. It was just hard."

The Holly King gathered me in his arms and hugged me.

"I know, Sweetheart, and I am sorry. I should have told you myself. I wish I had now."

Chapter Thirty-Six

Genius

We talked some more and decided it would be best to address the whole school in an assembly. "Those girls who drank the elixir and attacked you are probably part of the Oak King faction," Father said.

Oh, lord.

I felt very weird: I'd started out in the same dorm room as Jessica and Naomi, and now they'd been expelled for trying to kill Chance and me.

There had been others on their side. I hoped the others would not hurt anyone.

"They'll probably be so taken aback by the Holly King's assembly and the news that Jessica and Naomi are in prison awaiting trial, they'll be too afraid to do anything," Chance said that morning. "Besides, it was those two girls who've been the worst, by far. The rest of them seemed to just be hangers on, like a clique."

We all sat in the lunchroom together, Chance, Renée, Liesl, and me. Father was being briefed before he addressed the whole school.

"Oh my God, you guys, my parents shit a brick when they were told what Naomi had done. I swear, she is lucky she's behind bars, because my parents are ready to kill her, ha ha ha!" Renée said.

I froze. "Not ... not literally, right?"

"Ha ha ha, no, Holly, not literally. But they are really furious," Renée said.

I looked at her. "Hey, you knew about my father, didn't you?"

Renée became sober. "Yes," she said in a quiet voice. I'm so sorry. I was bound by a Secrecy Spell, remember? The headmistress herself placed it on me."

I grinned. "That's okay, I understand."

Renée looked so relieved it seemed like she might faint.

"Hey, don't forget about me," Chance said, waving his hand. "I knew, too!"

"Maybe I should beat you with a wet noodle," I said.

He grinned. "We were just keeping you safe."

"Now what are you going to do, Holly? Isn't the news out now?" Liesl looked concerned.

"Hmmm, I'm not sure. But I'll bet they'll cook up something good," I said.

"Come on, finish your breakfast. It's getting late," said Renée. "We don't want to miss the assembly!"

A few minutes later, we walked over to the Assembly Hall and found seats. The place was packed. Even the professors were there to hear the Holly King speak.

We could overhear the hubbub all around us. Some of it was hilarious.

"Look! The guards are here, too. Everyone wants a glimpse of the king!"

"Then who's guarding the school?"

"Nobody," a boy said solemnly. "We'll likely be attacked."

"Idiot, the king comes with his own entourage. He's got more guards than the whole school put together."

"All right, all right, don't shove."

"You started it."

I glanced at Renée and giggled silently.

After about ten minutes, the headmistress came on the stage and called for quiet.

"As you know, the Holly King is here for a visit," Professor Ó Baoghill began. "What you probably did not know, is that there was an attack on two students late last night. We suspect the students who did this, excuse me, *former* students, were in cahoots with the Oak King faction that bombed our school just a short while ago."

The hall erupted in voices.

It took several minutes to quiet everyone.

"Settle down! Settle down!" The headmistress kept repeating. Finally, everyone quieted and began to listen again.

"We have been up most of the night addressing this latest issue," she continued, "And the culprits have not only been expelled, they've been removed from the school and grounds, and transported to the city prison, where they are awaiting trial on the charge of attempted murder."

The hall erupted into loud voices again, everyone standing in the uproar.

The headmistress walked off the stage, shaking her head.

The stage was empty for a few minutes as the jibber-jabber carried on.

Then another professor came onto the stage and stood at the podium, and everyone quieted and looked at him expectantly.

He uttered just one sentence. "Please join me in welcoming ... The Holly King!" and he walked to the side, clapping.

The hall erupted in cheers and screams and woots and clapping as my father slowly walked onto the stage. He was dressed in all his regalia, and from my seat, I could see that yes, indeed, he looked very much like Santa Claus.

An Irish Santa, to be sure. His outfit was green and white, and he even had on a pointed hat that matched his coat.

As he reached the podium, the hall suddenly fell silent. No one wanted to miss a word.

"Greetings, students, faculty, everyone. Thank you for that grand welcome. I am honored," the Holly King said. "I wish the circumstances surrounding my visit were better. I know how much you've suffered in the recent bombing. I am working with the headmistress to solve the crimes against the Academy and you, its students. Security will be increased, and we will get to the bottom of this, I assure you.

"I wish to have a minute of quiet to remember the student who died in the bombing, and the two students whose lives were nearly cut short last night." He bowed his head and fell silent.

The hall full of people followed his lead, bowing their heads and closing their eyes. I heard more than a few sniffles.

After a long minute, Father looked up once more and continued to speak.

"As you know, the kingdom has been embroiled in a war for a few years. It has now arrived at the boundaries of Titania Academy, and I couldn't be sorrier. You don't deserve this. None of you. This is an institution of learning, and your strongest concern should be your schoolwork. Not bombs and attempts on your lives.

"I want you to know exactly who the students were who nearly died last night, and how they survived. This is a lesson on respect, on culture, and on survival." He paused for a moment, and I felt a flutter of nervousness in my stomach.

He was going to tell them?

But Father was speaking again. "Late last night, two students were pushed off the highest western parapet, and thrown off the castle, in an attempt on their lives. The only reason they survived was because of the instinctive actions of one of their familiars. This hawk appeared as its master was falling to his death. The familiar used its instinctual magic to increase in size as it flew underneath the students, catching them on its back, and saving them from a horrible death."

The hall gasped in unison.

"The students in question are Chance Mac Craith and Holly Ó Cuilinn."

Those assembled in the hall gasped even louder, and voices rose in concern. I felt dozens of eyes on me and Chance.

"I would like to ask them both to stand at this time, so you can get a good look at them," the king said.

Chance and I glanced at each other, shrugged, and rose to our feet. Everyone started clapping and yelling out encouragements.

"You go, Chance."

"Bully for you, Chance."

"Holly! Yay!"

"Way to go, Holly!"

Chance muttered a spell, and his hawk familiar appeared on his shoulder, and the calls of approval rose even louder.

"WELL DONE!"

"LOVE THAT HAWK!"

"WHAT A BEAUTY!"

After a few minutes, we moved to retake our seats, but my father called out into the microphone: "Don't sit down just yet. Everyone, I have some news to tell you."

The hall went silent again, all eyes were on the king.

"Chance and Holly are in second and first year, respectively. They're great students. And Holly," he paused for a couple of beats, "Holly is my daughter. Holly Ó Cuilinn is my daughter. She is the daughter of the Holly King!" his voice rose at the end, in his own call of encouragement and approval, and his fist punched the air in triumph.

The hall went wild.

"OH MY GOD! OH MY GOD!"

"AMAZING!"

"HOLLY! HOLLY!"

"HOLLY: BE MY FRIEND?"

"HOLLY, YOU ARE AWESOME!"

"ROYAL HOLLY! ROYAL HOLLY!"

"WOOP! WOOP!"

It went on for more than ten minutes. Everyone was clapping, even my father.

I blushed furiously and tried to hide my grin.

Chance grabbed my hand and thrust it into the air, and I laughed.

The Holly King eventually called for order.

"Now, before I go, I want to ask a special favor of each and every one of you." When he said this, he pointed at various students, and his gazed was piercing. "I want you to do the Holly King a special royal favor. Will you do that for me? Will you do a special favor for your king?"

Everyone yelled out.

"YES!"

"YEAH!"

"I'LL DO ANYTHING YOU ASK!"

"WE LOVE YOU!"

"ASK US ANYTHING!"

"WE WANT TO HELP YOU!"

"YESSSSS!"

"WOOT!"

He put his hands up for quiet, and everyone hushed again.

He waited until every eye was on him, and it grew so quiet you could hear a pin drop.

He stepped close to the microphone and spoke in a low, almost conspiratorial, but deadly serious tone.

"I want you to guard my daughter."

The hall erupted in screams of approval. Everyone who could reach me put their hands on me in gestures of encouragement. Some just patted my back; others reached out and put their hands on me and uttered protection spells; still others called out promises to protect me. A few even cried out they would protect me with their lives. Over a thousand voices were crying out.

I started crying.

Chance put his arm around me.

"I'm fine, I'm fine. These are happy tears," I assured him. I'd never felt so overwhelmed in my life.

"The Holly King is a genius," Chance whispered in my ear. "Everyone has just been charged with this task by the king himself. No one will be able to touch you." Chance kissed my cheek.

Everyone had been staring at us. When they saw Chance kiss my cheek, they all erupted in applause.

As if I couldn't blush any stronger.

An hour later, we were all gathered in the guest quarters my father was staying in. We drank hot mead, and even the headmistress joined in for a half cup of the jeweled liquid.

"All right. I am hoping everything will be safe here from now on," said the Holly King. "We've placed extra spellwork and anti-curse charms over the enter castle, inside and out, on the grounds, in the forest, and these spells extend a hundred miles in every direction."

The headmistress nodded in gratitude. "We are so thankful for your intervention, my king."

My father turned to Chance. "My boy, I saw that kiss on my daughter's cheek."

Now it was Chance's turn to blush bright red.

"You take good care of Holly. I will be visiting regularly to check on things," Father said.

Chance nodded.

"Hopefully, with the whole school protecting you, knowing what your heritage is, you will be much safer, my daughter," the King said. "I must take leave of you now, and I am sorry I can't stay longer. It breaks my heart. But there is much work to be done, in this war, and concerning the attacks. And a boarding school does not need the distraction of parents hanging about."

I nodded, tears in my eyes. I couldn't speak around the lump in my throat. I was sitting between Chance and my father, and I jumped up and turned and fell onto the king in a huge bear hug.

"Oof!" he said, laughing. "Oh, how I love you, Holly!"

Dear reader~

I'm so glad you read Faerie Misborn and I hope you loved it. I do hope you'll consider leaving a review. It means so very much to hear what you think.

Get book 2 of the series!

Faerie Elemental
Coming out early 2020!

Here ends Faerie Misborn, the first book of the Titania Academy series. The second book will be called Faerie Elemental.

ABOUT THE AUTHOR

Samaire Wynne grew up in a lot of different places, and now happily resides on the East Coast, laboring away at writing stories every day. She is an animal lover with far too many pets, yet she still muses how she'd like to add even more. A lover of all things night and gothic, she also loves to read and reread her favorite books. Owned by a cat named Tyrion, she can be found haunting the shadows and mists that hang low over the hills of southern Virginia.

Made in the USA
Middletown, DE
30 October 2023

41592388R00265